BOONDOCKING

Also by Tricia Bauer

Working Women and Other Stories

BOONDOCKING

a novel

Tricia Bauer

Bridge Works Publishing Co.
Bridgehampton, New York

Published in 1997 in the United States by
Bridge Works Publishing Company,
Bridgehampton, New York.
Distributed in the United States by
National Book Network, Lanham, Maryland.

First Edition

Library of Congress Cataloging-in-Publication Data

Bauer, Tricia, 1952–
Boondocking : a novel / Tricia Bauer. — 1st ed.
p. cm.
ISBN 1-882593-19-7 (hardcover)
I. Title.
PS3552.A83647B66   1997
813'.54—dc21   97-13325
CIP

10 9 8 7 6 5 4 3 2 1

Book and jacket design by Eva Auchincloss
Jacket Illustration by David Gothard

Printed in the United States of America

For Bozzone

CONTENTS

With special thanks to Barbara and Warren Phillips,
and to Bobbie Ann Mason

BOONDOCKING

I

SYLVIA

ONE

———◆•◆•◆———

Sylvia and Clayton sat in a shiny travel trailer in front of the house that for thirty-one years had been theirs, and peeked at the new owners opening windows and repositioning furniture.

"I swear she's moved that damned couch five times," said Sylvia. She drew hard on her cigarette.

"Must be a perfectionist," Clayton said, dismissing Sylvia's concern. He told her she worried over the most insignificant things. Last night when Sylvia said she thought the woman was wearing her yellow print blouse, the one his mother had given her two birthdays ago, Clayton shook his head. The blouse was among the many possessions Sylvia and Clayton had boxed and left in the cellar for the new home owners to do with as they wanted. Sylvia and Clayton's decision to move into a trailer and begin what he jokingly called, though in fact it was no joke, "life on the road," left little room for most of what they'd accumulated over the years. The necessities, which Sylvia had

3

culled from all their belongings, now squeezed into place in the twenty-four-foot trailer like pieces of a puzzle.

Sylvia kept on about the blouse until Clayton reminded her that she was a good thirty years older than the new woman and about twice as large. Sylvia wasn't really fat but what Clayton usually referred to as ample. He told Sylvia he didn't consider that criticizing. "There's just no way you and — is her name Debra? — would ever wear the same clothes," he'd said.

"I should have cut the lawn the other day like I wanted to," Clayton said, shaking Sylvia out of her reverie.

Sylvia stopped glaring at the furniture moving inside her old living room to concentrate on the grass, long and shaggy around the base of the red Japanese maple, and along the azaleas concealing the foundation of the two-bedroom brick ranch house. The trim and shutters of the small building were painted such a bright white that the cement sidewalk leading to the front door appeared gray in comparison.

"That's up to them now," said Sylvia. "The headaches are all theirs," she added, thinking of other chores she and Clayton would no longer have to perform: snow plowing, leaf raking, lawn watering and seeding, flower feeding, house painting. The list was lengthier than she'd anticipated.

"I know," said Clayton, "but as long as I got the time, I wouldn't mind."

"They said they didn't want you to," Sylvia reminded him sharply.

"They were being polite, Sylvia."

Sylvia stared at her husband, at fifty-nine almost totally gray. She didn't mean to squawk at him; she was nervous, that was all. She was nervous, and he was itching to get on with things. With anything other than sitting and watching out the window as if it held one big television rerun of their life.

A week earlier, Clayton, William Clayton Vaeth on his bi-

4

weekly paycheck, had taken early retirement from Evergreen Inc., a power tool manufacturing plant and the major employer in the area, an hour northwest of Baltimore. Clayton had worked the eight-fifteen in the morning until five in the evening shift ever since his promotion to line supervisor six years earlier. Employed by the company thirty years, and before that subcontracting carpentry jobs in the plant as it was being built, Clayton had spent well over half of his life at Evergreen Inc. His coworkers had sneaked beers into the cafeteria on his last day and presented him with his own bowling ball. "Clay Ball" was engraved onto the smooth blue and white marbled surface.

Sylvia knew Clayton couldn't imagine his life apart from Evergreen. But then, neither of them had envisioned life without Janice. And here they were.

Sylvia could tell whenever Clayton was thinking of their daughter; he didn't sit still and mourn the way Sylvia did. He had to get up and move around so that his sadness didn't settle in one place, like his head, and give him a headache, or his chest, and give him a gas pain. In the small quarters of the trailer, he walked past the kitchen area, the bathroom, up to the double bed, then back again. He told Sylvia that this spread his feelings through his body until they dispersed the way the tail end of a beer did if he poured it into the Little Pipe River when he was fishing.

"Why don't you go get us some ice cream," Sylvia said, sensing her husband's restlessness. He was tall and big-boned, and when he paced through the trailer he made her think of an animal in a too-small cage.

When Clayton stopped and looked right at her, she touched her hair, dyed to match the blond color she'd had when he'd met her. Now she was fifty-eight, round and soft, her former firm curviness hidden in the added pounds.

"Well, I'm glad you're not worrying about calories tonight," he said. Sylvia was known to say, "I shouldn't, I really shouldn't," to a stack of cookies before downing it, and then moaning over the weight she never seemed able to lose.

"If you're going, get a move on," she said. He appeared glad of the excuse to propel himself out of the trailer and on a specific mission.

"OK," he said, "but don't you go anywhere." Yesterday she'd teased him by saying that if he wasn't home in time for dinner she'd find some new man to hook up the trailer and drive her and everything she owned off into the sunset.

In general, Clayton appreciated Sylvia's suggestions. He was the one to sense when things were wrong, when one of them needed something, but Sylvia pinpointed precisely what could be done to remedy difficulties or to forget about them. Sylvia had recommended a vacation after their only child, Janice, died. "Get away from it all," had been Sylvia's exact words, sounding like a TV commercial. Clayton had not only agreed with her but, after weeks of tearful, late-night discussions, proposed that the vacation become a permanent leave-taking. From the day they'd met, Sylvia had accused her husband of wanting to go too far, but this was actually the first time she'd allowed him to act on his excesses. Maybe she finally believed there was nothing left to lose.

She heard Clayton start the pickup, its cap-enclosed bed packed with possessions they wouldn't need easy access to: winter clothes, tools, emergency food supplies, and the sky-colored bowling ball. She pictured him easing down Garden Road and, as he pulled onto the main road, slipping into third gear. With all the weight in the truck, he'd be driving carefully, practicing for when the whole house moved behind them. Sylvia imagined the few remaining thoughts of Janice blowing away from him, replaced by possible ice cream flavors.

With Clayton's truck out of sight, Sylvia stole another look at her old house. Debra and Rodney Pinch had drawn the filmy off-white cotton drapes in the living room, but Sylvia could still make out their dark forms pacing off the room, and, most likely, suggesting decorating ideas to each other. The young couple from the Washington suburbs had ended up paying an extra two thousand dollars above the house's selling price for most of the Vaeths' furniture, appliances, curtains, and other paraphernalia. Sylvia had been glad of the way things had turned out, after spending many sleepless nights picturing the contents of her home splayed across the front and back lawns like a huge ravaged body, its most private secrets picked apart and dragged off by strangers in search of tag-sale bargains.

The only piece of furniture the young couple hadn't absorbed was Sylvia and Clayton's bed. Two days ago, the newcomers had struggled out the front door with the mattress and box spring, and leaned them lengthwise against the garage walls. Sylvia had felt peculiar watching something so personal being discarded. Clayton had said to her, "Maybe they're getting a waterbed." His voice was all practicality, having not the slightest catch of nostalgia. "Let me know if you see them tossing the new toilet seat," he'd added. "I'll switch it with the one in this bathroom if they don't want it." She thought he'd been trying to get a laugh out of her, but when she studied his expression, it was completely serious.

When the Pinches had asked why the Vaeths were moving, Sylvia explained, firmly and without emotion, the facts surrounding Janice's death. Sylvia felt that the couple, who might make a guest room or a nursery of Janice's old bedroom, should be informed that the accident hadn't happened *inside* the house.

Less than two months earlier, Janice and her husband, Melvin Kondrake, and their nearly four-month-old baby, Rita, had been driving half a mile from their apartment in downtown

Baltimore when their car veered into oncoming traffic. Melvin later confessed he'd taken angel dust sometime before the accident (he couldn't remember exactly when) and told the police he wanted to drive over the approaching cars, which appeared to him as a colorful metallic bridge to another dimension. Janice had died instantly, Melvin suffered a concussion and two broken ribs, and the baby survived without a single bruise on her pale pink skin. She hadn't even been secured in a car seat. Somehow, enveloped by the miraculously protective curve of her mother's body, Rita had been unharmed by the accident. No one at the hospital could believe the baby was intact when she arrived in the emergency room, covered with her mother's blood.

When Sylvia finished telling the details, the Pinches said nothing. Sylvia had never felt her house so quiet. Debra picked at her thumb. Rodney tilted his head back and appeared to search for a pattern on the textured ceiling. Even the perky real estate agent, Mrs. Goodhue, was speechless; Sylvia suspected the woman had never heard such a straightforward story.

There were a few facts Sylvia didn't reveal. She hadn't told the young man and woman or Mrs. Goodhue how Clayton had wanted Melvin prosecuted for murder. She hadn't explained that the court had sentenced him not to the Maryland Correctional Facility but to a private psychiatric facility, which his parents agreed to pay for. Sylvia especially didn't want the couple to find out that Melvin hadn't held a steady job in the three years that Janice had known him, or that Janice had supported her family on her salary as an aide to a veterinarian.

The Pinches went off silently with Mrs. Goodhue between them. Although Sylvia hadn't noticed the three talking among themselves, as many other prospective buyers did once the car doors closed, the Pinches put a binder on the house that day, and the mortgage was approved before the custody of little Rita Kondrake was determined.

If only the courts were half as decisive as the Pinches. More than anything, Sylvia wanted Rita as far away as possible from the influences of Melvin's family. The baby was staying with Samantha, Melvin's sister, who made her living doing women's nails and hair in her kitchen. When Sylvia imagined Rita's tiny fingernails painted bright dots of orange, she wanted to scream.

"I got rocky road," Clayton said, opening the door to the trailer. Poco, the little black dog Janice had named when she was taking Spanish in high school, jumped and snapped at the air near Clayton's hand.

Clayton's voice startled Sylvia. "Sorry I scared you," he said, putting his cold, ice cream hand on her neck. Since they'd moved out of the house, Sylvia sensed Clayton had become more thoughtful of her, almost understanding how vulnerable she sometimes felt without the buffer of a house and all its trappings.

"Rocky road sounds like it's right up our alley," she said. Clayton picked up Sylvia's reading glasses to study the writing on the container. As he bent forward to turn on the television, Sylvia leaned over him and retrieved two red plastic dishes for their dessert. They'd replaced all their china dishes after the trailer salesman told them plastic would "travel better."

"I ran into Les from Evergreen," Clayton said.

"How's Jeanette doing?" Sylvia asked. She hadn't seen the couple in months, not since Jeanette's hip operation.

"She's OK, I guess," Clayton said. "Les caught me looking at a damned stuffed bear."

Sylvia took her husband's hand. She understood exactly his

impulse to grab at anything that reminded them of their granddaughter.

"It was a cute little bear," Clayton said as he spooned himself some rocky road. "I didn't want to jinx anything by buying it."

"I'd have hit you if you'd bought it," Sylvia said laughing. "Me trying to get rid of things, not take new ones on."

All along, the process of pressing a houseful of belongings into a new space the equivalent of two closets and a dozen good-size dresser drawers had been difficult. Before moving out of the house, Sylvia went through their possessions. Each item that she picked up and studied, she sorted into one of three piles. As expected, the accumulation of yeses and maybes initially far outnumbered noes, and soon Sylvia had to debate over the piles of clothes and jewelry and kitchen utensils a second and then a third time.

Those nights of Clayton's last days at Evergreen, Sylvia had stayed up all hours deciding what would come with them. When she finally did fall off to sleep (once in the living room on a pile of sheets and comforters), her dreams featured bizarre images — throw pillows turned into faces demanding to be taken along, the kitchen step stool walking on its own out the front door.

As hard as Sylvia worked to pare down her life, she felt constantly challenged by Clayton's words: "Sylvia, we don't have room for the waffle iron; it's something we use once a year, tops," or "You've got to be kidding with this stuff. We're not moving into a bigger house, for God's sake! We're moving into a trailer." She often found herself on the floor in the middle of one of their rooms, sobbing over a glass lamp that had never strayed from her bedside or something as inconsequential as a barrette in the shape of a pineapple. Every little thing she left behind could remind her of pieces of Janice. But she kept on, instinctively knowing that only a stripped-down life would eventually enable her to stop mourning. Whenever Clayton came into the room unexpectedly, she told him she had a cold. More than once Sylvia thought of throwing herself onto the "no" pile, of saying to Clayton, "Leave me here, too. That way you'll have twice the room in that stupid trailer."

After they finished the ice cream and watched the news, Clayton set his nearly empty bowl on the floor for Poco. Sylvia moved the two boxes she had yet to sort through from the middle of the floor to the bedroom at the rear of the trailer. Her final task: two remaining boxes that had to be reduced to one. Sylvia had saved the hardest chore for last. The boxes overflowed with photos and mementos.

"What you doing back there?" Clayton called. He liked her sitting with him to watch television.

"Never mind," Sylvia hollered. "I'll be right out." This was one of the disadvantages of a trailer that she'd have to get used to, everything pressed up against everything else so that you could hear the other person even from behind a closed door. With Clayton retired, she could see herself going crazy without a few hours completely to herself. Instead of spreading out into activities and projects he'd never before had time for, Clayton would be jammed right next to her.

A bathroom fitted with a small shower divided their new living space. The bedroom and its many hidden storage areas were located in the rear of the trailer; the combination kitchen and living room was situated up front. The kitchen featured a double sink, a couple of large cupboards, a tiny refrigerator with a freezer area the size of a shoe box. Clayton had mounted the TV and radio so that both could be enjoyed from the two easy chairs off to the side of the kitchen table. The facing benches on either side of the table converted into a second bed. Every inch of available space was accounted for.

The two boxes in front of Sylvia weren't huge, but there was

11

space for precisely one of them, not both, in the back of the pickup. Sylvia opened the first box, filled mostly with photographs. Stuffed along the sides were a high school diploma, a diary, and, near the bottom, a bowling trophy, some medals, a couple of stray markers from old board games.

Sylvia spotted a photo of Janice as a newborn. She lay in a carriage in a white dress and a tiny white-ribboned bonnet. The dress had been pulled up to the baby's chest to announce her sex. Clayton had taken the photo by standing on a kitchen chair above the bassinet. They'd been giddy with pride. Sylvia remembered the moment Clayton had taken the photo so precisely that she could recall the scent of hamburger frying a few feet away.

Sylvia and Clayton had Janice relatively late in life (Sylvia had been thirty-seven and Clayton a year older. "Two years shy of forty," he always said when marking that time), after ten years of not conceiving, followed by four miscarriages. For most of her pregnancy, Sylvia had stayed in bed while Clayton pampered her with hot cocoa and cheeses, old favorites, and with newfound cravings like black olives and cantaloupe.

When she'd first brought the baby home, Sylvia had been afraid to breathe around little Janice. Even Clayton whispered when he approached the bassinet. All their care, all their precautions, and Janice had died in such a reckless way. Sylvia was certain that, even though Janice had always been an inquisitive child, she hadn't known anything about angel dust before she met Melvin.

Sylvia came across a picture crayoned on thick white paper of a tree and a house, and three figures inside, each looking out of a window. But the fourth window, with windowpanes outlined in the green color of the tree, was without a face. Sylvia thought of the beginning of Janice's imagination, when the picture had been drawn. What could have been going through her daughter's mind as she tried to figure out her brief place in the world? Sylvia longed to fill that one empty window with a face. She had lost Janice, but there was still Rita. She ached for the touch of her granddaughter's soft skin and chubby legs.

"Sylvia," Clayton called. "There's a movie coming on."

Sylvia quickly gathered up the physical evidence of her memories and stuffed them into the two boxes. She wiped the tears from her face and, holding the containers before her husband, said, "I just can't do this now." She was tired of making decisions, of throwing things out. How could one little box make so much difference?

"Well, pack one and hold one on your lap," Clayton said, reaching for her.

"I'll hold one on my lap," she said with resolution, not as if she were repeating him, but as if that idea had just come to her.

Before Sylvia and Clayton had finished reading the *Morning Sun,* their neighbor from two houses down, Marlene Hinthorne, knocked on the trailer door. Weeks earlier, Sylvia had asked if Marlene would forward mail and keep an extra key to their safe deposit box at Maryland National while she and Clayton were on the road. Although the box wasn't all that necessary now that Sylvia and Clayton had no deed to a house or title insurance, there were the wills as well as a passbook for their special emergency account, and the diamond engagement ring that had been Sylvia's mother's. Until she met Melvin, Sylvia had planned to present the ring to Janice.

"Well, I wonder who this could be," Clayton said, looking over his reading glasses at Sylvia. "Maybe it's Pinky Thompson come to pay me back that five dollars he borrowed in 1953," he said, repeating what had become a joke over the years. Pinky was probably dead by now.

"Good morning, you vagabonds," Marlene called. "The guardian of your valuables is here," she said as Sylvia opened the door. On the word *valuables,* Marlene winked.

Just the possibility that she and Clayton might one day buy another house had made Sylvia keep something from Clayton: she had stored her grandmother's dining room table and chairs in Marlene's basement. She'd felt guilty, burdened by the deception at first, especially when arranging for Marlene's brother to move the furniture while Clayton was at work. But Sylvia knew she'd have felt worse if she'd left the family heirlooms to strangers.

Marlene handed Sylvia a crumb cake and mentioned that she'd left a full water jug outside. Their neighbor was younger than Sylvia, only about fifty, but appeared older. She was chunky, and her short hair was totally white except for a four-inch underlayer of black at the nape of her neck. When talking, she frequently pulled at the remains of dark hair, as if they held some strength from her youth that was still reliable. Marlene's husband had slipped through her net of warnings and precautions when he'd had a heart attack three years earlier. And Marlene's three children, whom she'd once confessed called her neurotic, seldom visited. Although she was sure to miss Sylvia and Clayton, Marlene was obviously anxious to begin her new job for the couple.

"That's a cute blouse, Marlene," Sylvia said, knowing she seldom received compliments. The shirt had a pattern of tiny pink and yellow flowers with bright green stems. Most of Marlene's shirts and dresses were decorated with emblems from nature — flowers, birds, acorns, sweeps of wild grasses. Sylvia found Marlene's choices in clothing odd, because she was the only person Sylvia knew with an aversion to nature. Marlene openly confessed to hating "the feel" of grass or animal fur or even dandelions gone to seed.

14

Because Marlene preferred tax forms to a colorful pile of October leaves, she was the perfect person to sort through their bills and junk mail. She claimed not to know the difference between a gladiolus and a daylily, but Marlene had no trouble fingering an advertising gimmick cleverly housed in an official-looking brown envelope.

"When's the big day?" Marlene asked. Her dogged concern over the date of the hearing to determine Rita's custody made Sylvia think of someone going daily to a lost-and-found to seek a missing glove.

"Far as we know, it's still a week from yesterday," Clayton said, without looking up from the paper. Sylvia knew he quickly tired of this nervous woman who would have preferred walking through a tunnel to her car and to the other houses on Garden Road rather than expose herself to the elements. "She should try working thirty years in a machine shop. Then she'd appreciate the fresh air," Clayton had once said to Sylvia.

"I'm just glad Mrs. Santos visited us *before*," Sylvia said.

"Who the hell's Mrs. Santos?" Clayton asked.

"The family court lady," Marlene answered. She looked at Sylvia and shook her head.

"*That's* right," Clayton said.

The family evaluation had taken place prior to the sale of the house, when all of Sylvia and Clayton's trappings of stability were still intact. The court wasn't likely to sympathize with grandparents who were about to take to the road, no matter how honorable their intentions.

Marlene sat down next to Sylvia on the bench seat opposite Clayton. Sylvia caught her studying the kitchen table between them. "This makes into a spare bed, right?" Marlene asked. Sylvia explained how the table collapsed and the two benches flopped out into a double bed.

"Gosh," Marlene said, "everything in this place folds up or pulls out."

"Not everything," Sylvia said, though the former owners had customized many of the trailer's features, and Clayton had mentioned a few of his own plans to make the most of what space they had. "I'll show you later," Sylvia promised. Marlene had already cooed over the clever, practical features of the trailer the first time Sylvia had shown her around. The slide-out bread board, which the trailer's previous owners had extended and converted into a fold-away ironing board, particularly impressed her. Marlene appeared not to hear Sylvia say, "The brand-new trailers are even more amazing."

"Well, I'm going to leave you ladies to your talking," Clayton said, folding the paper and slowly getting up. Sylvia noticed that since they'd moved into the trailer, Clayton had become more careful, not only around her but also with the things he used. Folding items to their smallest size, stashing them into drawers, he denied his old sprawling self, which once allowed papers and clothes and dishes to pile up haphazardly.

Clayton explained that he wanted to pick up a fire extinguisher and a replacement piece of carpet. "This place smells like a kennel," he said to Marlene, leaving Sylvia to explain how Poco had had a couple of accidents their first nights in the trailer.

When Sylvia had noticed Poco sitting in front of the refrigerator unit or the closet door, she'd simply ignored him. Now she wondered if the little dog hadn't wished that one of those openings led to a different place entirely, and not, like the trailer door, to his old yard, which was now patrolled by a sleek black Labrador.

Clayton rapped on the window and called, "I'm going to run by the plant and see when my pension checks kick in, too."

When the truck started up, Marlene took his seat, opposite Sylvia. "It's good he's got that pension," Marlene said.

16

Sylvia explained that by taking an early retirement, Clayton wouldn't get the full amount of his pension. But supplemented with the money from the sale of their house, their income would be sufficient.

"Well, they look pretty settled in," Marlene said, peering out the window.

"They should be," Sylvia said. "We left all the basics in the house. And then some."

"Did they ask you over yet?" Marlene asked.

Sylvia nodded. The couple *had* been generous in offering to let Sylvia and Clayton keep the trailer parked in front of the house while waiting to hear about the custody arrangements.

"Debra asked me if I wanted to use my old sewing machine," Sylvia said. The young woman had mentioned that Sylvia might want to make curtains or something for the trailer on the Singer in the basement.

But in the five days since the closing, Sylvia hadn't been able to bring herself to return to the house, which would smell of strangers and be arranged in a new way. She imagined herself bumping into the furniture like an old woman who'd suddenly lost control of her sensors. Sylvia wondered whether Debra's generosity would allow for use of the old place for a few hours if Mrs. Santos needed to make a return visit. The whole idea sounded like a predicament from *I Love Lucy*.

Although Sylvia hadn't gone back into the house, she'd watched it. Rodney left for work between eight-fifteen and eight-thirty each morning, Debra anywhere between nine and nine-thirty. Meetings after work as well as stops at the grocery and hardware stores (Sylvia recognized the different shopping bags) made the couple's evening arrival unpredictable. But within a year, Sylvia guessed, the Pinches' lives would be synchronized to a schedule you could set your watch by.

17

"I don't know," said Marlene, returning to the monetary discussion. "Even with the pension, a medical emergency could wipe you right out. Then you might never be able to buy another house."

Sylvia knew that Marlene's warning wasn't meant to be cruel. Marlene was only voicing her own concerns, which were always on the brink of being verbalized. "What if" preceded most of Marlene's worries, even though for a good part of the time "what if" never happened. It merely froze you in one place, where about all you could do was eat and watch TV and answer the telephone, which, hopefully, didn't bring bad news.

"Now, if it was me," Marlene said, pulling a few hairs at the back of her head, "I'd take a nice leisurely drive out to the Midwest. Blow all of this nonsense with Melvin clean out of my mind. And settle down in Chicago."

"Chicago?" Sylvia asked, suddenly paying attention.

"Isn't that where your people are from?"

"Milwaukee," Sylvia said. "A small town outside Milwaukee," she clarified. Marlene tapped herself on the head. Sylvia did plan to visit her hometown, but settling there was not an option. Sylvia had rejected a life working on her uncle's dairy farm, as well as marriage to Barry Wilcox, a cheese packager, forty years ago. She'd always felt out of place there as a girl, and returning now, at fifty-eight, with a house on wheels, would confirm far more than years of gossip about her whereabouts could have predicted.

"Oh, I don't know," Sylvia said. Marlene's stoic practicality made Sylvia rebellious. This must have been the way Janice had felt when she'd once talked to Sylvia about college experiences. When Janice met Melvin near the end of her first year of college and subsequently taunted Sylvia with new theories on everything from unisex dorms to "God is dead," Sylvia had felt forced to hold up the conservative side of each argument. Now she sensed herself opening up to accommodate a more liberal stance. "Maybe Clayton and I will never settle down again," Sylvia said. Sylvia stressed "settle down," as if that phrase were one Marlene had invented.

"Don't go getting crazy ideas," Marlene said. Sylvia was certain that Marlene forgave the strange ideas because of all the trouble with Janice. "Especially if you have that little baby with you," Marlene added.

Sylvia couldn't explain that her every child-rearing practice, which stressed the importance of safety and stability and consistency in punishments and bedtime hours and meals, had been jolted loose when Janice died. If from the start you weren't sure your body could carry a child carefully enough, and if after she'd been born you'd given her the most attentive upbringing, how could you understand when that child was freakishly shattered against a windshield and propelled to her death? How could you ever again believe in your own ability to protect? Because Sylvia couldn't say these things to Marlene without breaking down, she simply shrugged at the woman across from her.

"We'll see," said Sylvia, feeling the way she did when she was nervously awaiting that one card to win a gin game.

"I hope he doesn't get out," Marlene said.

"Who?" Sylvia said, looking toward Poco.

"Melvin," Marlene said softly. Sylvia often ignored Marlene's paranoia, but this she paid attention to. She lit a cigarette.

Sylvia wished she could tell the court that if she and Clayton were allowed to raise little Rita in the trailer, the girl wouldn't necessarily have a room of her own or a backyard or constant playmates, but maybe she would have something better. Maybe she'd never stay in one place long enough to grow so bored with it that she'd resort to drugs and the wrong kinds of boys, or so familiar with it that she'd become falsely confident of sharp turns in a road she knew by heart.

After dinner, while Clayton installed a smoke detector above the kitchen area, Sylvia measured the floor space so they could cut the new rug first thing in the morning. "Before Miss Crumb Cake shows up," Clayton had stipulated. Sylvia had given him one of her "you'd better watch it" looks, but then smiled. Marlene could distract you from chores all morning if you let her.

Clayton had taken Sylvia's suggestion and kept a list of jobs that needed completing before they took off. By selecting a couple of items to concentrate on each day, he stayed occupied and seemed not to fall into moping about Janice so frequently.

Sylvia hadn't shown herself to be the best example of her own advice. Many times when she was absorbed in packing up the old house, Clayton had come on her exhausted and wet-faced. But lately, now that most of her work was done, she was less likely to give herself over to the sadness. Sylvia's relief from depression would come not with the distraction of work but with the physical leave-taking.

If Sylvia blamed Clayton for taking her suggestion of a vacation way too far, she never totally rejected his plan to leave their old home behind. All their married life, Clayton had agreed to Sylvia's decisions about the house — how they should decorate it and arrange its interior, what they should bring into it and remove from it, what they should eat and wear in it. Sylvia had surrounded the three of them with possessions. Objects and clothes had grown up around Sylvia's family like layers of insulation against the outside world. Sylvia had been a hoarder since she was a girl, saving every ticket stub, dried corsage, and old doll loved to a fragile mass of limbs. After she married and they bought the house, everything assumed a place, even the cork from a bottle of champagne opened on their fifth wedding anniversary. But Sylvia hadn't been able to save what she treasured most of all, her daughter.

Sometimes when she had sat alone in the house, after-noons back when Janice had first left to live with Melvin and Clayton was still at work, Sylvia felt numb. Surrounded by an excess of appliances and clothes — two televisions, eight saucepans, sixteen pairs of pants — she'd lost track of who she was. Clayton had made her realize that she'd held on to objects unnecessarily, unconsciously. Until she was in the middle of getting rid of them, Sylvia hadn't recognized how many things she and Clayton actually owned.

When Janice died, Sylvia became aware of a drastic change taking place in the house every time she moved, even slightly. The books on both shelves in the living room, the English tea set, the furniture throughout the rooms seemed to go slack. Janice had been the core, the force keeping every physical detail tautly in place. The initial thought of her, of a family, had been the reason they'd bought the house in the first place.

Clayton had started the discarding. One morning after Janice's accident, but before they'd thought of selling their house, Sylvia awoke to find every belonging of their daugh-ter's moved to a neat stack in the garage. She was surprised to see how much stuff Janice hadn't taken to the Baltimore apartment she'd shared with Melvin — old records, paper-backs, near-empty bottles of perfume, heaps of colorful clothes. Piled all together in the garage, Janice's property was substantial. When the items had been dispersed throughout the room in their appropriate places on shelves and in drawers and a closet, they hadn't affected Sylvia so strongly.

"I'm going to get somebody to help me with her bedroom furniture, too," Clayton had told — not asked — Sylvia that

21

morning. But before his friend Bud Harper arrived, Sylvia discovered Clayton struggling with Janice's old bureau himself.

Sylvia was used to Clayton tossing things. If he was cooking eggs and they didn't look just the way he wanted, he'd been known to throw them out, pan and all. Later, when everything had cooled off, she'd retrieve the pan. Clayton would never have the ingenuity to save a meal that wasn't turning out right, even with hungry dinner guests waiting in the next room. Once, when the Orioles lost four games in a row, Clayton didn't scream and curse, but the next morning he told Sylvia they needed a new clock radio and promptly got rid of the old one. While Sylvia had tolerated Clayton's casting off food, a toaster, a pair of shoes, a faulty yet usable lawn mower, she wasn't quite sure how to deal with his reaction to death.

After Janice's possessions disappeared behind the heavy doors of the Goodwill truck, the room that had once been filled with dolls and music and giggling telephone conversations was painted white. It stood empty, full of echoes and smelling of paint. The room reminded Sylvia of a scar, pale and shiny compared to the other rooms. The house had suffered a wound at least as large as one of its rooms.

But Janice's empty room had only initially debilitated Sylvia. Gradually the white space had made her feel light, free of something. And she thought she had come to feel what Clayton had always known.

Sylvia hadn't cried at Janice's funeral. The closed casket covered with hundreds of pale pink roses had taken her breath away, but she hadn't cried until she'd begun to sort her household goods with the same resolve that Clayton had demonstrated when he'd emptied Janice's room. With each possession that was dropped onto one of Sylvia's piles, another sensation seemed to return. She was amazed that discarding something as inconsequential as a small, silver-plated hand mirror could make her cry for a good half hour.

Although the individual decisions about what to keep and what to leave in their house had been difficult, Sylvia eventually felt relief. When she'd finished choosing among her belongings and thought of her new, uncomplicated life, she was full of energy. At nearly sixty, she and Clayton could start over, return to the time before they'd thought of buying a house or conceiving Janice, before they'd even kissed. Only now, if everything went as Sylvia hoped, they'd have Janice's baby, Rita, as proof that once they'd lived like everyone else.

"Well, that's done and out of the way," Clayton said, pointing at the smoke detector. He sidled up to Sylvia. "The farther we go, the better it's going to be," he said softly.

"As long as we have Rita," Sylvia said. She felt Clayton squeeze her hand.

Sylvia thought once again of the way retirement would press her and Clayton together. She hoped that they wouldn't be in each other's way too much. Clayton told Sylvia stories about a couple of his retired friends from Evergreen, who'd relayed their wives' complaints. The women resented their husbands' need for a specific schedule, which, for years, the workplace had required — what time is lunch? what time are you leaving? what time are you getting back? Fred Walker said that his wife had started drinking and then answering all his routine questions with, "When I finish my drink, that's when." Sylvia suspected Anita Walker had been drinking all along, and that Fred just hadn't noticed until he really spent some time with her.

Sylvia figured that she and Clayton could work things out so long as they had little Rita in one of those special car seats when they pulled away from Garden Road. When she'd finished writing down the measurements of their floor space, she opened the trailer door and looked out. She turned and said to

Clayton, "It just gives me the creeps. Them in our old house."
After a puff of cigarette, she said, more to herself than to him,
"Them in our old clothes."

"Then stop looking the hell over there," Clayton said.

"Want to go for a walk?" Sylvia asked, throwing the cigarette
down. The last thing she wanted was a fight with Clayton that
would leave her nerves jangled for the next couple of days.

They hadn't walked together in years, but Clayton didn't ask
questions. Setting his screwdriver on the small countertop, he
immediately followed her outside. Poco trotted behind them,
his tail stiff between his legs.

After Janice had been born, Sylvia had coerced Clayton into
walking with her because she'd wanted to get back into shape.
They'd taken turns carrying the baby as they walked past the
houses on their street and the beginnings of houses on the next
street over. In spite of all the exercise, Sylvia never did regain
her figure; Janice had added permanent inches to her body.

Besides Marlene, the neighbors seldom talked to her and
Clayton these days. Without stopping, they'd merely nod in
acknowledgment on their way to and from work or the store, as
if they were afraid grief and abandonment were as contagious
as a virus. The neighborhood was filled with a great cloud of
silence, like the time the apple-spraying plane, manned by a
drunken Terry Wurms, had mistakenly flown beyond the
bounds of Mr. Fritch's orchards and sprayed two rows of
houses. For weeks after, the blocks remained silent of birds and
insects and even voices. Only the occasional slam of a car door
broke the streetwide stupor.

Sylvia was certain that as she and Clayton walked hand in
hand, inside each of the lit houses neighbors talked about
them. They used adjectives like *sad, crazy, surprising, out of character*. But from where she was, Sylvia could hear only the mum-
bling of window fans, the clashing of dinner plates, and pans

being washed and put away. Each brick house with painted trim was an echo of the one preceding it, a prediction of the one beyond. Sylvia wondered if the neighborhood understood what she and Clayton had recently come to believe: the security that everyone had tried to establish on these streets just wasn't reliable. Jobs with hospitalization and pension plans weren't safety nets. Nothing was guaranteed.

When she and Clayton had first bought their house in 1949 in the middle of a line of twelve, no other streets existed in the neighborhood. "Give it time," Clayton's sister, Lucille, had said. She lived in a Baltimore neighborhood thick with houses. And year after year more houses and streets had popped up all around Sylvia and Clayton, as if the twelve original ones had seeded themselves and spread. Now the streets of houses went on and on like a great field of corn.

Although it was only mid-June, trees stood dense and still with summer. The two honey locusts Sylvia had nursed into fine, twenty-foot trees mocked the small house below them. She wondered if she could ever give up on her neighborhood entirely — its dull continuous cackle of TV, its smell of cooking that in summer extended into the squares of backyards smoky with barbecuing meat, its above-ground pools whining like huge mosquitoes in the background.

Though they didn't speak of the situation, both Sylvia and Clayton were nervous about the question of Rita. So long as no one at family court found out about the travel trailer, Sylvia figured she and Clayton had a good shot at getting custody. The trailer stood before the neighborhood day after day, with its aluminum reflecting sunlight like the bright yellow of a permanent caution sign in the road. Sylvia hoped her neighbors wouldn't give her away if Mrs. Santos came back unannounced.

The iffy situation reminded Sylvia of the tenuous time before Janice was conceived, when every aspect of her life seemed to have some influence on what would happen — if I step on a crack, if there's no mail today, if a squirrel runs up Karen Walsh's front step — and was a sign of their success at reproducing. Each month she felt Clayton want to ask but not ask, "Are you?" "Will we?" and Sylvia prayed ("Please make this happen") that the beginning of a baby had taken hold inside her. And would continue beyond six or eight weeks.

Seeming to sense her mood, Clayton squeezed Sylvia's hand. "It'll all be fine once we get on the road."

"We'll see," said Sylvia, breaking the moment between them. She thought Clayton was right, but she didn't want him assuming she was entrusting herself to him altogether. She wanted to be able to blame someone if things didn't work out.

"You know, Sylvia, we can go anywhere you want. We can head for the West Coast." Other than a couple of trips to Sylvia's hometown in Wisconsin, Clayton had never left Maryland.

The idea was suddenly as intoxicating as Andy Schaeffer's honeysuckle bush just ahead. She'd been concentrating more on what they were leaving than on where they were headed.

"Florida?" she asked. She thought of beaches and fresh oranges and young women with blonde hair. If she was going to give up most of her stability, it wouldn't hurt to have predictable weather at least.

"It could be Florida. Texas. Could be anywhere." She knew he was figuring that if they got custody of their granddaughter, they'd want to be moving as far away from Baltimore as possible.

"Everything will work out," Clayton said again, this time, she thought, more to convince himself than her. "One way or another," he added.

Sylvia would be willing to live in the Ozarks if she and

Clayton could have Rita. "Rita, my little senorita," Janice used to say. Sylvia sighed. "Well, I just hope the tomatoes come out good for the Pinches. After all the bragging I did on Maryland tomatoes." Sylvia had started the plants from seeds months before Janice's accident.

"Tomatoes always taste good."

"Some years you can get too much rain and then they go all mushy inside."

"I don't know what the hell you're talking about, Sylvia." He put his big arm around her and forced a laugh.

TWO

―――――◆・◆・◆―――――

"C ome on, Sylvia. Let's get this show on the road," Clayton called from the window of the truck cab. It *would* be a show, Sylvia thought, the securely hitched trailer rolling out into the world for all to see.

Clayton had filled the truck with gas the night before, and she'd heard him cleaning the windshield before she'd even slipped out of bed. He'd told her he wanted to get an early start before the day heated up to the hellfire weather they'd been having lately, but Sylvia had become involved with one thing after another. She'd said, "Right after breakfast, Clayton, and we can take off." Then later, "Right after lunch, Clayton."

After lunch it was 95 degrees. Clayton complained that the fresh, pastel plaid shirt he'd put on after his morning shower now clung to him like another skin. Sylvia conceded that it *was* a little sticky. These days she could deal with the heat better than Clayton — and she from Wisconsin, where she remembered once ice skating in May. As he made a fifth "final check" through the trailer, Clayton said that with all of the postponements of the hearing, all the lawyers' rigmarole delaying, starting, then putting off once again the proceedings to "protect little Rita Kondrake's interests," half the summer was gone.

"Sylvia," he called, "I'm going to just take off with you back there."

"It's against the law," she yelled out the closest window. Sylvia had researched state regulations.

"How's anybody going to know what's going on back there so long as you don't hang your feet out the window?"

"In a minute," Sylvia hollered. "One more minute and I'm ready." A frown crossed baby Rita's forehead, and she prepared to cry, but Sylvia hushed her while securing a fresh diaper. Sylvia already found she had to adjust almost every habit now that Rita was with them — her tone of voice, her reaction speed, the time she went to bed and woke up.

The cute, round face of her seven-month-old granddaughter reminded Sylvia of Janice, but she couldn't remember if Janice's hair had been so dark. Summers before she started school, when she played by herself in the sunny, fenced backyard, Janice had perfectly straight hair that was practically white. Rita let out a squeal, catching Sylvia's attention. Rita's eyes were blue; Janice's had been gray. Sylvia had heard somewhere, maybe from Clayton's sister, who wasn't always reliable with facts, that all babies had blue eyes. Sylvia hoped that Rita's eyes would stay blue or turn gray like Janice's.

Melvin's eyes had caught Sylvia's and held them when she'd spotted him in court. They were black as two bottomless holes. Sylvia had read about black holes. Although she'd been fanning herself with a piece of newspaper in the stuffy courtroom, Melvin's stare had given her goose bumps.

Over the years, Sylvia had spent countless hours puzzling over what a girl as pretty as Janice saw in Melvin. Melvin was six feet and lanky, his forehead shone with oil; and he wore his pants too short and his hair too long.

On her back, Rita cooed and reached for her feet. Despite having Melvin for a father, the baby was perfect. Her tiny fingers and toes, arms and legs amazed Sylvia. But there was no telling if even a perfect baby would be prone to drugs or boys or other trouble later on. So many things couldn't be predicted. Only last week, Sylvia had read about a teenage boy who'd murdered his parents and hidden them in the basement freezer.

Clayton was always telling Sylvia she read too many far-out stories. He'd said they'd do their best with Rita, which was all that could be expected. Besides, now that they were hitting the road, there was no telling about anything — who they'd meet, if their pension would hold out, if they'd be able to find a doctor when they needed one. Clayton had said he could go on, but there was no sense bothering over things that couldn't be counted on to happen.

"What's going on back here?" Clayton said as he opened the trailer door.

"All set," Sylvia answered.

She wondered if he could tell from the tone of her voice, from the fact that she avoided looking at him directly, that she was a little emotional about finally pulling away from Garden Road. Clayton sat on the corner of the kitchen bench, his body bent forward, his hands on his knees, ready to spring into movement as soon as she gave the signal.

"You grab Poco," she said.

If it wasn't for Clayton insisting that their life change drastically, Sylvia would have taken a two- or three-week vacation and then returned right here to go on making her small adjustments to situations. Already she'd become friendly with the Pinches, inviting them for a stuffed pepper and mashed potato dinner in the trailer a few nights ago. Just last week, Clayton

30

had said he didn't think anything could destroy a resilient person like Sylvia. Then he'd proceeded to confess that he'd never had enough strength himself to stay and bear a situation out.

He reached up and put his arm around her waist. "We can't sit here forever, Sylvia."

"I know that," she said stiffly.

"We do have a baby to think of," he said as she positioned Rita on her hip.

Clayton stood up and tickled Rita under the chin, and the baby laughed and pulled into herself.

"Poco," Sylvia said to remind him of the dog thumping his black tail in front of the refrigerator.

"Before we take off," Clayton said, "let me show you something."

"I thought you were in such a hurry," Sylvia said, though she knew it irritated him when she turned his own words back against him. Her nervousness made her testy. But what would be the point, she told herself, in getting a nasty little disagreement started just as they were ready to embark on their adventure? An argument now would be a pretty bad sign.

He led the way outside to the back of the trailer, where he had drawn a good-size outline of the United States, with each of the states carefully delineated. Clayton patted his back pocket, which held a pack of permanent markers for coloring in the states as they passed through them. Maryland was already distinguished in bright red, such a small achievement in relation to the whole silvery country. The color made her think of the accident, and she gave Rita a little hug. What had Clayton been thinking, choosing red for Maryland?

The colored shape of Clayton's home state was the first item in an agenda to be ticked off, like a list of chores or groceries. And when the tasks were completed, the map shaded with color, they'd have completed whatever they were now setting out to do. And then what?

"Don't we at least have to stay overnight before we color them?"

Clayton shook his head slowly. "I haven't decided yet," he said.

"One more minute," Sylvia said, handing Rita to Clayton and rushing off to find her camera. Then she took photographs of the old house, the trailer, the trailer with the house showing in the background, Clayton holding Rita and saying, "Enough."

Finally in the cab of the truck, Sylvia secured Rita in the car seat between herself and her husband. Poco curled up by Sylvia's feet and began whining the way he did when he was on the way to the vet's. When Clayton started the truck, the sadness of inevitability passed through Sylvia's body and caught in her throat. It reminded her of the day she'd dressed Janice for her first day of school. She had studied her daughter in her new blue dress and dark red shoes knowing that Janice was taking a first step without her. That was the start of Janice meeting teachers and other students who would influence her; her little girl no longer belonged to her and Clayton exclusively.

Today Sylvia considered herself. Traveling away from the place that had been her home for so long, she imagined bits of herself dropping off and remaining on the trail of colored states they left behind. She would no longer be a person defined by her house and backyard. If she was frightened, she consoled herself with the fact that now she would see some of the places she'd only read about or that Janice had told her about. Feeling her face going out of control as tears filled her eyes, Sylvia turned from Clayton. Staring out the truck's passenger window, she watched houses fall away and become smaller and smaller, almost toys. The things that stayed close to you, you didn't think about losing: the house, the lawn, the neighbors. You worried about smaller things then — a burned-out light bulb, a leaky pipe in the basement, an overdone roast.

Rich people could take chances with their lives because they could afford to, and poor people could because they didn't have anything to give up, really. The middle class, thought Sylvia, valued things that could vanish with carelessness. That blanket of safety, flung over first-mortgaged homes and dependable cars and the buffer of neighbors keeping watch over everything, was revered. It was not something to be thrown off lightly if you got a little too warm.

"We're going to have a great time," Clayton said. Sylvia thought he sounded too enthusiastic, as if he were trying to convince a child. "Just take it easy, Vee."

In all their years of marriage, Clayton had never called her anything other than Sylvia. Not "honey" or "babe" or one of those terms of endearment she often envied. Vee, the middle part of her name, sounded light and cheerful, and Sylvia found it fitting that she should have a new, abbreviated name at a time of such great change in her life.

"I'm so glad," Sylvia said, holding on to one of the baby's kicking legs.

She didn't have to finish her sentence. She was sure Clayton knew. They were both relieved to have gotten custody of the child easily, to have kept the secret about their plans to travel and avoided having Mrs. Santos from family court see the trailer.

They had been ecstatic in the courtroom when they were awarded custody of their grandchild. Clayton had taken Rita from Sylvia and would have tossed her in the air like a winning football if Sylvia hadn't restrained him. She'd scrutinized the dark, somber eyes of Melvin's relatives and the polished dark wood in the courtroom before turning toward the door. Looking back on the situation, it really wouldn't have made any sense for Melvin's sister, Samantha, to keep Rita. Besides working on women's nails and hair, Samantha tended bar nights. Sylvia would tell anyone that Samantha wasn't capable of making a decent meal. And yet the threat of Samantha's wanting Rita, coupled with the Vaeths' plan to pull up roots, and, Sylvia had to admit, their age, had worried her up to the last minute.

Even though Janice had once said that Melvin and Samantha's parents didn't like being referred to as grandparents, Sylvia had also fretted over the couple's ability to deliberately complicate the situation. But the Kondrakes had appeared relieved when Sylvia and Clayton left the courtroom with Rita, almost grateful that some uncomfortable part of their life was finally over. And Sylvia's other worry, that the court would determine a foster family to be in Rita's best interest, had been unfounded as well.

What Sylvia hadn't anticipated was that after the court formalities, Melvin, who even clean-shaven somehow looked scruffy, would approach them, bend to Rita in Sylvia's arms, and kiss the baby gently on the forehead.

"Sweetheart," Melvin said so softly it sounded like an exhalation. Sylvia hadn't imagined the weird man capable of such tenderness.

"Come on, son," Melvin's father had said, clearing his throat and leading Melvin off.

Clayton had said he didn't care if Rita grew up to be the wife of a chicken farmer so long as she was happy. Sylvia decided not to press Rita to attend college as she'd done with Janice, or to pin her down with questions like, "What do you want to *do* with your life?"

Sylvia wasn't sure Clayton would know what she was talking about if she tried to explain what she'd learned from Janice: you shouldn't have children just to live out the dreams you weren't able to realize yourself. Clayton would tell her that kind of talk was just her feeling guilty, somehow blaming herself for what had happened to Janice. All Sylvia knew was that it would be different with Rita. Rita was their second chance.

Rita's eyes began to droop and her head sank toward her chest; the excitement of leaving Garden Road had exhausted her.

"It's the truck moving that does it," Sylvia said. Clayton nodded and adjusted the radio dial. Sylvia wanted to say, "Remember when Janice would throw one of her fits when she was going through the terrible twos, and the only way I could calm her down was to pack her into the Oldsmobile and drive out to the lake? She'd fall asleep before I ever got there." But Clayton was humming along with a song on the radio, and Sylvia didn't want to disturb him.

The motion of the truck, the warm air fast on her face, didn't make Sylvia sleepy. It invigorated her. The familiar neighborhoods were well behind them now; the highway stretched far ahead. Clayton stepped hard on the gas, and the rig surged forward. Sylvia looked over at her smiling husband. He'd told her he'd always wanted to run away from home, and finally, at fifty-nine, that was exactly what he was doing.

The first time he'd told her about his family, she got tears in her eyes. Clayton's father had abandoned his family when Clayton was four and his sister, Lucille, had just started to walk. Clayton grew up feeling that his mother and sister aligned him with the runaway father simply because of his sex. And when he married Sylvia and moved an hour away from the family house in Baltimore, his sister and mother twisted the relocation into desertion. He'd told Sylvia that unless he had a few too many beers, the bounds of their nagging were never far away.

Clayton's mother had so favored Lucille, especially when it came to schoolwork, that Clayton finally gave up trying to please. He dropped out of school when he was sixteen and began running errands for a couple of builders. When he handed over his meager "contribution to the family household," as his mother described it, she would cluck her tongue, not with thanks, he said, but in acknowledgment that his debt as a man was paid, at least for one more week. Sylvia hoped that all those years of his mother's pressure and Lucille's self-righteousness, which she wore like bad makeup, were peeling off Clayton as he drove west.

"Slow down," Sylvia said, not wanting him to get too crazy. "You can't stop this load on a dime." Clayton checked the speedometer.

He drove into the Allegheny Mountains, the cooler air refreshing them. "Let me know if you want to make any side trips off of here," he said.

"I'll tell you the exit," she said. He would follow the main highways; she would urge him off their straightforward route and onto narrow roads pointing deep into the countryside and mountains. Although he was the one who had originally wanted to travel, Sylvia saw herself, now that she'd gotten started, as the more curious explorer of the two, getting them lost and then, in their bewilderment, leading them to an unexpected treasure.

Included in the box of mementos on Sylvia's lap was an accumulation of newspaper and magazine clippings, some dating back before she was married, the latest featured in the *Sunday Sun* just the week before. She was glad this collection hadn't gone the way of her stamps and matchbooks and salt and pepper shakers. Maybe she'd always suspected that one day she would travel the United States and put to use the articles, pictures, and mere mentions of interesting places. These weren't routine tourist attractions like Kennedy's grave — though she wouldn't mind seeing the eternal flame — but odd and bizarre sites. Sylvia's favorite, the one she wanted most to see, was the Talking Animal Farm in Illinois.

Sylvia was more interested in traveling to the Gourd Museum and the Hot Dog Capital of the World than to the U.S. Mint or the Metropolitan Museum of Art. Even Clayton had become intrigued when she showed him a story mentioning Weeki Wachee in Florida, where mermaids swam underwater and drank Cokes at the same time. And these were just the places Sylvia had learned about. There was no telling how many more coves of craziness lay tucked away in towns with names revealing few clues to their strangeness. Baldwin, Blue Earth, Sumner, Durant, Troy. Sylvia hoped that she and Clayton wouldn't run out of unusual places to visit, and at the same time have a chance to see them all. Especially the many weird attractions they were sure to find in California.

Rita fussed and Sylvia opened the fully stocked diaper bag in search of a bottle of juice. Rita's tiny fingers grasped the bottle along with Sylvia's. The infant gazed into Sylvia's face, then was distracted by movement outside the truck.

"The Freshwater Fisherman's Museum is just outside of Pittsburgh," Sylvia said. She was certain Clayton would appreciate the collection of lures and photos of amazing-size trout and bass, as well as the world's largest night crawler, preserved in a fish tank.

"Just give me some advance notice," Clayton said.

"OK," she agreed, supporting the bottle with one hand and with the other sifting through the many yellowed clippings for places located on their way to Milwaukee.

"Oh my God!" said Sylvia.

"What is it?" Clayton said, instinctively looking toward the baby. Rita twisted and frowned at the confusion.

"I thought that was Melvin's car," Sylvia said, squinting in the direction of a dark blue Ford.

"For Christ's sake, Sylvia. Forget about Melvin. He's in the booby hatch." He said her "Oh my God!" made him think of crib death, even though he knew the baby was fine beside him in the car seat.

"We've got the courts on our side," Clayton said, after a minute. "We've got custody, don't forget. It's all legal." After another minute he said, "Besides, his car wasn't blue, was it?"

Sylvia settled back into her seat, unable to tell her husband what she had tucked in the box with the clippings of possible places to visit: a letter from Melvin. The letter had arrived ten days before, during the hiatus before the rescheduled hearing, and it read, "Dear Grandparents, I'll get her no matter what." It was signed in Melvin's tight, obsessively regular handwriting, the letters pressed even closer together with the aid of a felt-tipped pen. Sylvia didn't want to think of what Clayton might do if he knew about the letter. When she'd first read the letter, she shook. The carefully written words were full of all the determination Melvin had shown when he'd started going out with Janice. Then, his facial expression had said, "I'm going to marry your daughter whether you like it or not."

Janice hadn't taken drugs before she met Melvin; she hadn't ever been a bit of trouble. Oh, she and Sylvia had normal, mother-daughter squabbles about makeup and clothes, but no major differences while Janice was learning to assert her independence. Then Janice met Melvin and college plans were exchanged for marriage ones as easily as different dress sizes.

The few times that Melvin and Janice had eaten Sunday dinner at the Vaeth house, he'd told outlandish stories, such as the one about his four-year-old cousin lifting a station wagon. Janice hadn't questioned Melvin's statements — "I ate one more hot dog than the guy in the *Guinness Book of World Records*.

Trouble was, I didn't have a witness" — but merely giggled at the assertions. Sylvia had held back from embarrassing Melvin with remarks like, "Come on — you don't expect us to believe that, now do you?" She had simply smiled politely and insistently passed him seconds, as if the platters of steaming-hot meat and vegetables would coax him back to reality.

Sylvia hoped that Rita would never succumb to such lies. She prayed that all ties to Melvin would be cut as easily as she planned to drop the child's last name. When introducing her to people on their travels, Sylvia had decided to call her grandchild Rita Vaeth.

"Oh no," Sylvia said. "You'd better pull over. I think Poco's getting sick." The little dog's body heaved back and forth; its mouth pointed at Sylvia's sandaled feet, which she pressed up against the car door.

"I've got to find a spot," Clayton said, sounding annoyed. He told her easing back into traffic once they got the dog straightened out would be a pain in the ass.

"Clayton," Sylvia pleaded, "just stop. You're not selecting a house site, you know."

"Jesus," said Clayton. "You'd think I was driving a Volkswagen." Sylvia was astounded that, even in his fit of frustration, he'd allowed the word *Volkswagen* out of his mouth. He didn't look over at Sylvia. Janice had driven a Volkswagen — light blue, secondhand, with a sunroof that Clayton had installed himself.

"Forget it, Clayton. Too late," Sylvia said just as the sharp smell reached Clayton's nose.

"Shit," said Clayton, exiting the highway. He slowed to a crawl and pulled into a diner at the end of the ramp. He was driving the way he might if he were hauling something as huge and priceless as a dinosaur. Cars honked and flustered him.

"Forget about those morons," Sylvia said.

Just as Clayton shut off the truck's engine, Rita began to cry. "Oh, baby," Sylvia said, reaching for Rita while carefully avoiding the orangish puddle on the floor. Holding Rita and dragging Poco by his leash, Sylvia headed across the parking lot and into a field behind the diner. She walked in the grass, then deep into weeds that stretched above Poco's head. She kept moving until she was out of view of the diner's customers and Rita had quieted. Poco trotted out in front, breaking through the sea of tall grass. For a while, Sylvia simply followed, glad to be moving her legs, stiff from so much sitting. She imagined that animal instinct had given Poco the urge to lead her to a special, maybe picturesque, place. But when the dog finally came to a stop at the edge of the grass, they stood merely opposite the far end of the diner. Weathered garbage lined the boundary of the parking lot.

From where she was, the trailer resembled a miniature version of the diner. Sylvia took the lead across the blacktop and back to the truck. Clayton stood in the parking lot talking to a man in khaki pants and a matching shirt, which looked like some kind of uniform but wasn't.

"Earl, this is my wife, Sylvia," Clayton said. Earl nodded at Sylvia, then reached over and tweaked Rita's cheek with his thumb and forefinger. She hoped Clayton wouldn't say that Rita was their granddaughter; then they'd have to tell this stranger the whole story. But Earl didn't focus on Rita. As Sylvia studied Earl, he pushed his glasses up the bridge of his nose three times. And when she freed a hand to shake his, he held the glasses up all the while with his left hand.

"Earl owns the diner there," Clayton said. All three of them turned to look at the large, bullet-shaped building.

"Earl says we can stay in the lot for the night," Clayton said. Sylvia noticed that Earl's forearms were blue with tattoos.

"There's storm warnings out for tonight," Earl said.

She smelled Lysol coming from the truck as Clayton explained they could get free parking for the night in return for helping Earl set up and serve a dinner of hot turkey sandwiches to the members of the Calvary Presbyterian and Community United Methodist church baseball teams.

"There's a dinner like this nearly every month. Usually, I call on a few extra waitresses. But I figured you folks might want to work something out." He took a deep breath, as if he'd just surfaced from a dive. "Plus, I can give you a good price on the dinners for yourselves. After we're done serving, you understand." He looked at Sylvia and added, "All you can eat." He laughed. "Provided the Bible thumpers don't finish it first." He went on to explain how the team from Redeemer Lutheran had eaten 140 meatballs one Sunday in May.

Sylvia didn't like Earl's take-advantage attitude.

"Can't beat that can we, Sylvia?" Clayton asked.

"That's nice of you, Earl, but I thought we'd try to make it to the campgrounds. It should only be a couple of hours away," Sylvia replied. She shifted the baby to her left hip. What exactly did he think they'd do with Rita while they were serving all-you-can-eat to the church-going athletes?

Clayton acted surprised — maybe that instead of pulling him aside first, she'd spoken directly to Earl. He shrugged his shoulders.

"Suit yourself," said Earl, obviously disappointed.

Sylvia guessed from the ruddy color of his face that Earl would spend half the night drinking, maybe even here in the trailer with Clayton. Earl looked like a man who lived alone and preyed on the ears and kindness of strangers.

"Good luck outrunning the storm," Earl called as he headed back to the diner.

"What's got into you?" Clayton asked. "He was a perfectly decent man."

41

"Clayton, you know we've got reservations at Deer Hill."
Clayton didn't answer. The brightly colored brochure sat directly in front of her on the dashboard. She'd studied the folded glossy paper for weeks — the aerial shot of 400 campsites winding like a wide river along boundaries deep green with trees, the picture in the center of a huge blue swimming pool, and the smaller photos of people playing volleyball, square dancing on a hardwood floor, fishing in shiny lake water.

Even without the reservations, Sylvia didn't want to be setting up for the night right off the highway like a huge, silvery sitting duck. At a trailer park or campground they could blend in with other travelers. Although she was probably being irrational, she didn't feel far enough away from Melvin to be able to relax in the open. Earl's slippery nose had even put her in mind of Melvin's oily face.

"Well, let's get moving then," Clayton said.

She heard irritation in his voice. Their first day on the road and things weren't going nearly so smoothly as she'd anticipated. She had to worry about the baby now. Under different circumstances she might have gone along with Clayton and put up right here, had a nice hot turkey dinner — the two of them for under ten dollars — and then later maybe a drink with Earl.

"Let me feed the baby before you take off," Sylvia said.

"Can't you feed her while we're moving?" She made Clayton wait until she found a bottle, then he put the truck in gear and drove back toward the highway. Sometimes it felt as if she'd just cleaned up after feeding Rita and the baby would be ready to eat again.

"How come the only time men really get talking is after they've had a few drinks?" Sylvia said, trying to make conversation and heal over his annoyance at her.

"Hmm," he said. It was more a noise than an answer.

Rita flailed her arms and let out a scream.

"Whose side is she on?" he asked, and Sylvia smiled.

When Clayton was still working at Evergreen, he'd stop by the Crow's Nest tavern a couple of times a week after work. Every once in a while he'd tell Sylvia what his coworkers talked about. It could be anything from safety regulations at the plant to POWs. In between opinions, Sylvia pictured the men gently aiming their beers at their mouths. One of the men, Sylvia thought his name was Dan, talked about Vietnam when he got drunk. Sylvia couldn't imagine what she and Clayton would have done if they'd had a son sent to a foreign place to fight. She wondered if it would have been harder to have had a son vulnerable to the horrors of war than to suddenly recognize that tragedy was everywhere, as Janice had demonstrated.

Now that Sylvia and Clayton had Rita, they'd decided not to worry about the pervasive danger of motoring, because Rita had already survived a major car accident. Sylvia took her cue from the immune system; if you had German measles as a kid, you were unlikely to get them again.

Sylvia opened the window. If Melvin left them alone, the images of the accident and the anxiety of the court hearing would soon disappear as easily as stale air from the truck. Sylvia looked straight ahead into the evening sky, going gray before her eyes, and at the highway connecting at some very distant point with the gray. If you drove far enough you could drive into the sky, and then up, and then there was no telling what road conditions would be if you ran into a cloud. She felt good just letting her mind go all crazy like that.

Poco trembled at Sylvia's feet. He stopped shaking only long enough to lick at his lips.

"What's he going on about?" Clayton asked.

Sylvia checked to be sure that Poco hadn't messed the floor

well again. That was all she needed, another fragrant cleanup job.

"Must be that storm Earl warned about," Sylvia said. At the time, she'd thought that Earl had made up the whole business about threatening weather just to entice them to stay on at the diner.

"How in the hell he can sense a storm so far off beats me," Clayton said, shaking his head and glancing at the dog.

"Maybe he can smell it," Sylvia said, offering information from a television show she'd seen on the amazing abilities of house pets. Poco got shook up when he did something wrong and anticipated the consequences (a swat from a rolled-up newspaper) and, like Sylvia, when he sensed trouble.

Poco had never liked Melvin. Janice would have taken the little dog when she married except that he voiced his stubborn disapproval of Melvin. The first time Janice brought Melvin to Garden Road, Poco had jumped onto Melvin's lap. Melvin's immediate response was to stand up and send the confused animal tumbling to the floor. Later, Poco made off with a snapshot of Melvin from Janice's room, took it under the bed, and proceeded to tear it apart. Sylvia didn't let on that she'd shaken the photo in Poco's face to get him worked up. After that, the only time Sylvia heard the animal growl was in Melvin's presence. Poco didn't let up snarling until Melvin was well out of sight.

The baby appeared to pick up Poco's anxiety and began writhing in the car seat. Trying to distract her, Sylvia held up a rattle shaped like a crab. Sylvia wished she could shake off her own worries like the dog, just vibrate until they lost their hold and fell right off her. The first major stop on their travels would be outside Milwaukee, and although it was a couple of days away, she was already concerned about the visit.

Sylvia's parents were both dead, but her brother, Tom, and

sister, Claire, still lived less than a half hour from the family house, which hadn't sold in the three years it had been on the market. When Tom and Claire first heard about the Vaeths' plans to move from Garden Road, they'd suggested that Sylvia and Clayton move into the family house. Now that they were getting older, Tom and Claire wanted a reminder that their older sister was still among them; everyone claimed that Sylvia was the likeness of her mother. Clayton had said, "Don't get any ideas. This is going to be a visit. Two weeks tops."

Sylvia had assured him that she didn't intend to move back to Milwaukee, where she felt claustrophobic whenever she neared the neighborhood. At the thought of the box-size rooms with their dark upholstery and thick rugs, she fretted that she would sink into the heavy armchairs and not be able to get up. Still, her best intentions could be chipped away by a well-meaning, if selfish, family. Sylvia most feared that she'd be eighteen again, on her way out the door to catch a train that would take her far away from predictability, and that this time she'd allow guilt to lasso her.

"Jesus," Clayton said when the first crack of thunder surprised him.

The wind picked up, thumped the truck, and pressed at the load they were hauling. Leaves on the roadside trees flipped over to reveal pale green undersides. Small twisters of ground leaves and trash spun along the roadside.

"Look," Sylvia said softly. She wanted to get Clayton's attention but not distract him so that he lost his concentration entirely. Sylvia pointed out a birch bent halfway to the ground, its leaves rattling in the fast air.

"Earl sure called this one right," Clayton said as if he'd known the diner owner for years. He flipped up the tinted lenses attached to his glasses. "It's darker than a bitch," he said.

"Should we pull over?" Sylvia asked. Poco was whining now,

45

short bursts of dog fear. Rita kicked in her seat and didn't smile even when Sylvia shook the crab rattle again.

"You don't want to push on to that campground?" Clayton called over the thunderclap and Poco's whining. She knew he was thinking about the deposit they'd put down.

"I don't know," Sylvia practically screamed. "Will we make it before the storm starts?"

"Maybe it'll blow over," Clayton said. Even as he spoke, Sylvia saw the pelting rain that would soon force them to roll up the windows.

Sylvia patted the dog's head again and sang, "Don't Sit under the Apple Tree," turning first to Rita and then to the dog. Rita soon grinned at her grandmother, and even Clayton smiled when Sylvia ran out of real words to the song and sang, "Don't sit under the apple tree when the angels start to pee." In the distance she noticed a line of laundry waving against the dark sky.

Sylvia was at her best in the throes of a difficulty. After a crisis, when things were calm again and silently fitting back into their routine, she sometimes fell apart. Though she and Clayton had been married almost thirty-five years, she knew her initial control as well as her delayed emotional outbursts could still unsettle him.

A ragged line of light split the sky, and rain seemed to pour through the opening. Clayton turned the wipers on high. The wipers slammed back and forth so frantically that Sylvia feared they might break loose and fly off into the turbulence. But for all their swiping, the blades couldn't keep the glass clear for half a second. Rain beat against the roof of the truck like enemy fire.

"We might have to stop and wait it out, Clayton."

"I want to at least see a sign so I know where the hell we are."

"What's this coming up?" Sylvia asked, squinting at a large light-colored rectangle. "My God," she said. A tractor trailer lay on its side, jackknifed in the exit. Far off Sylvia heard the wail of an emergency vehicle.

"Take the next exit, Clayton."

"We'll see," he said. His hands looked white with squeezing the steering wheel.

Sylvia felt the wind pulling the trailer over the lines in the road. The rain didn't let up, and they were soon on top of an exit without ever having seen a sign warning of its approach.

"All right, all right," he said, leaving the highway. "I don't know where in the hell I'm going to pull this baby over though."

"What's down that way?" Sylvia asked, trying to keep one hand on Rita, the other on the dog, as she leaned forward and then to the side, and peeked out the opaque windows.

"I can't see shit," Clayton said.

Sylvia could barely make out what was ahead of them. The windshield wipers continued to press at a steady, high gear, but were no competition for the rain that seemed thrown directly, even deliberately, at them. Clayton hunched forward, his face practically in line with his hands on the steering wheel. Sylvia watched the huge wet smear in front and behind them. For all she could tell, theirs was the only rig on the road. Sylvia wanted Clayton to pull off to the side, but he explained that he couldn't tell where the edge of the road was. He might hit a soft shoulder and get stuck.

"Besides, with this visibility, somebody's liable to drive into our bedroom," Clayton said.

"Here, try this," Sylvia shouted above the rain. She pointed at what appeared to be a break in the line of metal fence.

"This is somebody's driveway, Sylvia."

"If anybody's got a driveway this big, they can afford to have company."

47

"You mean they can afford to have us shot." Despite his own objections, Clayton made a wide right turn down the roadway Sylvia indicated.

"Did you see what the sign said?" Clayton asked.

Sylvia shook her head. She had no idea what they were coming onto. The driveway, or whatever spread before them, was wide enough for two cars, but Clayton wouldn't be able to turn the rig around if he had to. She didn't mention this particular problem. Just as Sylvia sensed that they'd come into an open space, Clayton cut the headlights and ignition.

It was so black, Sylvia couldn't make out the steering wheel. Clayton softly told Sylvia the last time he'd seen such darkness was a few months after his father had left, when his uncle took him on a fishing trip. The cabin they'd stayed in had no electricity, and his uncle had said something strange like, "This is as black as it gets."

Clayton half-turned the ignition key, just until the dashboard lights went on and the red dot on the radio glowed. He fooled with the dial. Sylvia shook her head but didn't comment when he settled on Peter Allen's "I Go to Rio." She draped a light blanket over the baby's legs.

Years ago, pausing outside Janice's closed door, Clayton had often eavesdropped on her music. Sylvia had caught him a couple of times. And when he'd come back from the Crow's Nest after a few beers, he wanted Janice to tell him the names of the groups she was listening to. Once in a while he'd call, "Turn it up, Janice," and then he'd try to get Sylvia to dance with him in the living room.

Gradually the rapid-fire rain eased into a rhythmic tapping, and when it turned to drips, they decided to make their move back to the trailer. Clayton turned off the radio and the space around them went pure black. He flashed the headlights on a huge, empty parking lot.

"This should be OK till morning," he said. "I've had enough driving."

"What about the reservation?" Sylvia said, suddenly remembering Deer Hill.

"Can we get our money back?"

"I don't know. I should have called and told them we couldn't make it."

"They've figured it out by now," Clayton said smiling. The fact that he wasn't overly concerned surprised her.

Their first night on the road and they had stopped in some unknown place. Sylvia had pictured pulling into the campground, hooking up to the electric power, filling the water tank, then inviting a few of the other travelers for a drink before dinner. She flicked on a light in the trailer.

"Isn't this great?" Clayton said. He went on about the benefits of the small gas-powered generator. Sylvia had to admit she was glad to be through with drawing power through the gizmo he'd hooked up to the Pinches' house. Even though they'd made good on the Pinches' electric bill, she was relieved that the huge umbilical cord stretching between the old address and their new home was part of the past.

Clayton's enthusiasm about the generator warmed Sylvia. "If we lived here in a house," he raised his eyebrows at the word *house,* "we'd probably have had our power knocked out in the storm." Sylvia didn't mention that people could get generators for houses. Marlene, for instance, would have one if they weren't so expensive.

Sylvia and Clayton heard the distant high-pitched scream of sirens. Looking out the small curtained windows of their new home, they couldn't see another light.

"This is kind of scary," Sylvia said. She was still standing and holding Rita. "Feels like we're at the end of the world or something."

"Nonsense," Clayton said. "This is fun. Our first night. Let's get out the cards and have a game of gin before dinner."

Pulling through the storm seemed to have energized Clayton. In the truck, even here in the trailer, he said, they were closer to the raw way things worked than they'd ever been. She understood that from now on they would need to use instinct and skill to stay on top of situations.

"Let me feed the baby first," Sylvia said.

"Well, we might as well eat, too, then," Clayton said. He wasn't used to the routine with the baby yet. Sylvia felt him studying her as she prepared to heat a bottle.

Sylvia wished she could have cooked hot turkey sandwiches just to make up to Clayton for nixing his plans at the diner. Instead she prepared spaghetti, one of his favorites. After she settled Rita in Clayton's arms and handed him the bottle, she stirred the spaghetti. Rita watched the activity until the bottle was well past half empty and she became visibly sleepy.

The baby fell asleep just before Sylvia and Clayton were ready to eat dinner. Clayton continued to hold Rita in one arm and use his right hand to awkwardly twirl and eat the spaghetti.

"Did you burp her?" Sylvia asked.

"I forgot."

"Well, you'd better." Clayton lifted Rita to his shoulder as Sylvia started the dishes.

After the dishes had been washed and put away and the table wiped clean, Clayton sat Rita in her baby seat beside him and dealt the cards for 500. He looked over the top of his glasses at the cards on the table, and through his glasses at the cards in his hand. Back and forth, he regarded the different groups of cards from the appropriate perspective.

Not wanting to encounter the rain again by retrieving her reading glasses from the glove compartment of the truck,

Sylvia squinted and held her cards at arm's length toward the floor and away from Clayton's view. She bent toward Rita and then kissed her soft baby face.

"Should we get the kerosene lamp, Clayton?"

"For what?"

"To save some electricity." She imagined waking to a dead battery, even though Clayton had explained about the generator.

"Sylvia, that's for an emergency."

"This is an emergency," she said. She looked over at Rita whose face was becoming red with strain.

"Play your cards," he said. After another hand he said, "Sylvia, this was no emergency. This is the way it'll be a lot of the time." He paused. "RVers call it boondocking." He explained that they couldn't always afford to be staying in fancy camps with hookups that could power everything from an air conditioner to an electric can opener. Sylvia was a little unnerved. This was the first she'd heard of boondocking. But she'd lived with Clayton long enough to know that this boondocking business would wear off the first time he didn't have any clean clothes.

"Loser does the dishes?" Clayton asked. He liked a little stake in any game he played.

"I already did the dishes," Sylvia said, not looking up from her cards. She picked up a line of new cards, but before she'd incorporated them into her hand she quickly set the whole run back in place. "I thought that was a six," she said.

"A card laid is a card played."

"I didn't lay anything. I picked up by mistake," Sylvia said, becoming frustrated. "Loser changes Rita's diaper," she said. Clayton agreed. She knew what he was thinking: the way she was playing, he'd beat her in two more hands.

After Sylvia won the second hand, Clayton grew irritated at

Sylvia's difficulty in making out the cards. "I'll go get your damn glasses."

"No, don't bother. I'm doing just as well without them."

"That's what worries me," Clayton said. From where she was sitting, Sylvia could smell the faint yet unmistakable odor of baby shit.

Just as Clayton announced that he was going to play standing up in order to change his luck, Sylvia said, "I'm out." She placed her last two cards on a run of Clayton's.

"Damn," he said.

Clayton shut Sylvia out at the next round, stranding her with four face cards, but he couldn't catch her lead.

"You win," he said, pulling his lips back in a phony smile. She knew he was waiting for her to relent and say, "I'll do the diaper. You go walk Poco."

"Where's Poco's leash?" she asked instead, reaching for a flashlight. Sylvia would rather have changed Rita than walk around in the pitch black, but she thought it was good for Clayton to learn to care for their granddaughter. Plus, just picturing what he was doing made her victory sweeter — Clayton staring at Rita for a few minutes, then placing her on her back on the changing pad. The baby cooing at him and kicking the air to turn herself over. The sudden scent of baby poop hitting Clayton in the face, causing him to turn his head away as he held Rita in place.

Clayton hadn't handled Janice very much, not in practical ways; Sylvia didn't remember him ever changing a diaper. Walking Poco over the expanse of parking lot, she gave Clayton plenty of time. When they finally reached an edge of blacktop where wisps of grass came up against the hard surface, Poco pulled hard on the leash.

Walking carefully with her flashlight picking out, then avoiding, the puddles she came upon every couple of steps, Sylvia considered that she might not always be around if something came up and Clayton had to deal with Rita alone. Sylvia couldn't imagine where she'd be, but she still felt that Clayton could use a little baby training. She turned the flashlight off so that everything around her became black as a well. Poco steered her around the puddles. When she heard Rita crying, she walked deeper into the darkness.

Poco growled and pulled forward. The sound startled her. The farther Sylvia walked from the trailer, the closer the old fear came. She felt it settle on her, then travel out along her arms and legs. It meant Melvin, his eyes moving in the wet blackness, seeking her out. Skulking around for little Rita. Anybody with half the persistence Melvin had could escape from a mental hospital. Sylvia had read about it happening many times. On a dark night in the middle of nowhere, an old couple was asking for trouble. When Poco rubbed against her, she jumped and took the lead, heading back toward the trailer.

Sylvia opened the door and found Clayton grinning weakly. His head and shoulders pressed against the wall, he looked exhausted. Rita whimpered softly in his arms. Sylvia thought she could see baby powder hanging in a cloud over the kitchen table. She imagined, too, the question on Clayton's mind — was he too old not only to raise a child again, but also to learn to do all the things he'd missed the first time around?

"Everything OK?" she asked. She decided not to mention the band of silver duct tape at the baby's waist.

"Under control," he said. He added, "One more hand before we turn in." Sylvia put the sweet-smelling baby to bed with the last of the bottle she hadn't finished as Clayton dealt the cards. Then the rain started up again. A crack of thunder set Poco trembling and pacing anew. But even with the revived noises of the storm, along with Clayton's exclamations at the cards, Rita dropped off into a deep sleep.

53

"Are we in the safest place or the most dangerous for a thunderstorm? I forget which is which," Sylvia said. She was still thinking of Melvin, but knew if she brought up his name she'd dampen Clayton's mood.

"Don't worry about it," Clayton said, smirking at his cards. Then he said, "I almost forgot," and retrieved a bottle of champagne from the refrigerator. "For our first night," he said. The cork smacked the ceiling of the trailer and liquid spewed over the lip of the bottle as Sylvia went for the plastic glasses.

Sylvia knew they wouldn't go to bed until Clayton won a satisfactory hand, but she didn't make it easy. As cards clicked and slid on the Formica tabletop, points amassing for one, then the other, the rain drumming steadily just above their heads, Sylvia thought of how the trailer had looked from outside when she'd stood at the edge of the wet grass. The safe squares of warm window light came out of nowhere; they appeared suspended in the thick black that spread in every direction. But while the lights seemed as if nothing held them in place, she could see the dark figure of a man and the smaller silhouette of a baby in his arms, inside the glowing space.

"Well, Vee, let's call it a night."

Sylvia studied him. She wasn't sure why he was now, after all these years, calling her Vee, but it felt right. Finally he'd branded her with his own name for her. She liked its intimacy.

"Any chance of finding that little lamp I used to keep in the basement?" He meant the gooseneck one they'd once bought Janice; she'd used it for only one semester of college.

"No," said Sylvia. "That stayed with the Pinches." Some other time she might have been pleased to tell him it had been left behind in his crazed rush to eliminate so many of their possessions, but tonight she teased him by gently pinching his arm.

Clayton put his other arm around her and said, "That's OK.

54

I'm not really in the mood to read anyway." Despite the dark, she thought she saw him wink.

A loud sustained whistle like an air raid siren shook them awake. Rita wailed, and Poco jumped on the bed and barked in their faces.

"What the hell's going on?" Clayton asked Sylvia.

"How should I know?" she asked back, getting out of bed and hurrying to Rita. Her first thought was that Melvin had tracked them down, and involved every emergency vehicle within 500 miles of Baltimore.

Clayton pulled back the orange and brown curtain over the bed to reveal hundreds of men carrying lunch pails and hard hats. In their work clothes, the men in the distance didn't stand out against the blacktop or the background at first glance because the sky was still dull with night. "What time is it?" he called. The flood of men moved toward the trailer and then broke to pass by on either side. They stared at the vehicle smack in the middle of their path to work, and a few laughed.

"Sylvia," Clayton said, "we've parked at some kind of factory." She saw the outline of a pale building not too far off, but couldn't make out the signs.

Sylvia knew her husband wanted to put on a pair of chinos, wave good morning to the men, and explain that he was retired but had once, like them, started and ended each workday with the scream of the factory whistle announcing it owned precise hours. Before he'd dressed, though, a knock came at the trailer door and Sylvia, in her bright pink robe, answered it.

Two men in suits looked up at her. The men were indistinguishable except for their height. The taller of the two took a deep breath. While he searched for a way to begin, the shorter man spoke as if he encountered a trailer at the factory daily.

"Morning," he said, nodding at Sylvia. The taller man smiled obligingly at Rita.

"There's a slight problem," the shorter man said.

The other man then moved immediately to the point. "You're covering our parking spots."

Clayton followed the men out into the parking lot and began to explain. "That was some storm," Clayton said. He ran his hand through his hair, like when he was ready for a conversation, but the tall man simply pointed underneath the trailer.

"Would anybody like a cup of coffee?" Sylvia called.

They ignored her and walked around the outside of the trailer. In the dark, Clayton had parked over the spaces of the company's top employees, supervisors who'd earned parking places with their last names painted on the black topping — Davis, Thompson, Horn, Buckley.

"What does that one say?" Clayton asked. From the nearest window, Sylvia watched Clayton bend to get a better look around a trailer wheel.

"Fryer," the shorter man said. "That's me. That's my spot."

"Jeez," Clayton said, "that 'r' needs a little touching up." When the man didn't reply, Clayton said, "I'm sorry about this."

The two men went back to their cars and idled their engines while Clayton called in to Sylvia to sit down just until he moved the rig a few hundred feet out of the way. Before Clayton opened the door of the truck cab, she saw him wave to a couple of the workers, men who'd probably had to park in a field half a mile away.

Slowly Clayton turned the vehicle. Holding on to Rita, Sylvia watched out a window as he took care not to tag the expensive cars parked around them. Then he drove toward the crowd of working men. Their momentary shock at seeing a trailer there, out of place, disappeared as soon as Clayton passed by. For inconveniencing the factory managers, for concealing their privileged places, the workers should pat him on the back. If he'd done something like this at Evergreen, someone might have called him a hero and bought him a beer after work.

When Sylvia felt the rig come to a halt, she dressed, stood up with Rita in her arms, and Poco at her heels, and grabbed her purse. She locked the trailer door, and opened the passenger side of the cab. As she settled things in place, she wondered if every morning would begin like this: in an effort to outrun danger, they would wake up in the middle of other people's lives.

II
Clayton

THREE

————◆————

By the time Clayton pulled the trailer into the outskirts of Dixie Camperland south of Daytona, a red sun was starting to make its way into the sky, and the Indian River smoked as though a bunch of small fires had almost burned themselves out. The parking brake ground in the silence. Clayton surveyed the sleeping sprawl of mobile homes and RVs littering the banks of the river. The closest RV wore a bumper sticker announcing "Sea Esta."

The last time he'd driven all night was nearly six years earlier, when they'd finally left Milwaukee. Their first destination after taking off from Maryland had turned into a genuine roadblock. Just as they'd begun their traveling, Sylvia had been ready to settle down again. Clayton had been anxious to get as far away from Sylvia's hometown as was physically possible. He'd never imagined having to practically pry her fingers from the wrought iron banister of the house in which she'd grown up. After they'd gotten some distance from the place, he concluded

61

that Sylvia felt safer back in her hometown, the memory-laden house of her childhood, with her brother and sister, though aged, still protecting her against her biggest fear: Melvin. Clayton pictured Sylvia's extended family like the group of wildebeests he'd seen on TV, all backed into a circle and defiantly facing out at the enemy.

But it wasn't long before Clayton understood that Milwaukee was only the beginning. Those first years on the road in the early eighties, Sylvia went through a routine of crying every time they pulled away from anywhere — trailer parks, campgrounds, or the parking lots of churches and Elk or Moose lodges, wherever they'd stopped, even if they'd only stayed overnight. He had endured her sobs and nose blowing the way he might if she had a long-term illness. But when Rita started getting carsick at the same time Sylvia was carrying on, he put his foot down. "You're the one making her sick," Clayton had said. Sylvia argued that car sickness was a physical condition, which every female in her family had suffered and outgrown, not some emotional response. Even though Sylvia's theory had proved right, he was glad when she quit her crying.

Clayton opened the door of the truck cab, stretched, and took a deep breath. His first visit to Florida was nothing like the colorful travel brochures his old coworker Bud Harper had once planned a vacation around. Clayton could still detect, almost taste, the bitter scent of the brushfires he'd tried to outrun. He seemed to be constantly in flight from something. If it wasn't the thought of Melvin, now it was these damn fires.

Clayton compared Melvin to the arthritis that had started years earlier and then gathered strength and settled in a vulnerable spot in his body just as he was growing older and weaker. You never forgot about the condition, but sometimes you imagined the inflammation, anticipated your body's reaction, before there was any actual reason to respond.

Sylvia called and wrote to their ex-neighbor in Maryland regularly. Marlene kept them informed about Melvin's mental state, his trips out of the institution, and his activities inside it. Clayton wasn't sure how Marlene obtained such specific information, but Sylvia assured him the woman "had her spies." He didn't dismiss the idea that Marlene made up stories just to ease Sylvia's mind.

Clayton hadn't been truly calm since they'd left Maryland. They could be sailing along a flat-out band of roadway in the heartland of America and Sylvia would imagine the one car they passed in twenty minutes to be Melvin's. Or Clayton would spot a hitchhiker with an uncanny resemblance to Melvin's sister. Marlene routinely picked up Clayton's mail from the couple who'd bought his house; the Pinches kindly allowed them to continue to use the address. Odd bits of mail sometimes came forwarded in Marlene's packages — bizarre newspaper clippings and cartoons. And once they received a manila envelope full of promotions for children's toys, which Marlene swore *she* hadn't collected. The outside label had been typed.

With the exception of one letter sent shortly before they began traveling, Clayton didn't have any concrete evidence that Melvin was still a threat. And yet instinct told him otherwise. That was the kind of irrational position he'd once accused Sylvia of.

Clayton had never seen a ghost himself, but he didn't disregard them entirely either. At times, Melvin seemed to be a voice audible only on sensitive recording devices, the cold rush of air in a strange room, the movement you felt but knew was not a logical gesture from this world.

Clayton tilted his head back and sniffed. Wildfires, they were called on the news. The fires had pressed him off course and threatened his schedule to reach Las Vegas by the end of

August. Sylvia would tell him not to get all worked up over a couple of lost days, but he wanted to get to Texas ASAP. He'd told his sister he was already there. By suggesting that they meet her in Las Vegas during her honeymoon, he had avoided attending the wedding back home in Baltimore.

Clayton thought it fitting that Lucille had selected Las Vegas as her honeymoon site, since he'd said back when he was a teenager that he'd give odds on his hard-nosed sister *never* getting married. Lucille had beaten Clayton's odds. She planned to marry "a younger man," Eddie Mindell, fifty-four and twice divorced. There was no telling what she'd do at the slot machines.

The other reason Clayton favored catching up with Lucille in Vegas instead of Baltimore was that he didn't want Sylvia pulling some stunt in Baltimore the way she had in Milwaukee six years ago. Making him look like the bad guy just because he preferred to press on. They hadn't been back to Maryland since they'd left, and Clayton wasn't especially anxious to see how they used to live. Plus Baltimore was Melvin's turf.

Clayton could hardly remember what it felt like to be from a place that stayed the same day after day. By marking off a small space in the world with a chain-link fence, a person took a stand. And yet, uncertainty kept him alert. He couldn't allow the numbing drone of a television program to become a life-style the way most of his old neighbors in Maryland had. Sometimes Clayton fantasized that the United States was one big game board, and he and Sylvia were hard plastic markers constantly directed by a roll of the dice.

The distant smoke distorted the scent of salt water. At places in Georgia, the smoke had swarmed thick as fog across the windshield. Instinctively, Clayton had turned on the windshield wipers and the defroster. Nothing worked against natural disaster but distance. For a time, however, Clayton worried that the fire was moving faster than his 60 miles per hour. And then the smoke detector had gone off in the trailer and Clayton had to pull over, guessing at the limits of the shoulder, take the batteries out of the damn thing, and work his way back into traffic like a blind man. The wildfires made his eyes water and his throat tighten. What had been worse than the smoke, though, was the idea that the pervasive grayness was only the afterthought of a fire burning continually out of control. Clayton had never actually seen flames, but he could picture them crackling a path toward him.

Sometimes Sylvia experienced a burst of fear, but Clayton had become the constant worrier, the one with a continual low-grade fever. She could sometimes panic at the thought of Melvin appearing, but the possibility didn't seem to eat at her the way it did him. He guessed it all had something to do with the decision to sell the house and become rootless. That kind of change had different effects on people. Concern settled and took hold on Clayton these days, reverberating out to his fingertips and facial expressions. Worry shook him; his body's reaction to trouble was to try to throw it off.

It was June. Because the Titusville area had seen no rain in nearly seven weeks, the brush beneath Clayton's feet was brittle, dangerously close to igniting with the slightest spark, maybe even the heat of the sun. He walked around the outside of the trailer; he couldn't have parked any closer to the Indian River. On the back of the trailer, thirty-one states on the U.S. map were filled in with bright colors. This dull, scrubby section of Florida wasn't a place Clayton considered they'd stay for longer than the time it took to assign the state a color. The fires had literally pushed him to the edge, less than fifteen minutes from the Atlantic.

Clayton caught a distorted glimpse of himself in the reflection of one of the trailer windows. When exactly had the lines on his face thickened and lengthened and deepened? The time his license plates had been stolen? The day Rita choked on a cookie and he had to turn her upside down after Sylvia's attempt at the Heimlich maneuver failed? Or was it the long stream of nights broken apart by baby cries?

Once he had concerned himself mainly with parts of power tools and machines. Metal and plastic. Pieces clearly assembled right or wrong. Pieces of something larger. If he'd kept on at Evergreen, focusing on machines instead of a grandchild, maybe he wouldn't have aged so dramatically. Still, it was miraculous to have actually raised a child to school age. And that he'd seen so much of the country in the process.

"Where are we?" Sylvia called to Clayton from the bedroom area. He peeked into the RV where she was fixing Rita's hair. The child's long, dark braids were so fine that by the time Sylvia worked down to the ends, her fingertips looked large as sausages. Sylvia licked the tips of her index fingers to help her secure the tiny braids with rubber bands smaller around than dimes. Normally Clayton didn't interest himself with his granddaughter's hair, but today Sylvia was making quite a production out of it.

"Be still," Sylvia said several times to Rita, who looked like she couldn't wait to get outside. When Sylvia finished, Rita reached back and gently squeezed the braids, then rushed out to Clayton.

Rita was pretty, her hair darker than that of her parents, olive-colored skin, and blue-gray eyes. She was smaller than Clayton remembered Janice being before she started school. Once when Sylvia had been mad at Clayton for no particular reason, she'd accused him of causing Rita's petite size.

"How do you figure?" he'd asked. Sylvia had pointed at the impatiens, which she kept by the kitchen sink. The plant produced beautiful red and white blooms in its little pot in the trailer. But she said when she'd planted a similar one every summer out in front of the house, the plant had spread all along the bushes to the side of the front steps. "It was your idea," Sylvia had argued. "This trailer business. There's not room enough in here for anything to grow."

After she'd made the accusing remark, she'd recoiled, although he'd never once hit her. He'd taken a deep breath and said, "Sylvia, sometimes I think you packed your mind in one of the boxes we left with that young couple." But her remark had started him fretting. Was Rita's growth really stunted? Before Clayton retired, if something got to him he simply rid himself of it, instead of allowing it to root inside him. But Melvin had shown him that not everything could be tossed off or paced away.

Clayton considered that maybe the traditional arrangement of men going off to work and women staying home with the children was put into place by someone who knew a secret: given full-time charge of domestic responsibility, men were much bigger worriers than the ladies.

Rita was at the core of all Clayton's anxiety, but she was his diversion from it, too. She was the payoff. Watching her laugh, witnessing her learn to talk and walk and figure things out, filled him with happiness. The day she'd learned to recognize numbers, first following the numeral three with her index finger than holding up three fingers to announce her age, he'd been so astonished he was afraid he would weep right in front of her.

If Clayton's independent new life were to grow from a simple idea and finally take on the shape of a person, it would look like Rita. On quiet nights when Rita and Sylvia were sleeping or afternoons when they were dozing to the hum of the road, thoughts of Rita could amaze him. He and Sylvia had nurtured and protected her all the while she was growing into a little girl. He'd no sooner get the routine of the diapers down, or the tiny jars of baby food, than she'd have passed through that stage and on to another challenge he would have to figure out. He'd question more than complain to Sylvia, "I thought she liked peas," and Sylvia would simply shake her head.

"Florida," Clayton said instead of good morning.

In their rovings, things changed, literally, overnight. His windshield vision of the world could switch from farmer's meadow to major metropolitan area, from apple-picking camp to pig farm. In a couple of hours, yesterday's Georgia back-woods had transformed into a slow-moving river lined with fish camps and trailers. He couldn't say exactly why, but Florida had a look and smell and feel different from every other state they'd visited.

"You smell anything, Sylvia?" His nostrils flared and he looked at her.

"Very faintly," she said. "Clayton, you've asked that question at least a hundred times since we first heard about the wildfires." The Florida air reminded him of the way their living room on Garden Road had held the cigarette smoke of a party from the night before.

"Nice spot," Sylvia said. The majority of trailers clustered together farther down the river.

Clayton could tell she was glad he'd loosened up and paid a camping fee. Although they'd done their share of boondocking at roadside restaurants and in public parking areas, Sylvia always argued for settling at a designated camping area with telephones, laundry setups, and disposal facilities for holding tanks. These were places where they could stay for as long as they wanted, which generally meant until Clayton thought they were spending too much money. He knew she used the money angle to coerce him into staying put for a while. To get him to remain places longer than a few days, she would mention what

68

a bargain the monthly rate was. Not long after they'd initially set out, she'd used the price of gas as an argument for settling down.

For six years they'd been moving around the country. Sometimes Clayton felt he was running so hard he couldn't catch his breath. Days became a smear of green and brown and blue across the windshield. At times he was afraid Sylvia would outright hide the truck keys from him, especially that time he felt chest pains. The symptoms had turned into a panic attack instead of a heart attack, but from then on, Sylvia liked to set up in places reasonably close to a hospital.

The frantic traveling was exhilarating, too — looking at real mountains for the first time, outrunning a thunderstorm blowing across the prairie, tracking down a family who'd stolen a friend's ham radio. He never could tell what phenomenon, what people, even what local brand of beer they'd come on from one stop to the next. It was a job driving, an interesting job, but work nonetheless. And at the end of each day he felt a sense of progress that he'd never experienced at Evergreen.

"I hear the ocean," Rita said, jumping up and down.

"That's only the traffic on 95. The ocean's over that way," Clayton said, gesturing in the opposite direction.

"When are we going there?" she asked insistently. He didn't reply.

Since they'd had Rita, he'd amassed a hell of a lot of child-rearing experience that he couldn't imagine ever having to use again. That irked him a little, like watching Sylvia toss out a few leftover beans or tomatoes that could have been added to a next-day sandwich or soup. Before Rita, he'd never given a second thought to saving things.

An odd noise, half scream, half gasp, startled him. He couldn't tell if Rita or Sylvia or maybe both of them had simultaneously let out the sound.

Suddenly, as if it had fallen from one of the palm trees nearby, a large brown and white dog charged at Clayton.

"Get down," Sylvia yelled. She was about forty feet from the trailer and about half that distance from him. Her arms instinctively enveloped Rita.

"What in the hell?" Clayton said. He automatically started to run toward Sylvia and the trailer but quickly saw that he wouldn't make it in time.

"Pretend like you're eating," Sylvia hollered.

"What?" Clayton couldn't make the leap between danger and eating.

Poco barked from inside the trailer. Sylvia dragged Rita to Clayton's side. "*Down,*" she said as she lowered to her haunches. She tightened her arms around Rita, then made loud munching and slurping sounds.

Sylvia was acting crazy. Too scared to pretend to do anything, Rita reached a hand out for Clayton. He held her hand, pressed her tiny fingers into his palm.

Clayton copied Sylvia because she seemed to know what she was doing, ridiculous as it was, and because there wasn't time to do much else. Baring huge yellowed teeth, the dog circled them, growled, looked at Rita quietly crouching with two fingers in her mouth. The three of them hung together, he and Sylvia dramatizing an exaggerated eating frenzy. Studying Rita's face, Clayton was relieved that their bizarre behavior didn't appear to upset her. Her reactions astonished him. A dangerous scenario with a dog she could roll with, while his refusal last week to stop for Charm Pops or some other goofy candy had sent her into a tantrum. Machines and tool parts were so much easier to understand than a child's psyche. Metal pieces fit neatly together. As Sylvia and Clayton emphatically gobbled the air around them, the dog stopped barking, growled softly, then ran off.

When the animal was out of sight, Clayton laughed with relief and rolled onto his back. Sylvia opened the trailer door and Poco ambled over to Clayton, then began licking his face. "Where did you learn that trick?" he called to Sylvia. Clayton looked up at the sun, a lovely red, smoke-covered wafer. He wished the technique would work with Melvin. He'd gobble the air twice a day, three times if necessary, to ward off Melvin. At the sound of his voice, Rita turned to Clayton and fell against him. He caught her by the shoulders, pulled her down, then ran a hand over her head.

"I read it in the paper," Sylvia said.

"All I know is, you don't read the same paper I read." Clayton laughed again. He put his hands over Rita's ears and said to Sylvia, "I told you we need a gun."

"We don't need a gun," Sylvia said. Sylvia said the word *gun* softly.

"I'd like to buy one while we're in Florida," Clayton said. There had been a couple of times when they'd been boondocking in unofficial camping areas when he was sure Sylvia would have felt more secure having a handgun. Still, she maintained her argument that a gun was a magnet for trouble.

"It's good to have some protection," he said. He was thinking of Melvin chasing them down, running them up against a precipice or a wall or an ocean, then making off with Rita. A gun in a situation like that would give you a little say in the outcome.

Rather than waiting for Sylvia to contend, once again, that guns were illegal in certain states they were sure to pass through, he asked, "How about some real food?" If Clayton didn't create a few diversions, Melvin could occupy his thoughts for hours at a time. "Hungry, Rita?" he asked.

"Do you want to try to get a little sleep first?" Sylvia answered.

71

"How can I sleep when the welcome wagon just passed through?"

Leaving the house behind had switched everything around between him and Sylvia. On Garden Road, the many drawers and shelves which had separated their belongings and different domains seemed to Clayton to have defined their personalities as well. Sylvia had been the one to fret over a situation until it blew up to an impassable obstacle, while Clayton had always shucked off little issues before they bloomed into trouble. In the rig, with their possessions all mashed together, somehow their character traits had stretched and turned inside out.

The longer he and Sylvia traveled, the easier it became for Sylvia to forget details that once had stacked up against her. All that concern had to go somewhere. Clayton figured it had settled on him.

After breakfast, as Sylvia straightened up the trailer, she talked to Clayton about possible side trips on the way to Las Vegas. He reminded her to make sure the places still existed before he went to all the trouble of tracking them down. Last month, on the recommendation of a twenty-year-old newspaper clipping, they'd traveled to a sausage museum that had, at some point after the article was published, become the site of one more Home of the Whopper. Rita, of course, had been delighted.

"I'll call ahead," Sylvia suggested. She was probably right that the most interesting things went on well off the main roads. Sylvia never believed in traveling the shortest distance between two points unless you happened to be in an ambulance. Clayton hoped that if Melvin pursued them he'd stick to the interstates.

"Clayton," Sylvia called as she pulled up the bed covers and secured a couple of books in the grooved ledge he'd constructed on one side of the bed. "How does the National Atomic Museum in Albuquerque sound?"

Clayton grunted. He was in the middle of mounting Safe Distance, a radiation detection device, possibly the most important new piece of equipment on the wall.

"Maybe if you spent half a day in the museum, the obsession with fallout and nuclear winter and fission and all that stuff would blow out of your system."

"It's not an obsession, Sylvia. It's called planning ahead."

"Boring," Rita called from the bathroom. She seemed to have just learned the word. Clayton had heard her use it half a dozen times already this morning.

"And not too far from the Atomic Museum there's London Bridge that somebody moved to Arizona," Sylvia said.

"Calm down, Vee," Clayton replied. It didn't make sense to see a landmark in Arizona that belonged in England.

Clayton had to reposition a couple of Sylvia's framed samplers to make room for the Safe Distance detector. After he screwed the metal holder onto the wall and stepped back to look it over, he smiled at his wife's cross-stitched poems on either side of the new installation. The poem on the left read:

> We thought we could settle
> for Florida sun.
> To hell with that crap
> it's time to have fun.

And to the right stood another of Sylvia's creations:

> We don't have an attic.
> We don't have a cellar.
> But I've still got a stove
> and my wonderful feller.

The new thingamajig, as Sylvia called it, would help Clayton sleep. During the time they were traveling out west, Clayton had been thinking and reading and worrying about nuclear power and nuclear weapons. Sylvia told him he was a good twenty-five years too late to start concerning himself with nuclear, but he was convinced that it was when you thought there was nothing left to worry about that you were probably in the most danger. At night, he imagined a muffled underground explosion whenever he heard a crack of lightning.

He couldn't imagine that work had once so absorbed him that he hardly paid attention to what was going on in the world. Every anxiety that had once bypassed him now seemed to haunt him. He worried, too, about Rita — that she could be mowed down by a force she had no understanding of. Some nights he dreamed that the inside of the earth was riddled with secret nuclear passageways where broken atoms had burned right through generators. He would wake sweating with fear that the earth was doomed with an irreversible cancer. It was sort of like the wildfires, only you couldn't ever see or smell the danger.

Clayton would never tell Sylvia about the kind of samplers he thought up:

> We took off from home
> to leave Melvin behind,
> but the farther we go
> the more danger we find.

He propped that thought up against his mind twenty-four hours a day.

Sylvia said his preoccupation with nuclear danger had all started with Alvin Spalding, a bland, puffy-faced man they'd met in Michigan; he'd taken a suspiciously early retirement from IBM. Alvin had equipped *his* RV with a darkroom that doubled as a fallout shelter, complete with emergency food and water rations as well as blankets and two rifles. Alvin had shared what he said was privileged information with Clayton — details about IBM's contracts with the Defense Department, and photographs, which he said identified a complicated network of major companies comprising a "nuclear ring."

Alvin would sit back in the webbed lawn chair he'd positioned outside his trailer near Grand Rapids and say to Clayton, "Name something. Give me the name of anything." Whatever Clayton replied — from "Triscuits" to "electric razor" — Alvin traced the product to what he called its "nuclear principle."

Sylvia said the man was nuts, but Alvin's paranoid logic had fascinated Clayton. Alvin's body was so attuned to radiation, he said he could anticipate it: the dark hairs on his forearms would stand straight up. When Clayton explained the amazing physiological warning, Sylvia had said, "If the hair on his arms stands up, then what does he need a machine for?"

When he wasn't spouting his nuclear theories, Alvin recited poems he'd written while working on IBM's computers. The computers all had code names, which Alvin insisted were genuine: Plesio, Snipe, Schooner, Ketch, Midway, Flewaffta. Clayton listened politely to Alvin's odes and couplets, but his mind was occupied with the man's theories on the pervasiveness of radiation, and how it would affect Rita.

Clayton didn't tell Sylvia that he'd paid nearly $300 for the Safe Distance radiation detection unit, which Alvin said within ten years would be standard household equipment, more essential than a smoke detector. Most of the money had come from the time Clayton bought shrimp on a pier in Louisiana and then sold it in a wealthy suburb of Dallas. He and Sylvia and Rita had made the trip practically nonstop, with Styrofoam coolers of iced shrimp piled in every available space between the kitchen table and the bedroom.

As Clayton admired the newly mounted device, Sylvia muttered, "Snake oil salesman."

"Come on, Vee. Let me show you all the maps I got with this thing." One located U.S. commercial nuclear power stations; another was a world map pointing out power stations, and a third delineated the directions and speeds of annual U.S. winds. A paperback entitled *Guide to Fallout Survival* accompanied the maps.

"I don't know, Clayton," Sylvia said finally, as she attempted to bend one of the maps back into its proper folds. "I mean, if there's a real accident, aren't we all going to die anyway?"

Clayton couldn't believe Sylvia spoke so openly around Rita. Sylvia didn't have to go to the extremes she had long ago in trying to protect Janice, but it wouldn't hurt for her to be diplomatic on occasion. Rita might stop eating again, the way she had nearly a year ago. She'd suddenly refused every meal Sylvia or Clayton offered, even favorites like spaghetti, and macaroni and cheese. Sylvia had used every means she and Clayton could think of to coerce the child to eat, even offering mere tablespoon-size portions of warm mashed potatoes and peas in doll dishes. After lying awake nights frightened that his granddaughter would whittle away to the size of a doll herself, he had taken Rita to a doctor who said simply, "She'll come around when she's ready to eat."

Finally, after six weeks of Clayton fuming about the incompetence of doctors and watching Rita pick at a few vegetables or lick a spoonful of some once-favorite pudding, she began to eat again. Now, to Clayton's relief, Rita ignored Sylvia's remark about nuclear tragedies and looked over the maps. "Where are we?" she asked.

While Sylvia reached for her bifocals so she could answer, Clayton lifted and hugged the child. Janice had never been so inquisitive. Their fair-haired daughter hadn't questioned where they lived or why they chose a certain place to visit on a particular weekend. Janice had accepted everything Sylvia and Clayton did — until Melvin came into the picture. Clayton promised himself he would never let some boy take Rita over so completely.

"What does it do?" Rita asked Clayton as she pointed at Safe Distance.

Sylvia said softly, "I think it makes Clayton feel secure."

"Drop it, Sylvia." He didn't need her playing junior psychiatrist again and telling him that he was really worried not about radiation, but about Melvin.

Rita studied the new equipment sharing the valuable space on the trailer wall along with Sylvia's cross-stitchings and a number of household utensils. While other children might have been dissuaded from getting some toy because of its price, Rita's obstacle to new toys was space. "Rita, honey, we just don't have the room," Clayton told the child repeatedly. In an average home, she might have fantasized about having life-size doll furniture, a fire truck, and a real pony, but Clayton saw that, from necessity, Rita had come to value smaller, obtainable things: a gold ring decorated with three forget-me-not flowers, a four-inch doll with a stream of fuzzy red hair. When Clayton took her shopping for a treat, it touched him that she knew to select some tiny item that wouldn't make him shake his head sadly at its size.

"If it starts flashing and making noise, that means we're some place where we could get sick. Then we have to drive away until the detector stops making noise," Clayton explained as he set her down and knelt to Rita's height.

"Like you told me to keep away from Jerry when he had a cold?"

"That's right," Sylvia said, rolling her eyes at him.

*   *   *

77

"Let's go play bingo," Sylvia called to Rita, who was stuck in front of the TV with Poco.

"Come on, Rita," Clayton said, flicking off the television. "Come along and bring me some luck."

Rita stood up, then tromped over to Clayton and took his hand. She had chocolate on one side of her mouth and a smear of it on the front of her T-shirt. Sylvia noticed the stains too, and went off to find a fresh shirt.

"That's my girl," he said as Sylvia tucked Rita's clean shirt into her shorts. Both of them looked up at him.

Under a blue tent just outside the community building, floodlights lit a swarm of picnic tables and a raised platform in the center, where the bingo caller stood. Marked white balls popped in a machine.

"By George!" An exaggerated English accent took Clayton by surprise.

"I thought I saw that ole U. S. of A. map on your jalopy. I said to Dot, 'That's got to be none other,' " said an immense man wearing a bright green shirt.

Sylvia and Clayton had met Charles and Dot Pike in Indiana three years earlier. The couples were about the same age and had discussed their unconventional retirement between games of gin and pinochle.

At first Clayton hadn't believed it when people said, "See you around." But Pikey wasn't the only person they'd run into again at a different trailer park.

"We saw Pete and Luanne in Pennsylvania," Sylvia said. "What was that park called?" she asked Clayton. They spent half their time helping each other recall the names of things.

"Was he still whittling ducks?" Pikey asked.

"He was doing a groundhog last we saw him," Sylvia said.

"Road Haven," Clayton said, remembering the name of the park.

Sylvia told Clayton that meeting up with people again was proof that coincidences were all around them, just waiting to happen. Clayton felt that maybe they weren't coincidences at all.

"I'm surprised we don't run into folks we've seen before more often. I mean, there are just so many trailer parks, so many people driving rigs from one to the next," Clayton said.

"And so many states," Pikey added.

So many states. That's what worried Clayton about Melvin. A man less than half their age could slice through the country like a hot knife in butter, as Sylvia would put it.

"Had any of the wildfires down here yet?" Clayton asked.

"Not so far. A little trouble near Orlando. But there's no prediction of rain any time soon, either." Pikey glanced overhead at the sun, then back toward Clayton. "Will you look at this?" he said, pointing to Rita.

In his amazement at how much the child had grown, Pikey seemed like a bachelor to Clayton, not the father of seven children and grandfather of twenty. Pikey's wife, Dot, had once shown him and Sylvia a family portrait of the entire clan in formation. It was easy to pick out Pikey and Dot's most noticeable features — wide-set eyes, long noses, almost nonexistent upper lips — repeated in muted variations among the offspring. Clayton had felt a twinge of jealousy just thinking of the noisy Thanksgiving table and the jokes of generations mingling in the air with the aromas of steaming food, a football game playing under all the voices. The Pikes' oldest daughter owned a 110-inch dining room table, Dot had once boasted.

Since they'd gotten custody of Rita, Clayton felt content that they were a family of three again. Some days Rita would do something so similar to what Janice had once done — blow bubbles from a wand and try to catch them, not with her mouth or hand but with the tips of her fingers — that Clayton would momentarily forget how much time had passed.

Pikey, Dot, Sylvia, and Clayton sat at a large picnic table with lines of bingo cards between them. Dot wore a white T-shirt with the words "Hog Tied" stenciled in red across her chest. Her large breasts pressed up against the edge of the picnic table as she leaned in to arrange her cards. Sylvia and Clayton were not small people, but sitting across from Pikey and his wife created a dangerous imbalance.

Clayton watched Sylvia hoarding a collection of red plastic circles in the palm of her hand. She alternated preparing her cards, talking to Dot, and watching Rita. After Rita had examined the bingo cards and markers, she concentrated on her coloring book. Although Clayton worried about Rita growing up without any children around her, mostly only retired people, Sylvia assured him that Rita was already an independent child with a firmly established set of likes and dislikes.

"Let's get this show on the road," Clayton said.

"We keepin' you from some other engagement?" Pikey asked.

"With the boob tube," Sylvia said.

"Don't listen to her, Rita," Clayton said, though Rita was preoccupied with a red crayon and an outline of a horse.

"Where you folks from?" a man from the next table asked Clayton.

"Baltimore. Originally," Clayton answered.

The small, white-haired man tilted his head back and put his right hand to his chin. "I-95 and 495 if I'm not mistaken," he said.

Clayton smiled, and the man's wife bent forward to explain. "He does this all the time."

"Danbury, Connecticut," Pikey said.

"I-84 and Route 7," the man answered quickly. His wife poked him and pointed to his bingo card.

"Man must have a map of the entire U.S. engraved on his

brain," Pikey said. Clayton pictured the maps he'd gotten with Safe Distance and wondered how long it would take to memorize all the danger spots.

When Rita interrupted with "Atlanta," which they'd bypassed a couple of days earlier, Clayton thought of Melvin — the subject that never left his mind for long. He wished the stranger had a location for Melvin that would never change.

Sylvia claimed that Melvin had probably lost interest in Rita after being in the institution so long, but Clayton knew Sylvia's tricks to calm him. Plus, he figured that all this time being confined could have made Melvin even more focused on Rita.

The bingo began. Although Clayton paid careful attention to his cards, he didn't come close on the first couple of games. Just when he'd think he was getting somewhere, a voice from deep in the crowd would put the skids on him winning.

"Bingo," Rita screamed, startling him. People looked around, confused by the shrill child's voice.

"By George," Pikey said. Clayton studied his cards to be sure he hadn't missed something, then stared at the others at his table. Nobody had a bingo.

"Hold your cards, ladies and gentlemen. This is not an official bingo," the caller said. The crowd grumbled. One man threw his card into the air as if it were a losing ticket at the race track.

"Shit," said Clayton under his breath. "Tell her she can't do that, Sylvia."

"You tell her," Sylvia said. Dot covered her mouth with her hand and giggled.

Clayton put his arm around Rita, but didn't take his eyes off the cards. After three more games passed, Clayton leaned toward Dot and asked, "Four corners?"

"Nope. Straight," Dot answered succinctly without glancing up.

"Bingo," Clayton yelled. After the caller awarded him the win, Clayton returned to the table with a crisp twenty, which he snapped proudly in the air. Rita laughed when he held it next to her eyes.

"Thanks, kiddo. You brought me good luck," he said to her.

"The crowd would have skinned you alive if it hadn't been a good bingo," Pikey said in a lowered voice.

Instead of addressing Pikey's comment, Clayton turned to Rita and said, "Don't ever let a crowd intimidate you, Rita." He bent over and kissed her on the forehead.

Midway through the games, a break was called. People in light blue caps collected money for new cards, while those in red caps sold refreshments.

"Anybody smell something?" Clayton asked, looking around the table.

"He's been going on like this for near three days," Sylvia said. "Clayton, I don't smell a thing."

"Let's stretch our legs," Pikey suggested, struggling out from behind the picnic bench. "Get me one of the special jackpot cards when the guy comes around," he said to Dot.

Dot said to Sylvia, but loud enough for Clayton to hear, "He's going to be checking on the RV. Ever since we got broke into, he's been a nut with keeping an eye on the rig."

"You got broken into?" Clayton asked Pikey. Every time he turned around there was something new to upset him. Pikey nodded and explained about a band of "rip-off artists" who preyed on elderly people in RVs.

"That's a damn shame," Clayton said.

"Shame? It was an outrage," Pikey said. "I kicked myself for being so hospitable to them."

"You met them?"

"I had them to dinner," Pikey said. He paused. "They were kids."

Pikey explained how the thieves had probably cased the rig during dinner, then returned the next day when they knew Pikey and Dot would be taking their morning walk.

"One of them shit on the floor if you can believe that."

"What?" Clayton had never heard of such a thing.

"Kids," Pikey said in resignation, then went on to reprimand himself for trusting people he met on the road. He said there was a tendency to share with other RVers, to think they were all good people.

"Animals," Clayton said, shaking his head. Melvin, Clayton had to remind himself, wasn't even a kid anymore. At almost thirty, he might be more destructive than Pikey's intruders.

With the women and Rita out of sight, Clayton felt free to talk about what he called "the situation" back in Baltimore. The Pikes were the only couple Clayton had confided in about Melvin.

"Any word about you know who?" Pikey asked.

Clayton relayed the information he'd received from Marlene. "He gets to come home on weekends now. Stays with his parents." Marlene had tried to assure them that Melvin was as harmless as a bug in a jar, but Clayton wasn't so sure. He couldn't imagine that Melvin would come looking for his daughter in a place like the bingo tent of Dixie Camperland in Florida; Melvin would think they'd be somewhere like the Ramada. Still, Clayton imagined Melvin searching for traces of Rita on the weekends, showing photos to strangers. He figured it was only a matter of time before Melvin manipulated enough people to gain access to his daughter.

"So, you all planning on seeing one of those shows like Liberace when you're in Vegas?" Pikey asked.

"I think Sylvia wants to see somebody funny," Clayton said, "to take her mind off certain things." Even as he spoke, he knew he was talking about himself and not his wife.

"Out there they're all funny," Pikey said. He suggested Digby's Silver Nugget as the best bargain for hookups.

"One of the big hotels gives coupons for a free blood pressure test," Pikey added. Clayton laughed.

Pikey and Dot were two of only a handful of people who knew about Rita's background. When Rita was still a baby, Sylvia had even told people Rita was their daughter to avoid repeating the details of Janice's death. Clayton remembered boondocking for three straight weeks — in a farmer's field outside of Knoxville, a bank parking lot in Chattanooga, a police station in Birmingham — after a particularly difficult stay next to overly inquisitive strangers at the Fairfield Trailer Park near Lexington, Kentucky.

Later, Sylvia modified her story and told strangers who asked that Rita was their adopted daughter. The explanation satisfied most, but Clayton didn't doubt that some people wondered what would ever possess a couple in their fifties to adopt a child. These days, though, Sylvia didn't say anything. She and Clayton just let people stare and think whatever they wanted.

Over the years, they'd talked about actually adopting their granddaughter, but in the end decided, in Sylvia's words, to "let well enough alone." There was no guarantee that outsiders deciding on Rita's future would understand the advantages of life in an RV over a more overtly stable environment manned by a biological father.

"Where can I buy a gun, Pikey?"

"You're in Florida, friend. You can pick one up most any place." Pikey stopped and took a deep labored breath. "Why do you want to go getting a gun?"

"Protection," Clayton said simply.

"Protection," Pikey repeated. He sighed and explained that it hadn't protected his rig from being ripped off. After a few minutes he said, "You want a .38. It's what the police use."

"What? Cops use a .38?" Clayton laughed at himself. Here he was thinking guns and Sylvia was probably chitchatting with Dot about recipes. If he reproached her for not being as concerned as he was, she'd tell him she'd done her share as well as his of worrying about Janice years ago.

Maybe Sylvia was right about him having the fire smell in his brain. Walking with Pikey, Clayton could have sworn he detected the odor of smoke, of wildfires on the way toward him. In some parts of Georgia, firemen had been fighting the fires for almost a week. Despite the trenches the men dug to try to control the fires, flames had sprung up determined and plentiful as crops, then grew all out of proportion. When Clayton had crossed the border into Florida, with the air growing increasingly warm, he'd worried they were getting closer to the core of the fire. Even though Sylvia had said, "It's Florida, Clayton. It's supposed to be hot, for God's sake," he knew she was trying to keep him from panicking.

"Wait a minute, Pikey," Clayton said, stopping. "I swear that's smoke. I can see smoke."

They quickened their pace and Clayton's heartbeat corresponded. "I'll be damned," Pikey said.

A gray billow of smoke veiled one of the trailers near them. Clayton's mind flipped to a scene where the entire trailer park was burning and people stood in the safety of the river, holding up whatever possessions they were able to save — TVs, radios, clothes, and jewelry. Clayton would have Rita in his arms. Not hooked onto his hips, but high overhead in both hands like a prize he'd just won.

"Looks like Evelyn's trailer," Pikey said as they neared the smoke.

"Who's Evelyn?" Clayton asked.

In addition to the smoke encircling the trailer, rusted barbed wire spun around the entire rig so that it appeared caught in an immense web. An elderly woman gestured behind a window and screamed something about bacon. While Clayton wrestled with the barbed wire near the trailer door, Pikey unhooked the rig's water tank, then fumbled his way inside to the kitchen area. Pikey doused the flames and Clayton opened windows.

"Near ruined my dinner," Evelyn yelled when the fire was finally out.

"Let us help you clean up this mess," Clayton offered.

"Get out of here!" Evelyn said. Clayton looked over at Pikey, who shrugged his shoulders. Once outside, Pikey explained that he'd gone through a similar routine with Evelyn about five months earlier.

"Her old man died," Pikey said finally, as a way of explaining the barbed wire and Evelyn's general defensiveness. Stuck in the ground in front of the trailer were signs that read NO SOLICITING and NO TRESPASSING.

"And now she's on the road by herself," Clayton filled in. He sucked his finger, which he'd cut on the barbed wire. He couldn't imagine Sylvia moving across the country if anything happened to him, and yet she'd have to if Melvin were still on the loose. Sometimes Clayton thought that their original plan to just drive off wherever and whenever they wanted had been shot to hell. Melvin made him feel he was running away instead of toward a specific destination.

Pikey shook his head. "She's got her spot here paid up for two years."

"Bet the owner of the park's kicking himself," Clayton said.

"Not really. He actually gets business out of this." Pikey gestured at Evelyn's trailer. "People pass the word about Evelyn and then folks end up staying here just to catch a look."

Clayton studied the trailer. He was surprised that they'd penetrated it so quickly.

"Now you might hear the rumor that she's still got the old

man in there with her," Pikey said as he shifted his weight from one leg to the other. "Not to be believed. I saw the ambulance. Five months ago it happened. The medics definitely dragged him out."

"You've been here five months?" Clayton asked.

Clayton recalled the theory that had been on his mind lately — that the RV lifestyle attracted odd types, mostly people who wouldn't be satisfied waiting patiently for death in the usual Florida condos. The retired people Clayton ran into these days had, all their normal lives, harbored the subversive plan to try to outrun death. Sylvia and Clayton had met people even younger than themselves who proudly announced that they'd taken off as soon as their youngest child graduated from high school. Stable, dependable neighbors turned off their televisions and took to the road to see everything they'd been missing all those years they'd dedicated to lawns and cars and kids. He envied their motives; they were free of his own complicated agenda.

As soon as Clayton felt the heat of the tent floodlights, he spotted Rita up on a picnic table, dancing to a fast tune. Rita swung her little arms and kicked her feet and laughed uncontrollably.

"I couldn't stop her," Sylvia said, smiling proudly at Clayton.

"If she don't look like that girl. What was her name, Pikey?" Dot asked.

"Shirley Temple," Pikey said.

"Shirley Temple," Dot said as if she hadn't heard him. "You ought to get this little gal into show business," she kept on.

Sure, Clayton thought. Sylvia would never have allowed Janice such freedom. Janice would have been in bed asleep at nine o'clock, not entertaining a bunch of old fogies. Sometimes it was hard for Clayton to accept how lax his wife had become.

Pikey said, "I don't know how you two do it." He shook his

head. "Don't get me wrong. I adore my grandchildren. But I love to hand 'em back, too."

Dot gave her husband an obvious nudge. "What?" Pikey asked, turning to her. "I'm just telling the truth."

Clayton didn't know how he and Sylvia kept up with Rita either. Always, the inquisitive, active child demanded most of their attention. And yet the alternative was unthinkable — that Melvin's family would raise Rita. Grandparents who would rather forget that their son had ever married in the first place. A wacky aunt who painted flags on women's fingernails. Clayton hoped he could teach Rita to think for herself before she ever — God forbid — encountered her father.

After a half dozen more games, Clayton said, "Well, let's call it a night before I lose any more of my hard-earned pension." He sighed.

"You won tonight," Sylvia reminded Clayton.

"Don't forget about the cards we had to pay for. And the snick-snacks," he said, doing some mental subtracting.

Sylvia put her arm through Clayton's. "He's getting so tight, I swear he squeaks when he bends over." She laughed and pointed at his feet. "He won't even buy himself a pair of summer shoes."

Pikey and Dot stared at Clayton's leather shoes with the part near the toes cut away.

"They suit me just fine," Clayton said.

"Air-conditioned," Pikey said.

"Air-conditioned," Rita repeated.

"You could get a pair of decent summer shoes for about ten dollars," Sylvia said.

"Ten dollars is ten dollars," Clayton said. He took Rita's hand.

Sylvia tried to minimize an expense by considering what she called the big picture. She said when you pulled back and evaluated how unimportant a ten-dollar bill was, you wouldn't worry. Clayton told her that kind of thinking could get them into debt. Up until a couple of years ago, Clayton hadn't seriously thought that their money was exhaustible, but now he wasn't sure. If something unexpected came up, say a fire, they'd have to dip into their modest savings.

Clayton liked to have a little money coming in, or at least the promise of money. He wanted to be able to show that he could support Rita if Melvin got some attorneys on his side. So he routinely picked up part-time carpentry work from the local unions and did small home-improvement jobs when they stayed in one place long enough to get responses from his newspaper ad.

Two and a half years before, outside of Cincinnati, Sylvia had worked afternoons in a library. She brought home reports of things she'd read and, of course, ideas for places they could visit. Sylvia's quilting had also helped them out. A woman in Dallas had paid eighty dollars for one of Sylvia's quilts. And Sylvia had told him it was just bunches of scrap material all sewn together.

"Do you ever do any temp work?" Pikey asked.

"Sure," Clayton said, elaborating about signing up with Senior Temporary Services in Ohio. He relayed to Pikey the interview with Cora Squabb, who had sat behind a messy metal desk. Her constant grin had gotten under Clayton's skin.

"Long-term temp, Mr. Vaeth, or day to day?" she'd asked.

"Pardon me?"

Cora had described the two long-term temporary jobs available. One job, working for an electronics manufacturer, involved dumping small containers of used oil into huge canisters. When he considered that job, he couldn't forget about Sylvia's comment that Melvin's eyes reminded her of the color of old WD-40.

The second job was disassembling ovens in a chain of bakeries that were being converted into rapid-lube franchises. Each of the positions had an indefinite closing date.

"Now in the short term, the jobs are more diversified."

Clayton had nodded, though he was still trying to picture himself shuffling around with containers of oil and running into months-old doughnuts that had fallen behind the ovens.

"Do you like children, Mr. Vaeth?"

"Sure," Clayton had said immediately. Didn't he spend all his energy on Rita — teaching her, warning her, protecting her?

"Well, maybe this would interest you. A Cincinnati department store wants a pumpkin to greet kids and push a new line of Halloween costumes."

Clayton had stared at Cora.

"We had one of our heavyset seniors play Santa last Christmas. He had a heck of a lot of fun. Quite a hit with the youngsters, too."

Clayton thought that if anyone at Evergreen, especially Bud Harper, saw him dressed as a pumpkin, they wouldn't let him forget it.

Clayton made a hundred dollars the week before Halloween, walking through Young's Department Store in orange tights and a great orange papier-mâché middle, his face and neck heavily made up like the stem of a giant pumpkin, his head topped with a green felt hat. That same fall he'd also painted a high school cafeteria and opened mail for a team of criminal defense attorneys, but neither job had been as fun or had paid as well as the pumpkin gig.

"Pikey would make a good pumpkin," Dot said as the couples split off on the way to their respective rigs.

Clayton said good night. The only problem with the pumpkin was that it had frightened Rita when Sylvia had taken her to

90

the store. As soon as she spotted the orange costume, Rita had begun to scream, and she couldn't be comforted until Clayton pulled off the hat, slapped at his chest repeatedly, and hollered, "Rita, it's me. It's only me."

Clayton stayed three days longer in Florida than he'd intended. He showed Rita the ocean, which got her squealing and made him hurry after her tiny figure racing along the water's edge. He bought a .38 one afternoon after Pikey gave him directions to a combination gun shop and used book store. Now, with Pikey and Dot leaving, there was nothing to hold him from pushing on toward Vegas. With any luck, he could still reach it before his sister.

Pikey honked and rolled down the window of his RV. "See you folks around," he yelled over the quiet campground. Pikey wasn't much for good-byes. "Have some of that fresh beef jerky for me when you get out west," he said.

"Where's Dot?" Clayton called back.

"Still sleeping," Pikey answered, "like half this dead-ass camp." He laughed loudly and waved good-bye to Rita.

"Will we see them soon?" Rita asked. Clayton rested his hand on her head.

Even though they didn't know Pikey's precise travel plans, Sylvia said she was sure that they'd eventually catch up with the Pikes again. The funny thing was, if Sylvia and Clayton still lived on Garden Road in Maryland, they probably wouldn't have socialized with the loud, sloppy couple. They reminded Clayton of people his family called hillbillies.

"When people retire, they all pretty much end up in the same backyard," Clayton explained, as much to himself as to Sylvia. He was drying dishes while Sylvia washed and Rita set out a game of cards. "Everything evens out when you're out of work." He alternated wiping silverware and playing crazy eights with Rita.

About an hour and a half after Pikey barrelled out of Dixie Camperland, dust billowing up around his rig as if he were driving a herd of cattle, Dot knocked on Sylvia and Clayton's door.

"Any idea where Pikey's got to now?" she asked a little impatiently. Sylvia and Clayton looked at each other.

"You can let me in on it if he's trying to pull one of his tricks or something." She held a large laundry basket full of clothes heavily scented with fabric softener.

Clayton felt Rita behind him. When she took hold of his belt, he thought of an anchor holding him loosely in place as he bobbed and swayed with different emotions.

"Dot, he left a while ago," Sylvia finally said.

"Did he say where he was headed?"

"I mean, he left. For Houston."

"I-10 and 45," Clayton said, but the women ignored him.

Clayton watched Dot's eyes grow wide. She pushed her lips together and out. He imagined Dot was debating between mistake and intention. "Jesus," Dot said. "I thought I told him I was going to do laundry first." By the time she actually entered the trailer and set her laundry basket down, her eyes had filled with tears.

"Now, Dot," Clayton said. "It's OK." Simultaneously he tried to comfort Dot and keep Rita from getting upset. "Why don't you go get one of your card games and play with Dot?" he asked Rita. "Old maid," he suggested.

"Old maid," Dot said and started to cry.

"Nice one, Clayton," Sylvia said.

"It's a card game," he said, flustered. He looked over at Rita, who was staring at Dot. Clayton hoped her little mind wasn't rooting into the mysterious territory of her father, imagining that Melvin had abandoned her.

Clayton couldn't believe a good-hearted guy like Pikey would actually leave his wife, especially with all those children and grandchildren to cement the relationship. But then you could never tell with people. He remembered Sylvia reading him a story about a woman who left scrambled eggs cooking on the stove when she started up her car and drove away from her three children.

Sylvia slapped the newspaper against a tabletop. "Let's go catch up with him," she said.

"Like hell. I ain't chasin' after him like some dog. No way. He can come back for me or he can keep on goin'," Dot said suddenly angry. "Whoever heard of a husband leavin' a woman with nothin' but a basket of *his* shirts?" Dot began to wail. "Son of a bitch," she managed to hiss.

"She's just upset," Clayton whispered to Rita. Insecure with all the commotion, Rita cuddled next to him at the table.

While Sylvia made coffee, Dot questioned Clayton. "Did he say anything to you about this?" Clayton shook his head, forced to a place he knew well — in cahoots with men who, without a word, left women and children.

"Well, you might as well make yourself at home here until you get word from him," Sylvia said. Dot turned on the television.

"Want to watch with Dot?" Clayton asked, but Rita shook her head. She seemed afraid to go near her now that Dot was by herself. Maybe Rita was afraid that being alone was contagious. A couple more years and Clayton figured he could be as good as any child psychiatrist in identifying moods, clues to problems.

"Clayton's got *Raiders of the Lost Ark* if you want to look at a movie," Sylvia said.

It was one big mess. People left people they had no business abandoning. Other people pursued people they should leave alone. All the pushing and pulling without a thought for the other person. Clayton was thinking again of Melvin, the man who'd grown into a phantom that never left his mind.

He could see that Sylvia was shaken, too, not only by the fact that Pikey had taken off without Dot but also by Dot's complete surprise. Sylvia had told him she'd been astonished at herself six years ago in Wisconsin, at her inability to move from her parents' house. She'd practically grown roots on the bottoms of her feet when she returned to the musty-smelling house going on forty years to the day she'd left. She and Clayton had assumed the opposing sides of her own internal battle — the dutiful, homebound Sylvia versus the adventurous, independent Vee. She said she wouldn't have wondered had Clayton driven away and left her standing in the doorway to her parents' house.

Once Sylvia got her senses back, as Clayton had put it, and left Topstone with him, they hadn't talked about the incident. The farther they drove from Wisconsin, the closer he began to feel to her. As he drove and the sun set across the prairie or first light bounced off low city buildings, what they had with each other came into focus. He suspected Sylvia hadn't even loved him at first. During the first months of their marriage, Sylvia had cried a lot. He guessed she was agonizing over whether she'd done the correct thing or merely the safe thing by marrying.

Sylvia had married at just about the same time as Pauline, her high school friend from Milwaukee. Pauline wrote Sylvia long letters on damp onion skin paper that might have been cried over. Pauline had fallen in love the way Clayton had read about it — suddenly, passionately, irrevocably. Pauline and her husband never had children, never wanted to upset the splendid balance of their relationship, and never fell out of love as their friends and even their families had predicted.

Sylvia bluntly told Clayton that their own marriage didn't have what she called "the intensity" of Pauline's. Still, the two young brides shared certain attitudes. While their friends talked endlessly of wedding details, Pauline and Sylvia viewed such flourishes as unimportant, trivial even, compared with the relationship itself. And when those same friends went through separations and divorces, Sylvia informed Pauline and said to Clayton, "I told you so."

Clayton had always thought that if Sylvia hadn't been so taken with Pauline's romantic onion-skin letters, maybe their own daughter wouldn't have lost her head over a loser. Probably he was being too hard on Sylvia. Most women had a hidden agenda of romance that seldom worked out.

About an hour before dinner, an RV horn blared loudly outside the trailer. Sylvia dropped the carrot she was peeling; Dot looked up from the TV; Rita stood up from her coloring book; and Poco began to piddle on the plastic in front of the refrigerator.

"Damn," said Clayton, watching the dog.

"Where the hell's my wife?" Pikey yelled.

Dot stood up quickly, spilling the seven and seven she was drinking.

"Pikey," Rita said loudly. Her expression looked more surprised than relieved, a picture of Clayton's reaction.

Sylvia put her hand on Dot's arm and said, "Let him wait a second."

"Like hell," Dot said. Clayton had never seen a fat woman move so fast. Sylvia's cigarette rolled out of the ashtray, across the table, and onto the floor. On her way to following Dot, Rita grabbed at the cigarette, but Clayton got to it first.

"Not so fast, young lady," Clayton said to Rita. He put out

the cigarette. "You stay here while we straighten things out," he said, but Rita kept on going. Impressed by Rita's judgment about when she could get away with ignoring him, Clayton trailed the women outside.

"By George," Pikey said enthusiastically as Dot came up to the rig.

"Forget 'by George.' Where the hell have *you* been?" Dot yelled. She wiped tears from her face.

"I was nearly three hundred miles down the road when I realized you weren't behind me." There was a surprised silence as Pikey and Dot stared at each other. "I thought maybe you bailed out at the truck stop in Mobile."

"I told you I wanted to do a load of wash before we left."

"I thought you were still in bed."

Clayton felt Sylvia at his side.

"How could I be in bed?" Dot screeched.

"I saw this big lump," Pikey said, his voice growing tender.

Clayton smiled when Pikey stepped down from the RV and grabbed his wife in an embrace. "What you gawking at like some teenager?" Pikey said to Clayton, then grinned.

Clayton held up his hand to the departing RV. Rita imitated him. A light rain touched his hand and cooled his face. Soon the only sounds he could hear were droplets tapping the brush and then the metal roof of his rig. With relief he watched the ground darken. He stood in the rain, the water delicately streaking his face and hands, spotting his shirt. He imagined a shower, then a downpour, that would rinse away the confusion of the afternoon, carry off all impending danger. Clayton didn't move until Rita's small voice jolted him with, "I'm getting wet."

He picked her up. She felt good and solid in his arms, despite the pain in his elbow, a spot arthritis had invaded. Sylvia pointed out a small garden that had been abandoned by some traveler.

"I didn't use to understand how a person could plant a garden and then not see it through," she said.

It still seemed odd to Clayton to allow strangers to pick the fleshy vegetables and tasty leaves you'd planted, but Sylvia said it was important to leave things for others. Except for Melvin. "I wouldn't leave a bag of garbage for you know who," she said.

Rita squirmed in Clayton's arms. Sylvia exhaled, directing her cigarette smoke away from them. It trailed off and disappeared before anyone who might have been following could possibly track them down.

Rita sat between Clayton and Sylvia. As Clayton drove, occasionally humming softly, Sylvia read a list of words aloud, and then turned the book toward Rita to display the corresponding pictures. Rita studied the bright images and the smooth curling letters that spelled out each word. Clayton listened to her say the sounds of the succession of letters. Rita appeared to like having Sylvia hold up the pages marked with letters so she could give each picture a name. Rita easily repeated words when they were displayed a second and third time. Sylvia explained they were getting a head start on Rita's first-grade education.

Clayton noticed that when Sylvia went too fast or when Rita wanted Sylvia's eyes fixed on her and not on something out the window, Rita purposely made a mistake. The kid was smart, knowing just how to capture Sylvia's full attention. He saw, too, that often Rita's concentration on the lesson was broken by a group of cows or a passing car with a noisy muffler or an odd-looking sign that would cause her to ask, "What does it say, Vee?"

"If she doesn't keep her mind on the book, she'll never learn to read," Clayton said, his tone blaming Sylvia. He'd advised

Sylvia any number of times that while they were traveling she should give Rita instruction in the evening, when they stopped driving and there were fewer distractions. Sylvia argued that the child was too tired by then.

"If you stopped driving at a decent hour, we wouldn't be so tired," Sylvia said.

"I thought we wanted to keep on schedule," Clayton said. He reminded her of the sites she wanted to see in Arizona and of the camping reservations they'd made in Texas.

Before Rita, Clayton thought that his and Sylvia's differences had evened out like a stretch of cultivated land. Each knew where the other's sensitivities lay, some of them as immovable as boulders farmers learned to work around. Rita had changed that, springing new issues on them ("Wasn't Janice coloring *inside* the lines by now?" "She does not need *another* stuffed bear!") that could set them squabbling for hours. The big fight these days was about Rita's education. The disrupted lessons did not bode well for Sylvia's plan to teach Rita first grade herself instead of enrolling her in school in the fall.

Sylvia usually had to beg Clayton to stay in one place more than a couple of nights. But the past few days he'd been reconsidering. He proposed putting up in a trailer park, at least for the duration of the school year, so that Rita could attend classes in a somewhat conventional way. All the interesting people and places they visited, Sylvia argued, were far more valuable than whole days wasted in crowded, increasingly dangerous classrooms. He had to admit that Rita seemed to love the steady stream of new locations more than either he or Sylvia. They'd no sooner settle down in a park or a church lot than Rita would inquire, "Where are we going next?"

While traveling *was* a positive learning experience, Clayton wasn't so naive as to believe it had anything to do with getting Rita an education. He didn't think it set a good precedent to begin her first year of formal schooling in the front seat of a truck. Lately Rita's education concerned him almost as much as the threat of Melvin.

Sylvia had sent off for a Learn at Home series of books and materials to supplement her own training and to avoid breaking the law. The only way that Clayton had gone along with the plan was by making Sylvia agree that if Rita didn't pass the test at the conclusion of level one, they would opt for "real education." Already he was beginning to doubt his judgment in temporarily agreeing to the home schooling.

Clayton admired Sylvia's faith that the six-year-old would have no trouble passing. The difficulty wasn't all Sylvia's fault. There were just so many distractions. Because Rita was interested in everything, it was often difficult for her to focus on any one thing for long. Today Rita was attempting to draw a full line of the correct number of balloons pictured in the book Sylvia held up.

"Clayton, do you know where my glasses are?"

Sylvia was just not organized enough to be a teacher. Clayton tried to picture a classroom of children Rita's age, with a teacher constantly misplacing the correct textbook or lesson plan. Vee hadn't always been so scattered. And he hadn't always been such a worrier. When they lived on Garden Road, she kept track of all their bills and appointments and knew where everything was, even a store receipt from months earlier. He actually could have done with her being a little more relaxed back then, when the slightest difficulty got into bed with them. But the way things worked, you got what you wanted either too early or too late.

"Whoa, get a load of this," Clayton said as he pointed out a billboard with thick black letters spelling "BIKINI TRUCK WASH, FIVE MILES AHEAD." Sylvia had been after him for the past month to get the rig washed. "What do you say, Vee?"

99

"Now who's distracting Rita?"

"What's 'distracting'?" Rita asked as Clayton downshifted and pulled his rig into the truck wash. One truck idled ahead of them in line.

Sylvia and Clayton and Rita watched the young women in colorful swimsuits, short shorts, and halter tops rub soapy sponges over the exterior of a tractor trailer. Two women stood on the top of the truck, three worked on the sides, and a sixth washed the front of the truck. Clayton noticed that the one at the front of the truck spent a long time on the windshield.

"I'll bet that water's freezing," said Sylvia. Rita laughed at the young women in tennis shoes jumping all over the truck, hopping up and down as if obeying some unheard command.

After the blonde in the black two-piece had squirted all the soap off her portion of the truck, the trucker stepped out of his cab and stood back to watch the others finishing off his rig. The sun made the water sparkle from the hoses the women held.

"I think you missed a spot," he advised when one of them straightened up from her work.

"This is a big truck, mister," said a redhead who hadn't gotten her hair wet. She wore a white T-shirt that clung to her breasts like another layer of skin. The trucker grinned.

"Just the truck, or the house too?" the girl in the black bathing suit asked Clayton. She wasn't teasing him the way she had with the trucker, but she still leaned over and pressed her breasts against the front of his truck.

Rita asked if she could put her bathing suit on, too. Ignoring his granddaughter, Clayton kept his attention on the young women now hurrying over the exterior of his truck and trailer. Two of them wore sunglasses. He heard the hard spray of water directed against the metal, then the swishing of soapy sponges. A black-haired girl wearing large gold earrings and an aqua bikini bent forward along Clayton's side of the front fender to clean a headlight. With her behind right in his view, all he could do was laugh, then look quickly over at Sylvia, who shook her head slowly as she allowed him this indulgence. Rita rummaged in the glove compartment to find her sunglasses.

Keeping his eyes on the black-haired girl, Clayton imagined what the others were doing. He wanted to stand back and survey the many hands and legs and breasts moving all over the rig, as the trucker before him had done. He was thankful that Vee hadn't made some crack like, "These gals could be your granddaughters," but sat silently without interrupting his fantasy.

Granddaughter. The word jolted him to remember the child next to him. He prayed he wouldn't spend his old age protecting her from her father, only to have her grow into a woman like her mother, who'd entice some man just as weird as Melvin. All the more reason to make sure Rita was educated enough that she wouldn't have to do some kind of sexy work for money. The absurd thought of Rita having a lover made him slightly dizzy.

"Clayton, I'm going for a cup of coffee. You want one?"

"Nope. I'm just fine here."

"I bet you are," Sylvia said. "Rita, you staying or coming?"

"Coming," Rita answered without a pause. Clayton watched Rita take Sylvia's hand, then look up at her. He was glad they'd left. A wave of guilt settled on him as obvious as the thick end-of-the-day clouds. "Female" meant the curvy, fleshy women against his truck — their swinging hair and brightly painted fingernails. But it meant his granddaughter, too.

When the black-haired girl moved away from his rig, Clayton looked out at the land before him, the road to his left. The gray strip shot straight ahead, then disappeared. With the sun descending, shadows grew across the landscape so dramatically

101

that he thought of those speeded-up films of flowers blossoming in seconds.

Sylvia hurried toward the passenger door, Rita in front of her as if her grandmother were pushing her. They didn't have the coffee. Her face white, Sylvia climbed into the truck and held Rita tightly on her lap.

"Have you paid yet?" Sylvia whispered.

Clayton nodded and said, "Just did."

"Let's get out of here," Sylvia said.

"Sylvia, what's up?"

When she didn't answer, Clayton knew she thought she'd seen Melvin again. She'd imagined spotting him a few months back, in a 7-11 outside Oklahoma City. Coffee had been involved that time as well. But then she'd gotten herself so worked up that she'd spilled the hot liquid all over herself.

"How can you even be sure what he looks like after six years?" Clayton asked now, though he knew he'd have no trouble recognizing his son-in-law. He wanted to go into the truck stop to reassure himself that Sylvia was mistaken, but he didn't want to encourage Sylvia's imagination by appearing to take her "visions" too seriously.

"Can we get going?" Sylvia asked.

"We didn't pay for my gum," Rita announced as she tried to unwrap the package of Wrigley's. She held it up to Clayton for help.

Clayton took the gum and was surprised he had trouble himself; his hands shook.

"I'll ask Mona," Rita said, pointing to the young woman in the wet T-shirt who was rinsing out a soapy pail.

"How does she know her name?" Clayton asked, but Sylvia was too preoccupied to answer. It concerned him that the child would just walk up and talk to anyone.

"Clayton," Sylvia said sharply, and he immediately started the engine.

"Vee saw a ghost," Rita said as she separated a stick of gum from its wrapper and folded it the way Sylvia did before sliding it into her mouth.

"A ghost?" Clayton said, feigning a playful tone. "Was it Casper?" he asked, and Rita laughed. He glanced at Sylvia, but she stared straight ahead.

Clayton got some speed up. He wondered if Sylvia could be right. It wasn't impossible. They ran into people they knew, like Pikey and Dot in Florida, who weren't even following them. Melvin could be stalking him and Sylvia, keeping his distance until circumstances were perfect, when they were isolated enough for him to snatch Rita and leave without a trace.

Incidents like this dropped Clayton into a fearful emotional place. He wanted to reassure Sylvia that Melvin was nowhere nearby, but he didn't know that for sure. Sylvia's reaction *might* be a premonition. Clayton had no practice in taking charge against danger. The exhilarating self-reliance that came from setting up camp disappeared when he was second-guessing Melvin.

"What say we give Marlene a call tomorrow?" he asked Sylvia.

"We'll see," she said softly.

"We'll give her the address of the campgrounds in Texas," he said. "She might have a little mail for us." Marlene sent on bank statements, and clippings from the local newspaper.

"I gave her the address weeks ago," Sylvia said.

"That's right," he said. More and more often he found himself forgetting details. "But we still should give her a call." Sylvia mentioned that she'd heard about phones you could use while traveling, but Clayton said the price was sure to be out of their ballpark.

"Let me talk this time," Rita said.

Clayton looked over at Rita, her mouth full of gum. She'd changed him, transformed him from a man who read the paper at precisely the same time each morning, went to work to make perfect power tools, and returned in the evening to the TV to forget about that work. He'd become a grandfather — more a father, actually; there was no other nurturing man between him and Rita. His life had become more dramatic than a movie, and he was determined to come out the hero.

FOUR

———◆•◆•◆———

Bob and Carol Melnick's two-bedroom brick ranch sat at the end of a row of others on Pasture Lane in Pleasant Valley, New Mexico. The collection of houses, clumped together in a huge expanse of scrub land, reminded Clayton of giant lawn ornaments in a desert yard.

The backdrop to the tidy domestic scene was a magnificent contrast of mountains. The proximity, the immense size of them, awed Clayton. And beyond lay more rises in the land, their blue-gray color appearing to be a shadow of the foreground. The enormity of this world was nothing like Florida. There, amid the strip malls and sparse patches of ground and trees, only the ocean's vastness had impressed him. For a minute he considered that the mountains here in the southwestern part of the state resembled waves caught and frozen at their crest — the motion of nature stilled.

Once Clayton had thought of mountains as topographical features stuck onto the ground rather than extensions of the

105

ground. Before he'd started traveling, he'd never imagined there were so many kinds and colors of mountains. They were brown, black, salmon colored, and tricolored. Sometimes they were white-topped with snow or dotted with brush to produce, at a distance, the texture of animal hide.

The Melnicks' trailer was nowhere that he could see, not even out back of the house in case someone had a change of heart. Sylvia and Clayton had met the couple the year before at Graceland in Memphis, when the Melnicks had just decided that, after ten years of RVing, they were ready to return to stationary living. The Melnicks were the only people Sylvia and Clayton had met who admitted to wanting to move back into a house.

The sole reason Clayton was stopping in town, and he hadn't told Sylvia this, was because Carol was a teacher. He needed some advice from a professional. In his pocket was a letter he'd picked up yesterday in Texas. It was from Melvin. The second one in six years — that he knew of. Sylvia had kept the first one from him for the initial three weeks of their travels. He didn't imagine his wife had held any others from him, but he couldn't be positive.

Carol Melnick was extremely tall, had unnaturally black hair, and wore black-framed glasses that curved upward to dramatic points. A foot shorter than Carol, Bob stood in his stocking feet behind her. Bob showed Sylvia, Clayton, and Rita around the house, pointing out fixtures that didn't need securing and knickknacks not glued in place on shelves. Bob opened the doors of the full-size refrigerator and stove in spite of Carol's protests. "They remember what a stove looks like, Bob," she said. He might have been an electrician, but Clayton thought Bob had overlooked his potential as a salesman.

The living room featured a long, modern-style couch. Folded across its low back was a green blanket decorated with crocheted yellow and pink flowers, similar to one Sylvia had made. The morning newspaper lay open on the floor. Momentarily, Clayton wished himself back where there was room for everything, where permanence meant more than pulling an awning out of the side of a vehicle and unfurling a length of artificial turf.

Yet, he'd come to accept that hooking into electricity and a honey wagon was his version of settling down, that he and Sylvia would never adapt to a traditional house again. It was hard to imagine their belongings unattached and spread loosely over shelves and floors. If the size of the trailer irked Sylvia at least once a day, he knew she liked the way everything fit perfectly into place, though Clayton would often remark that she had a habit of losing track of those places.

"I don't know about you, Clayton, but I used to wake up five or six times a night and think I'd fallen asleep at the wheel," Bob said. He laughed and rubbed at a place on the back of his head where there was no hair.

Clayton couldn't imagine not being able to take off if he felt threatened, like back at the Bikini Truck Wash. He truly didn't remember how it felt to just stay still and guard your turf. He was old, no match for a man Melvin's age. His only defense was to stay on the move.

"Any problems with nuclear testing around here?" Clayton asked as he fingered the letter in his pocket.

"For God's sake," Sylvia said.

Carol made a gesture of dismissal with her hand, emphasizing that she had no regrets or worries about giving up life on the road. "Feel free to use the washer," she said. "God knows, I remember how it used to build up when Bob wouldn't spring for stopping at a park."

Sylvia smiled falsely at Carol's offer. Clayton knew she

resented people with inside information on how her life worked, especially the troublesome parts.

"Look at her," Bob said, exclaiming over Rita.

The stove, the refrigerator, even the coffee table appeared to intimidate her. She walked slowly, stalking the room with her mouth slightly open. Clayton saw through her eyes that everything was bigger than necessary. Rita was probably considering the bathroom large enough for her bedroom. She hadn't seen the inside of a house since she was a toddler. "It's like a museum," Rita said, and Bob and Carol laughed.

"Sylvia's been dragging us to look at every collection of gewgaws in this country," Clayton said. Clayton was uncomfortable, though he couldn't pinpoint why. He felt like a kid who'd come in from a softball game and been told to take his shoes off at the door. He was glad of Bob's offer of a drink. "I won't say no," Clayton said. After shaking the whiskey off the cherry, he handed it to Rita.

"Don't you remember the King's house, Rita?" Bob asked.

"I wouldn't call that a house," Clayton said, defending his granddaughter. He was remembering the velvet ropes holding back Graceland's curious tourists, the displays of jumpsuits, and the long blue room lined with gold and silver records. "Do you have a jungle room, Bob?" he joked.

The couples laughed at Rita, her hands behind her back according to Sylvia's instructions, as she bent her head to look at everything. "Angelfish," she called excitedly when she spotted the fish tank. Then, as if prompted by Rita's comment, Carol brought out a tray of cold shrimp. As she set the appetizers on the coffee table, someone knocked on the front door.

"That has to be Molly," Carol said brightly, explaining about the neighbors' daughter they'd invited to keep Rita company. Sylvia and Clayton looked at each other as Bob opened the door to a plump girl with curly hair.

Bob and Carol had gone to a lot of trouble, but Clayton thought Rita didn't really need company. After Molly was introduced, she immediately took a seat on the floor directly in front of the shrimp. "Help yourselves, people," Bob said. He explained that he'd gotten up at seven o'clock to cook and clean the shrimp.

Molly grabbed a shrimp in each of her hands, gobbled the food, and reached for more. "Go ahead, Clayton," Bob said as he lifted the plate away from Molly and toward Clayton, then asked the girls if they didn't want to go outside.

Clayton had almost forgotten the civilities that came with houses. Politeness could grow so thick in a house it stifled the most forthright person. After all, you couldn't simply drive away from neighbors you'd offended; you had to live with them. Sylvia wouldn't put up with a little hog like Molly in their trailer. He hoped Sylvia was taking the situation in for the next time she wondered if Rita was missing something not growing up in a house.

"So where are you headed next?" Bob asked.

Clayton explained about Nevada.

"Were the Muddy Mountains in Nevada or Utah, Carol?"

"Money Mountains?" Clayton asked.

"Oh, Clayton," Sylvia said, and they all laughed.

Dinner was ham and scalloped potatoes, a Jell-O mold that would never have fit in a rig's tiny refrigerator, and a large bowl of peas dotted with pearl onions. A lace tablecloth draped over the table, and real silverware marked each person's spot. Carol had even lit two candles, although it wasn't nearly dark. Clayton thought of how frequently he and Sylvia and Rita ate off paper plates to conserve water.

"You shouldn't have gone to so much trouble," Sylvia said.

Everything Clayton touched felt breakable. The delicately flowered dishes, the tall water glass, the china salt and pepper shakers in the shape of windmills. Rita looked as awkward as he felt. She had an expression like the first time Sylvia had taken her to church. Clayton was glad Bob and Carol hadn't asked Molly to stay for dinner. He'd heard the kid ask Rita if she was a gypsy.

Sylvia had brought a store-brand cheesecake for dessert. He knew she wished she'd baked something, even cookies, just to prove you didn't have to give up cooking when you lived in an RV. Carol cooed politely about the dessert, but Clayton thought it didn't fit with the rest of the carefully prepared dinner.

After dessert Rita went into the living room while the others stayed at the table.

"I have to say, the good thing about traveling is that we never would have found this place otherwise. We're from Pittsburgh originally," Bob said.

Clayton asked if Bob didn't feel he'd lost some of his independence since he'd stopped traveling. Bob shook his head and spoke. It seemed he'd been waiting for just such a question. "There's something about having a well that makes you feel self-sufficient as all get-out."

Later, Clayton peeked into the living room, where Rita slept against a mountain of throw pillows. "There's something I wonder if you could give me your opinion on," he asked.

"What's on your mind?" Bob asked, but Clayton turned toward Carol, the teacher.

Sylvia gave Clayton a look like he'd just told the Melnicks the color of her underwear.

Looking from Sylvia to Clayton and then back again, Carol said, "Is this something you both want to talk about?"

"Clayton, I don't think —" Sylvia started to say.

"She's a teacher, Sylvia."

"I don't care. I think we need to talk to a counselor."

"Jeez," Clayton said, "a counselor." Clayton remembered Charlie Lee from Evergreen going to a counselor after his wife died. Charlie had said the counselor showed him a load of pictures that he couldn't make a bit of sense of, and asked questions he'd long since forgotten the answers to, like when was he toilet trained. Clayton could do without shaking old feelings loose.

"I'll make us some fresh drinks," Bob said, standing up.

Clayton kept one hand on the letter in his pocket. Forwarded by Marlene to the Roadrunner Camp Grounds where they'd stayed in Texas, the envelope was addressed to Mr. and Mrs. Clayton Vaeth at the house on Garden Road. Clayton had checked for a return address but found none. When he'd read, "Dear Grandmother and Grandfather," the letters squeezed tight together, his palms got moist, and the hair on his forearms lifted to imminent danger the way Alvin's stood up around radiation. The letter from Melvin stated that he hadn't forgotten about them or about little Rita, and that he would be "visiting" them as soon as he could.

Clayton pictured the man who had taken his daughter away. Then he looked at his sleeping granddaughter, so small and lovely. He stood up and threw Melvin's letter onto the center of the table. From the sound that came from Sylvia — like she was gasping for air — Clayton knew he'd made a mistake. Sylvia would recognize the peculiar handwriting; the bizarre lettering made them fearful of their own names. Clayton glanced into the living room to be sure Rita was still sleeping, then went to his wife and put his hands on her shoulders.

Sylvia told the whole story to Carol. She hadn't really talked about Janice in years, but the details came out just as Clayton remembered them. He could almost imagine she was relaying someone else's story instead of their own. When she verbalized the details of the car accident, she seemed to be detailing the plot of a high-action movie full of color and intensity. Each specific led smoothly into the next.

"I thought the best thing would be to wait until fall to enroll Rita in school," Sylvia finished, looking straight at Carol as if the remark were solely for her benefit. Then she added, "I figured it would be less traumatic that way. Less of a disruption if we forgot about kindergarten and she started out fresh at the beginning of the school year."

Clayton wanted to say, "This is news to me," but kept still.

"Gosh, I wish you'd come earlier," Carol said, pushing up the sleeves of her blouse — ready to dig into their life. "We could have gotten her into a summer program down the road here." Carol explained that it would be a good idea for Rita to get used to playing with groups of children.

"After Las Vegas," she went on, "I recommend you settle down for the time being. Give the appearance of providing a stable home for the child."

Carol invited Sylvia and Clayton to spend the night in her spare bedroom instead of the RV. The yellow curtains and twin beds, with their green and yellow spreads tucked tight against each pillow, did look cozy and inviting.

"Where did you get all the furniture to fill up the house so fast?" Clayton asked, curious to know if Bob and Carol had secretly stashed their possessions when they'd first taken to the road.

"Actually," Bob said, "we bought it from a couple planning to RV." He explained, "We put an ad in the *RV Times*."

Sylvia would be remembering all the paraphernalia she sometimes missed from their old home. She and Clayton had gotten into the teasing habit of pinching each other whenever they looked for something that had been left with the present owners of their house.

"So how about it?" Bob asked. "After all, when's the last time you slept in a real bed?"

"Why, last night," Sylvia said.

"Well, if you change your minds, I'll leave the door unlocked," Bob said.

Clayton carried the sleeping Rita out to the trailer.

"They don't have to be so uppity now that they have a house again," Sylvia said and lit a cigarette.

"They weren't uppity, Sylvia. You were the one who was snooty," he whispered. Clayton liked his own bed as much as she did, but he worried that, by refusing Bob and Carol's hospitality, he'd insulted them. One night wouldn't have hurt Sylvia. And Rita would have enjoyed the new sleeping bag all set up for her.

"Well, I guess I resent them telling us how we should raise Rita."

"Carol only mentioned that they have a good school system here, Vee."

Sylvia murmured that she didn't think counselors would offer such blatant opinions. She'd heard that professionals merely pointed you in the direction you wanted to go anyway.

Sylvia and Clayton argued as they helped Rita undress.

"Clayton," Sylvia whispered as they got into bed, "Rita has to fit in with *our* lives, not the other way around." Clayton supposed that Sylvia didn't want to abandon herself completely to Rita for fear that what had happened with Janice had been partly her fault — suffocating the child with too much attention, protecting instead of preparing her.

"But we don't want to lose her," Clayton reminded Sylvia, pushing their argument back out of sight, into the deep shadows and creases of the covers.

In a few minutes, Clayton envied Sylvia breathing steadily with sleep. He couldn't lose himself in dreams while nuclear power was brewing energy strong enough to destroy ranges of mountains and Melvin surely sat awake in a small room making plans.

Two days later, Sylvia stayed behind in the trailer to write a thank you note to the Melnicks while Clayton and Rita walked toward a shop called the Doll Hospital in an Arizona town called Tall Tree. Ever since Florida, Rita had not let Clayton forget about his pledge to get her doll fixed. Unlike her mother, Rita was not one to let a promise drop. When Clayton had planned to take Janice to the zoo on a future Sunday or to the drive-in movie, he had to be the one to remind her — "Do you remember what today is?" More often than he liked to remember, instead of looking forward to the promised treat, Janice had forgotten it completely.

Rita ran her finger along the cracked face of an infant-size doll that had once belonged to Sylvia — Vee-Doll. The soft cloth body and hard head and hands and feet, which clicked when touched together, spent every night on Rita's pillow. When the material across the doll's chest had worn thin, Sylvia sewed the doll a tight-fitting undergarment.

In spite of the doll's scratched face and its unnatural, painted hair, Rita favored it over all others. In Florida, a box had fallen onto Vee-Doll and her face had cracked down the middle into a scar from chin to forehead. Rita said she was glad Vee-Doll was going to the hospital instead of her. She hadn't liked the doctor Clayton had taken her to in Ohio a year ago, and she hated the tonic prescribed to stimulate her appetite.

The Doll Hospital was located between a carpet store and a bait and tackle shop on the town's main street. The town was small and quiet, and despite its name there was no tree in sight. Although the place seemed equipped with all the necessities, it wasn't a spot he would have stopped in had Rita not insisted

114

about Vee-Doll. Rita peeked around the sign announcing REM-NANT SALE on the glass storefront and into the carpet showroom.

"You don't need to be looking in there," Clayton said, reminding himself that their carpeting needs had been reduced to the size of a stairway runner.

He paused outside Pete's Bait, where the walls were lined with lures and traps of all kinds, stuffed animal heads, and long, waxy fish bodies mounted on wood. In spite of the fact that she appeared to be fascinated by the items covering every inch of wall space, Rita laughed and repeated, "You don't need to be looking in there," when she saw Clayton staring at a bright green and purple wiggler.

Doll parts filled the Doll Hospital. On one shelf Clayton spotted hundreds of doll arms, and on another, a mass of legs and feet pointed in all directions. A round wooden bowl on the counter nearest Rita held handfuls of shiny doll eyes. A woman with stark red hair, dramatic black eye makeup, and a tattoo of a ladybug on her right upper arm gently took Vee-Doll from Rita's arms.

"That's a darling little girl you've got there, mister," the woman said. Her voice was husky. "What's your name, honey?"

Rita stared at the unusual-looking woman. "Rita. What's your name?" she asked, without looking down or hiding behind her grandfather. The bright, dark-haired child was defiantly alive amidst the dolls. Her eyes looked especially blue.

"She's not shy," Clayton said.

"Don't you be shy, either," the woman said, more to him than to Rita. "My name's Beth." Clayton heard muffled thumps behind the far wall, and pictured the giant rolls of carpet pushed to the linoleum floor, then unfurled to reveal their individual colors and textures.

115

"What's your baby's name?"

"Vee-Doll," Rita answered. Clayton didn't mention that Vee was his wife's nickname.

"The day after tomorrow she'll be good as new," Beth said. She hummed softly as she slid the doll into a plastic bag, tagged it, and set it on an empty shelf. Then with one hand she offered Rita a red lollipop, and with the other she held out a receipt for Clayton.

He nodded and walked to the door as he took Rita's hand. He wondered what the woman meant exactly when she said he shouldn't be shy. Although he was almost sixty-five, Clayton was still handsome. He was tall, and his hair had grayed evenly. He imagined the red-headed woman was a good dancer. And there was something soft and susceptible about her that contradicted her appearance. He wondered for a moment what kind of grandmother *she'd* make.

That afternoon Clayton played blackjack in the trailer with Sylvia. Although Sylvia said they needed to get in practice for Las Vegas, Clayton had a hard time concentrating on the cards.

At bedtime, Sylvia wore her hair in one thick braid, nothing of the color and texture of Rita's two delicate ones. Over the afternoon, some of her hair had pulled loose, and the braid now looked frayed against her white pillowcase.

She'd worn what she called a French braid back when they'd met, more than forty years ago, and then her hair had been naturally blonde. He'd taken her out for a traditional Maryland crab dinner. Although he'd advised her to dress casually, she had appeared in a white cotton dress and silver earrings. He couldn't stop smiling at her that night as she gaped at the newspaper spread across the dining table and at the huge heap of red, steamed, and seasoned crabs in the center. She drank a beer with him and watched how he opened the first crab, lifting what she said looked like a tab on the underside, then prying back the whole shell.

He'd cleaned and eaten crabs since he was a boy, but that night he paid particular attention to each intricate step of the process as he demonstrated it to Sylvia. He scooped bits of yellowish goo from the inside corners of the top shell and then licked his fingers clean of the substance as he exclaimed over its exquisite taste. He removed the claws, sucking each one loudly after he pulled it off. The two largest claws he cracked with a wooden mallet. When he emptied one of the big claws of its meat, he pulled on a small white extension so that the claw opened and closed. As he put the claw to her face, she pushed away from him in mock fear. Then he broke the crab body in two and ran his fingers in and out of the shell dividers, producing huge clumps of white meat. He put a piece to her mouth while telling her what bait crabs favored — rotten chicken wings, almost anything that smelled. He held the lump of meat to her lips and knew that she would never again taste anything so delicious. He slipped the delicate, white flesh between her parted lips.

His Sylvia, so reluctant about things at first, and so resolute in time. She learned to make better crab cakes and crab imperial than his mother. And now she was forging ahead, dragging him into the damnedest places. Last week he had spent two hours with her in a building filled with chickens. Just when he was slowing down, Sylvia was slipping into fifth gear.

Her back was to him. He reached for her braid. The hair was thick as a climbing rope. He squeezed it because he wanted to feel something substantial in his hand. With his other hand he followed the line of her shoulder, her arm, to the place where her waist used to be.

"You thinking about those bikini girls again?" Sylvia said,

taking his hand from her side, but pulling it up close to her chin.

He tried to wriggle his fingers free to touch one of her breasts, but she held his hand closed. Finally, he turned away from her and told her good night, but she was already asleep. Clayton wondered if Rita was dreaming about the Melnicks' house. He hung his hand over the edge of the bed and waited to feel Poco's warm tongue. He tried to anticipate what the doll lady would say to him when he returned for Vee-Doll.

Sylvia suggested accompanying Rita to the Doll Hospital, but Clayton insisted on going. When Sylvia asked him what the attraction was, he shrugged his shoulders. On this trip, Clayton didn't bother with looking in the bait and tackle shop window. Even Rita seemed more focused on their mission.

The red-haired woman smiled widely when Clayton opened the door to her shop. She was just as attractive as he'd remembered. She winked at Clayton, then carefully fitted the doll into Rita's arms as if it were alive, revived from the dead. Rita glanced at Vee-Doll and then handed it back. "What's this?" Beth asked.

"That's not my baby," Rita said softly.

"Well, of course it's your doll, darling," Beth said.

Beth looked up at Clayton. Rita shook her head, her dark braids swinging to either side. "It doesn't look like my doll."

The scratches on the doll's face had disappeared, the chipped nose and crushed cheek now were smooth. The doll's face was orange and soft, as if it had caught some strange disease from the other sick dolls stacked against every wall.

With the doll in one hand, the woman nudged Clayton

with the other, and said to Rita, "I gave your baby doll a face lift."

"Your baby looks pretty now," Clayton said.

But Rita wouldn't touch the doll when Beth presented it to her again. Clayton took the doll and paid the woman.

"A plastic head will last forever," the woman called to Clayton as they left the store.

Clayton bought Rita and himself cones, and they sat down at a booth and ate the ice cream. Clayton knew his granddaughter was upset because she was pulling at her hair.

"What's the matter?" he asked. Rita swung her legs under the table.

"I don't want you or Vee to go to the hospital."

"Why would we? We're not sick."

"Don't go," she said. "You might look different when you get better."

"You don't have to worry about that. I'm strong as a mule."

His mention of a mule made Rita laugh. Then her smile disappeared and she asked, "What will my daddy look like when he comes out of the hospital?"

The question startled Clayton. He and Sylvia always tried not to mention Melvin around Rita. They'd been careful not to downgrade him. In her standard explanation for his absence, Sylvia said that he was sick and in the hospital, in spite of Clayton's protests that "sick" would make Melvin too pitiable.

They'd talked about Janice as delicately as they could. Clayton worried that if they told Rita too much, the child might somehow remember that night of the accident when she'd been taken to the hospital as bloody as when she'd been born. They'd shown her photos, of course, but were purposely vague about the details of her parents' lives. Usually Rita didn't pursue the topic beyond a couple of simple questions, which were quickly answered.

"What will he look like?" Rita repeated.

Clayton handed her a napkin instead of answering. Finally he said, "I don't think your daddy is coming out of the hospital. So you won't have to worry."

After a pause Rita said, "Never?"

"Come on, Rita. Let's get back. I think Vee wants you to help her with a sampler she's working on."

FIVE

The day before Sylvia and Clayton were expected in Las Vegas, Sylvia phoned Marlene in Maryland. They'd boondocked, with the owner's permission, next to a gas station. Clayton fooled with some trim on the truck while Sylvia talked on the phone. He heard her disclose their plans to settle in Colorado after the reunion with Clayton's sister, Lucille.

"Hold on, Marlene, he's right here." Sylvia handed the phone to Clayton. "She wants to talk to you."

Sylvia always did the talking to Marlene, but Clayton figured the odd woman had some gossip to tell him about Evergreen.

When Marlene spoke she sounded out of breath. Remembering his old neighbor's aversion to the outdoors, Clayton wondered if Marlene had found a snake in the kitchen.

"I thought it was best to tell you, Clayton. Sylvia gets so upset." Marlene didn't know that these days Sylvia spent more time calming him than the other way around.

"What's going on, Marlene?"

Marlene said, "He's out," and Clayton knew exactly what that meant.

"He went over to the Pinches first thing. Rooted through your old house like a wild hog."

Clayton could feel a prickling at the back of his neck. His hands were cold. Sylvia was instantly at his side, gesturing, wanting to know. He held his hand up to her. From the first letter they'd received from Melvin six years ago, the one Sylvia had initially kept from him in her shoe box — the paper now white and wrinkled as a piece of some ghost — to the one he'd picked up in Texas reiterating the threat, he'd pictured the confrontation scene in a thousand different ways. Still, he wasn't prepared for what Marlene was telling him. He wasn't ready to believe that what they had only imagined would happen now actually *could*.

"Where is he now?"

"With his sister, I think. But if the Pinches press charges, I imagine he'll wind up back in the hospital."

When he hung up the phone, Clayton imagined Melvin with his mousy-colored hair, maybe now tied back in a ponytail, entering the house on Garden Road that the Pinches had redecorated. He saw him moving through the rooms breaking ashtrays, knickknacks, planters.

Clayton imagined Melvin grabbing the Pinches' child by mistake, squeezing him until he cried, frustrated at not finding his daughter. He'd press the people around him for answers. Clayton pictured Melvin's handwriting, those thick fingers jamming letters together as he spread threats across the page. Clayton wondered how long they had before Melvin set off from Baltimore to find Rita.

"Clayton, what's going on? Why didn't you let me talk to her before you hung up?"

Clayton put his arm around his wife. "Where's Rita?" he

asked. After Sylvia assured him that their granddaughter was preoccupied in the back of the trailer, he relayed the news.

Sylvia hugged him, her head against his chest. "So much for my theory that he lost interest," she said into his shirt. She was trying not to cry.

A few minutes later, Clayton said, "I guess it's time to pick up." Sylvia didn't say much at all as they collapsed the trailer's awning and prepared to leave. Clayton and Sylvia were so used to the routine that they now quickly spotted a glass or dish that needed to be fixed to its proper place, a stray toy that required securing. With Melvin released from the Baltimore institution, he was like an article in the RV not tied down, sure to cause damage or even a bad accident if you didn't pull over and fix it.

Sylvia, Clayton, and Rita settled into the cab of the truck. Rita had begun calling Poco "Pokey," the old dog was now so slow. When the dog positioned itself at Sylvia's feet, Clayton started up the truck.

"So. Here we come, Nevada." Sylvia tried to sound enthusiastic, but she couldn't fool Clayton. The other week at the National Atomic Museum she'd said, "Clayton, this is so interesting," but he'd known she didn't mean it.

He reached over Rita and patted Sylvia's thigh with assurance. "First, we have a stop to make," he said, thinking of the gun hidden in the truck.

"What stop? We just got started." Clayton remained close-mouthed.

"Does it cost money?" Rita asked.

Rita would be thinking about the three dollars and forty-five cents, change he'd given her from the Doll Hospital. She'd squirreled it away in a bandage box in the medicine cabinet.

"No," Clayton said quickly.

At the first sign of desert, Clayton pulled off the road and drove a few hundred feet into the barren land. Rita giggled as the truck lurched back and forth, but Clayton worried about possible damage in the trailer.

"What are you doing?" Sylvia asked.

Without answering his wife, Clayton picked up Rita and carried her back to the trailer. "Now young lady, I want you to stay in here and don't go near the door until I tell you it's OK to come out." He turned on the radio. "I'm serious about this."

Rita nodded at the sternness in his voice. Sylvia watched as Clayton went to the truck bed for bullets, then produced the .38 from its hiding place beneath the driver's seat. He took Sylvia's hand and they walked into the desert.

"I've been giving it a lot of thought. You've got to learn to use this thing, Sylvia." He took a breath and said, almost in a sigh, "You need to be able to defend yourself in case I'm not here."

"Where are you going to be?" Sylvia stood with her hands on her hips.

"Jesus, Sylvia, I don't know. I might be in town getting a beer or something."

"Clayton, you always say it's cheaper to have drinks at home, especially when you count in the tip."

"Sylvia, please. Do this for me."

"I just know you won't be off in a bar."

"OK, so I'm not at a bar. Maybe I'm preoccupied," he said.

"Preoccupied," she said.

"Vee," he said softly.

Clayton wanted her to feel the hardness, the power of the .38 he placed in her hand. As she turned the handgun over, she asked how long it would take to warm the metal to the temperature of her hands.

"Don't worry about that, Sylvia." She came up with the weirdest ideas.

When he walked off to set up a target, she called, "I think this is a waste of time."

As he turned back and encouraged her, he felt a softness inside him gathering to one spot, into one hard kernel of assurance.

"Sylvia," he said gently when he approached her. He put his hand on her shoulder. "Chances are you'll never have to use this thing. But just knowing you *can* makes all the difference."

Clayton spoke so tenderly that she did not protest further. Shortly after they married, he'd taught her to drive. In back of an abandoned factory, he positioned pieces of wood and empty barrels to represent the location of other cars that he then coaxed her to park between.

As Sylvia held up the gun, Clayton pictured Rita inside the trailer, innocently dressing Poco in a pink hat and pale blue socks that belonged to one of her dolls. He imagined her urging the old dog onto her lap when the first shot sounded. He hoped that, with the music on the boom box, Rita wouldn't hear the gun firing. Otherwise, in his pastel outfit, Poco would cower by the refrigerator while Rita stood on her grandparents' bed to look out the window. But she wouldn't be frightened. She'd see him with his arms around Sylvia, taking aim at something so small in the distance that she couldn't make out what it was.

Clayton pointed out the different mileage signs to Las Vegas to distract Rita, who was getting cranky. They'd been driving for five hours straight. The problem with traveling so much was that it cost them a damn lot of money. Every time he put his foot to the gas he was pressing a little more money out of his pocket. That pocket had a definite bottom now.

Despite Clayton's distance announcements, Sylvia seemed to

be thinking of something other than the glimmering city of coins and cards and slot machines.

"What's on your mind?" Clayton asked. "You thinking about seeing your newly married sister-in-law?"

Sylvia shook her head. "The Miracle at Little Bluff," she said.

Every newspaper they'd read from each southwestern town they'd passed through had carried a headline about the recent visitation of the Holy Mother to Little Bluff, a town noted for its inordinately large number of cancer victims. Again and again the different newspapers reported that the Virgin had finally answered the town's many petitions for relief. Sylvia had read that the shadow of the Virgin Mary's garment had remained etched in the sidewalk as proof of the visitation. As a result of this divine intervention, people afflicted with any physical ailment, as well as the curious, journeyed to the darkened spot on the walkway near the precipice of Little Bluff.

"It would be something to see," Sylvia said, looking up from the most recent newspaper account, which, she announced, estimated weekend visitors to the site at three thousand. She said that a stop in Little Bluff would take them only about an hour and a quarter off course.

"It will be impossible to park," Clayton said, and Sylvia sighed.

"Plus they're probably charging an arm and a leg to get within a half mile of the spot," he said. A Chevy cut in front of him and Clayton honked.

"What do you think, Rita?" Sylvia asked.

"Don't go getting the child involved," Clayton said. Sylvia had mentioned to him in private the possibility of having Rita blessed at Little Bluff. Despite not taking Rita to church regularly, Sylvia argued that they should use all available safeguards. The sanction might give Rita an extra ounce of protection from Melvin.

"What's a miracle?" Rita asked.

"It's like magic," Sylvia said.

Clayton was about to advise Sylvia not to feed Rita any more crap when Rita said suddenly, "I want my daddy to appear. Like the Virgin."

Sylvia and Clayton glanced at each other over their granddaughter's head. Rita had this way of turning things around completely. Only a few minutes ago, parking had been the sole issue.

Clayton blamed himself for Rita's sudden interest in seeing Melvin. Becoming lax with their usual discretion, he and Sylvia had been talking about him for days. Although they'd tried to keep their voices down, privacy was not easily come by in the trailer. A man on a mission to find his daughter must have sounded appealing to a six-year-old who'd never seen her father.

"Some day you'll see him, Rita," Clayton said as matter-of-factly as he could.

"Now," Rita said defiantly.

"Not now," Clayton said. Anticipating Rita's next question, Clayton added, "He's too dangerous right now." He'd meant to say "too sick."

Sylvia cleared her throat. "Wouldn't you rather see a miracle, honey?" Sylvia asked.

"No," Rita said.

"Drop the goddamn miracle nonsense," Clayton said. That had got the kid worked up in the first place. Everybody was irritable with being on the road all day, and they were still an hour and a half outside of Las Vegas.

Clayton was just about to pull over to the side of the road, to stretch his legs and get Rita a cookie when they heard it. At first Clayton thought the odd noise was some kind of Nevada police siren. He checked his rearview mirror repeatedly in search of flashing lights, but spotted nothing on the horizon.

"What the hell?" he said. "The smoke alarm again?"

"Oh my God," Sylvia said.

"What?" Clayton's voice was uncharacteristically clipped.

"The detector," they spoke, practically simultaneously.

The words stung him. Clayton took his left hand off of the steering wheel and touched his forehead.

It happened when you least expected it.

The pulsing sound coming from the trailer didn't let up. Rita began to cry, and Poco, the barometer of discord, shook against Clayton's legs.

"Let's go west here and see if we can't drive away from it," Sylvia said.

Clayton obeyed her because he had no better idea of what to do. Taking short breaths, he envisioned the frightening air all around them. That was the trouble with this damn radiation stuff. You couldn't see it; you couldn't tell what you were up against. Out here somebody was always secretly doing some dangerous test, setting things loose that had no business escaping into the air normal people breathed.

Sylvia tried to comfort Rita, calm Poco, and tune in the truck's radio all at once for a mention of nuclear disaster. Hearing only twangy notes of country songs and announcements of sales, Clayton considered that he and Sylvia might be the first people to know about a disaster.

Sylvia said she didn't think the Safe Distance detector was working right, that Alvin Spalding could have sold Clayton anything.

"I'm not taking any chances," Clayton said.

The nagging blare continued behind them. As Clayton took the turnoff Sylvia advised, he flashed his lights at a passing car to warn of the danger ahead. Even as he did it, the action made no real sense. Sylvia retrieved a map from the glove compartment and figured out how to divert them from Las Vegas. Rita continued to cry. Poco now lay so motionless at their feet that Clayton feared the dog was dead.

Clayton was sweating. Great droplets of liquid rolled down his face and into the corners of his mouth and along his ears. The detector's blare was telling them of the dangers ahead and to the side. He tried to guess how long the batteries would last.

Suddenly Clayton thought of his sister in Las Vegas. Even if disaster struck the city, he was somehow more comforted to think of her in a carpeted room full of game tables, with her new husband, than in the Baltimore home where they'd grown up.

Clayton drove on, following Sylvia's hand motions to take that road, this highway, but the alarm persisted behind them whichever way he drove. Sylvia reached over and rubbed Clayton's shoulder. She said it wasn't good for his heart to be so upset. Clayton got the feeling she was urging him more and more in the direction of Little Bluff, home of the miracle.

They ran into traffic fifteen miles outside of Little Bluff, and Clayton pulled off to the side of the road and disconnected the detector. When he got back in the truck, Sylvia went on about bogus equipment until Clayton pointed out Poco, lying perfectly still at her feet.

Without saying anything, he motioned for her to pick up the dog. He knew it was dead. Sylvia held the animal on her lap, gently stroked his fur. He could see that she was pretending Poco was sleeping so as not to upset Rita further.

Clayton's head ached, imagining what he'd have to do with the dog. He'd picked the puppy from a litter of eight. Someone at Evergreen had left an announcement on the bulletin board. Clayton had carried the dog home to Janice in his jacket pocket.

Rita was exhausted from crying, and Clayton worried that she was still thinking about her father. Fear made him think crazy things. Melvin was the danger the equipment in the back of the truck had detected. They couldn't get away from him. He was everywhere.

III
RITA

SIX

—•◆•—

Bedtime," Clayton said. When Rita looked up and blinked, she felt her long fine bangs dipping close to her eyes.

"*Dukes of Hazzard* is next," she protested. *Dukes* was Clayton's favorite show and Luke Duke the character he liked most of all. Rita made a point of rooting for Cousin Daisy to make an appearance.

"You must have seen these shows half a dozen times each," Sylvia said.

"They're still good," Clayton said, looking at Rita instead of Sylvia. "I don't care if they *are* reruns."

He went on. "The show makes me think back on those first years of boondocking." He mentioned adventure after adventure he said could never have been anticipated from his easy chair in the brick house in Maryland. Those were incidents Rita couldn't remember herself — stopping at the Sears auto service center for water to flush the RV's toilet; encountering flash floods in Missouri; even leaving her behind in the reptile house of a Texas zoo when Sylvia became distracted remembering Janice's pet salamander.

"Least we never smashed up a rig like those boys do," Sylvia said, pointing at the TV.

As Rita scraped at the last trace of pudding in her bowl, Clayton said, "It's getting late, Rita. Besides, Vee and I have a few things to discuss." He looked over his glasses at Sylvia. Clayton's sudden switch from reminiscing made Rita imagine that someone had changed a television channel.

"Tomorrow's not a school day," Sylvia reminded him. Rita was confused by her grandmother's uncharacteristic alliance; usually Clayton was the one to take her side. Sylvia brushed the bangs back from Rita's forehead.

Clayton looked from one to the other and said it was impossible to win an argument when they teamed up. Then he went on about how females got together, even now, and made him feel small as the boy he'd been growing up, competing with his sister, Lucille, to win his mother's approval.

As the opening credits moved across the screen, Clayton said what he did during nearly every show. "You know, there's a town of Hazard in Kentucky. I bet that's where this takes place."

"Hazzard County is made up, Clayton. It's a TV town," Sylvia said. Whenever he or Rita became what Sylvia called, "preoccupied" with something, she tried to get them to concentrate on something new. Now she mentioned Phoenix's Mystery Castle, which an estranged father had built for his daughter, but Clayton ignored her. While Rita wanted to hear more about the weird place, especially the absent father with good intentions, she understood that her grandfather was not going to give up on Hazzard County.

"Some day I'll just have to point it out to you, Sylvia." He stopped, then winked at Rita. "But not anytime soon. I'm not ready to move on just yet."

For almost two years they'd lived in Augustine National Forest in eastern Texas. By working part-time picking up trash, providing campers with information, and replenishing supplies, Clayton earned rent-free trailer space and hookups.

"Clayton needs a white suit like Boss Hogg wears," Rita said.

"A hat is all," Clayton said. "Not a damn cowboy suit."

A couple of years ago, Clayton might have blown up at Rita's remark, but today he just shook his head. Sylvia had confided to Rita that Clayton had calmed down dramatically, his new slower speed seldom punctuated by the frantic pacing that had once identified rumbling anger or frustration. But if he had gained peace of mind more easily, he had sacrificed some of his precision. At Sylvia's prodding, Rita had noticed that Clayton was less exact with time, less careful with fitting every household item into its special place. He'd become more lax in his personal appearance as well, and had even taken up chewing tobacco occasionally.

Sylvia had reminded Rita, Clayton was over seventy and she was close behind. Sylvia tried to watch her weight and still dyed her hair blonde, although white roots seemed to appear in her hair overnight. Last week when Sylvia was in the bathroom with a package of Clairol, she'd told Rita that, just like with snow in her hometown of Topstone, Wisconsin, there was no getting ahead; you'd no sooner shovel out than a new storm would cover all your efforts. Clayton sometimes teased Sylvia that she was "spreading out," and blamed her added weight on their new RV. He said that she kind of grew into the more spacious, self-contained vehicle they'd recently bought from Pikey's sister.

While watching television, Sylvia worked on one of the cross-stitched samplers she hoped to sell and complained that her eyes were getting so bad she wouldn't be able to see the needle before long. In the new RV there was room to display

135

fifteen of the framed works on the walls. Ever since Clayton had advised that people would steal anything these days, poems included, Sylvia had been adding "© Sylvia Smith Vaeth" to the lower right corner of each sampler.

Sylvia looked away from the television screen and slid her needle into the word *map*. The finished piece would say:

> My husband's the driver.
> I read the map.
> But when we get lost,
> I take the rap.

People laughed at Sylvia's finely displayed thoughts and said that she was clever. "She's a card," people said, or, "How does she come up with these things?" The remarks made Rita proud of her grandmother. In the end, customers most often bought the samplers Sylvia described as her "heartfelt line," such as:

> Wherever we travel,
> From LA to Maine,
> We welcome our friends
> Again and again.

Rita enjoyed helping her grandmother come up with ideas for samplers. Sylvia said even Rita's thoughts had come to comply with RV life — pared down and to the point. Right now Rita was thinking:

> We don't rake the leaves.
> We don't push a mower.
> We just drive night and day
> And pray we won't have to tow 'er.

Sylvia never repeated a sampler unless she got what she called a firm, money-down request. When they had been traveling regularly, Sylvia had sold eight or ten samplers a week. Alvin Spalding, the ex-IBMer with the bizarre nuclear information, had generously paid $100 for her to cross-stitch his poem, "Minds of the New Universe." Sylvia told Rita that Alvin had probably felt bad about selling them that faulty radiation detector. Still, she hadn't charged him for the three planets she embroidered along the bottom border. Since they'd been camped in Texas, though, business had dropped off. Just the other week Clayton had told Sylvia she couldn't always rely on word-of-mouth advertising, and he'd proceeded to make her a sign: SYLVIA'S FAMOUS SAYINGS, STARTING AT $20.

"OK, Rita," Clayton said. *Dukes* had concluded and a New York crowd scene was featured in a news bulletin about a collapsed bridge. Rita was searching for an appropriate word to rhyme with Hogg.

"Just let me see who died," Rita said.

"Bed," Sylvia said emphatically, while pointing out the direction.

"OK, OK," Rita said. "Jeez. I'm twelve now. Did you forget?"

"You won't let us forget," Clayton said.

Something was up. Rita wouldn't have thought anything of being rushed off to bed if Sylvia hadn't made it such a big issue, all of a sudden bouncing to Clayton's side. Whenever her grandparents agreed this solidly on something, Rita knew it was serious. Holding the bathroom door slightly open with her foot, she washed her face and brushed her teeth.

"Isn't that him?" Sylvia was asking softly, and Rita knew they were looking at a person on TV who might be her father.

"His face is the size of a dime, Sylvia. How in the hell can you pick him out in a crowd like that?"

Rita couldn't hear Sylvia's response over the running water.

"Shit, Sylvia, you think every scruffy guy looks like Melvin."

"Keep your voice down."

Sylvia held her finger on a group of men and women on the

137

television screen. Rita heard her grandfather disagreeing as Sylvia attempted to differentiate victims, rescuers, and the curious. Although Rita squinted at the set, she couldn't begin to distinguish individual faces. Not that Rita would recognize her father; she'd seen only a few photos of Melvin Kondrake when he was much younger. She wondered if his face was as round and oily as Sylvia had once described. It wasn't fair for half the world to watch her father, or even someone who looked like her father, on a rescue mission while she wasn't allowed a glimpse. Rita thought about walking innocently back into the living room, but she didn't want to be blamed for a fight between her grandparents.

Sylvia *had* made a few mistakes. There was that time they'd stopped at a grocery store somewhere in Indiana and Sylvia thought she'd spotted Melvin at the frozen food coolers. Sylvia had been calm as she called Rita to her and took her hand. But when Sylvia saw that the man had blue eyes and heard his southern accent, relief so shook her that Rita had to carry the small bag of groceries out to the rig.

Sylvia and Clayton tried not to show how concerned they sometimes became. Rita wished she could tell them to relax, but that solid circle of fear never left her completely, either. For sure they didn't need to go to all the trouble trying to hide these things from her. She always found out anyway.

Last year during the parent-teacher meeting at Rita's school, Sylvia had pointed out that the science teacher had an uncanny resemblance to Melvin. Even Clayton admitted to the likeness, though he wouldn't agree to taking Rita out of that school, as Sylvia had suggested. Rita picked up the entire whispered conversation from her bed. Their concerns had wound through the living room and funneled right into her ears.

Claiming he had visitation rights, Melvin supposedly had been searching for Rita for at least the past three and a half years. Marlene was the contact. Although Rita had never seen Marlene, she'd talked with her on the phone. When Marlene worried that Melvin would try to coerce Sylvia and Clayton's location from her, she asked Sylvia not to call anymore.

Circuitously, Marlene's daughter Hannah in Georgia passed on the few bits of mail that still trickled to Garden Road. Rita wasn't surprised that the daughter lived hundreds of miles away from Marlene. Marlene was the kind of mother who constantly reminded her daughter of disaster — "If you don't get that lock fixed, all hell will break loose." Rita hoped Sylvia hadn't been that kind of mother; she wasn't that kind of grandmother.

Her father was uncanny. In one of his letters that Rita had seen, she read, "I know you're in Missouri," the week after they'd left that state. Clayton said Melvin had simply made a good guess, but Rita knew he didn't want to show how scared the letter had made him.

The thought of her father tracking her down worried her, but she was curious, too. It felt like the time she'd watched a scary movie from behind Clayton's favorite chair. At the most frightening parts, she had pressed her face into the soft upholstery.

Rita turned off the bathroom light and headed for her bed. She loved the new RV. She no longer had to wait for Sylvia and Clayton to make up the benches in the kitchen but could go straight to her sleeping loft behind a heavy plastic privacy curtain. In this RV, Rita found seclusion with a few books and her one remaining stuffed animal — a donkey Clayton had won for her at a firemen's carnival in Omaha.

Rita's bedroom even had a window that blended into a skylight, from which she could see the bright globe of the moon. If they ever took the new RV on a real trip, Rita would have a perfect view of the highway stretched out behind them like a lengthening piece of tape. She fantasized that if they drove too far away from their spot in the national forest, the road would run out and Clayton would drive straight up into the air. They'd be suspended so high that she could see all the places they'd ever lived. The towns and fields and parking lots and forests would look like one big campsite. She wondered if her father, the size of an ant, would be scouting out all the places she and her grandparents had ever stopped.

After Rita settled into bed, she listened to Clayton. He brought up once more the topic that had been a point of discussion for so long that it was now as accepted as an aging pet. Moving or standing still was the issue on which he and Sylvia differed, on which they'd even exchanged sides. Sylvia had mentioned "taking to the road" again when Rita got out of school for the summer. She was what Clayton called "hell-bent" on a trip to California, the only state not colored in on the old trailer's map when it had been sold.

"I'd like to see the homes of the stars, Clayton."

Rita pictured her grandfather shaking his head and simultaneously smiling weakly, the way he did to *her* when she asked for something — like a cello — that would never fit in the RV.

"I read where you can visit the famous TV family homes like the ones from *Ozzie and Harriet* and *The Beverly Hillbillies*," Sylvia went on.

Rita had to restrain herself from calling out, "What about *Happy Days?*" Sylvia had once told her that Fonzie had been one of Janice's favorite stars. Rita loved the episode of Fonzie spending Christmas with his stand-in family, the Cunninghams.

"We have such a perfect spot here, though," Clayton said. The part of the job he enjoyed most in Texas was pointing out special spots for tent campers and answering questions for RVers unfamiliar with the area. He knew the best places for fish, for views, and for hikes. At least three times a week he left his duties and dropped a line in nearby Lake Larson. Occasionally Rita went with him to watch the water ripple and hear the tiny nameless birds protest at his interference. Eventually she'd feel a tug at the bait. One day when she didn't have school, Rita made peanut butter sandwiches and she and Clayton had lunch at the lake. That afternoon he told her he'd never liked a spot as much in all their years of travel.

"I'm not going to argue with you about how nice it is here," Sylvia said. "But I don't see why we got this new rig if we are going to stay put for the rest of our lives. We might as well build a house." Sylvia was the first to admit that returning to her old life in a stationary house would be as boring as watching golf on TV, but once in a while she admitted she could do with a dose of regular people.

This time Rita couldn't resist offering her opinion. "We've been here almost two years," she yelled out. There was a long silence. She knew they were wondering how much of their conversation she'd heard. Rita wished she could just say that it was too late for them to worry about being quiet; she knew everything.

A few minutes later, Sylvia started again with her theory: without attics or basements or closet space for storing away their oddities, just about anyone was likely to become a little strange. The first time she heard that idea, Rita had said immediately, "What about us?" And Sylvia had replied, "Never mind about us."

"You can't build on a national forest," Clayton said in a lowered voice.

"You know what I mean," Sylvia hissed back.

They'd only had the nearly new RV on the road half a dozen times, but Clayton started it up religiously every morning. Sylvia and Clayton had acquired the vehicle after Pikey's brother-in-law died. Rita remembered Pikey as the fat man who'd mistakenly left his wife behind in the Florida trailer park.

Because Pikey had sold his sister's vehicle at practically the price Clayton ended up getting for their old rig, Sylvia convinced Clayton to purchase a used Rabbit, which could easily be hauled behind the new RV. Clayton drove the car to work and on errands.

"I'll make a deal," Clayton said. Rita peeked into the living room and saw Sylvia looking up from sticking her needle into a letter. "How about we spend the summer in California or wherever you and Rita want to go. My only condition is that we come back here in the fall."

Rita almost clapped, but then her grandparents' voices became so low she couldn't hear what they said, and that meant one thing. They were talking about her father again.

In her anxiety, Sylvia's voice rose. She was saying she couldn't promise anything. Melvin could run them down anywhere.

Every once in a while Clayton would let Rita start the RV, and sitting behind the wheel of the huge vehicle thrilled her. She'd watched Clayton often enough that she felt she could drive it, but he never allowed her to do anything other than turn it on and give it a little gas. When she twisted the key in the ignition, the power of the engine surged out to her fingertips. She always sensed possibility in the simple distance between her own two hands. Grasping the large steering wheel, she imagined driving her grandparents to a country where they'd feel totally safe.

Just as she was arriving at that sunny, imaginary land where they could drive forever, she'd hear Clayton say, "Well, young lady, that should do it." And the dream died with the engine.

SEVEN

————————◆•◆•◆————————

Rita sat at the back of the fifth-grade classroom and scribbled out a note to Libby Barnes: "Bat. Do you agree?" Rita watched Libby bend forward in her seat and begin giggling — confirmation that Miss Tompkins, the substitute teacher, with her tight cap of hair, dark angular brows, and eyes squinting with contacts, did resemble the animal.

Based on the pictures she'd seen of him, Rita thought about what animal her father looked like. Usually she decided on a weasel, something fast and sleek that could turn into a fierce fighter. But sometimes she'd picture a bigger animal she wasn't even sure existed. It was strong, slippery, and dark, and though the beast frightened her, she longed to get close enough to touch it.

Rita frequently entertained Libby with likenesses she discovered between people and animals or even between people and vegetables. Because Libby never initiated such comparisons herself, Rita sometimes became bored with her sole girlfriend.

143

But Rita did enjoy making Libby laugh, which was more of a response than she got from the other girls.

The clique of meticulously groomed girls, sporting perfectly coordinated outfits and subtle hints of makeup on their lids and lashes and cheeks, made faces of disgust if Rita cracked a joke. The more studious girls shied away from Rita. Their parents must have reminded them that she was the girl who'd been "held back" one grade, as if failure could be catching, like a cold.

Led by Pammie Squantz, the group of girls who actually started trouble didn't take Rita seriously. By their standards Rita was a runt — short and skinny and without even a nubbin of breast. Pammie's group sabotaged other students' lockers, cheated on tests, smoked in the bathroom, and talked constantly about boys. Rita couldn't imagine that the boys Pammie had pointed out as "good kissers" would have anything to do with someone as loud and pushy as Pammie.

Danny Wrigley sometimes invited Rita to eat lunch with him and his friends, Ira and Michael. During classes, Rita chose to sit at the back with the three guys, who got fair grades without acting like geeks. Like Rita, the three were scrawny, dark-haired standouts against the sunstruck look of the popular students. Rita suspected that Ira and Michael endured her company because Danny was interested in the RV she lived in.

Although Sylvia was always offering to be more than accommodating to Rita's friends, Rita did not invite Danny to the RV. For one thing, she didn't want to emphasize that she lived with such old people. The parents that Rita had seen meeting their children after school were young and aggressively friendly, almost like puppies.

In spite of her efforts to prevent Danny from visiting her, Rita liked being with him. And she liked his father, who was tall, smiled a lot, and had a very deep voice. Mr. Wrigley made a point of accentuating her name by calling her "Miss Rita." Danny was generous in explaining math problems that she had difficulty with, as well as accepting of her suggestions on compositions. Probably because he had two sisters, he wasn't shy around her, even if someone teased him about being in love. Until they showed the films, Rita had been perfectly relaxed with Danny.

Earlier that morning, Mrs. Zyper, the homeroom teacher with an amazing resemblance to a spaniel, had directed the fifth-grade girls to proceed to the gym and the boys to walk single file to the main assembly room. In their respective places, the students watched films entitled *Growing Up Female* and *Growing Up Male*. Afterward when the group, silent except for intermittent giggles, met back at the homeroom, Missy Perner had bragged that she'd sneaked into the boys' film. When Rita asked Missy about it, all the girl could say was, "Gross," in an exaggerated growl.

Since the movie, Rita had felt uncomfortable in Danny's presence. Sylvia had already told her all about menstruation and answered a few questions about sex. Rita now knew her first question to Sylvia had been silly: Did the number of children you had equal the number of times you'd had sex? But the film filled Rita with concerns. With its technical drawings and specific names for parts that couldn't be seen, the film imposed a new and strange importance on her body in all its complications. Whatever she shared with Danny, even if she finally broke down and took him to the RV, where he'd see her grandparents up close, she would still harbor the enormous secret of her own body.

Today Danny asked, "Want to have lunch with us, Rita?"

Ordinarily she would have said yes, but now she shook her head. If Danny wanted to see her RV, next he'd want to look under her clothes, to see for himself the insignificant beginnings of grown-up body parts, and the few soft hairs that had appeared, delicate as the first lines of spring onions in a garden.

"Next time then," he said as he went off to join his buddies. He must have said something to Ira and Michael, because they looked her way, then broke into a laugh. Rita supposed that from now on all the joking would have something to do with the differences between girls' and boys' bodies.

Rita walked to the cafeteria with Libby, whose figure was pretty much the same as her own. The girls carried their trays of chicken, peas, Jell-O, and milk to an empty table. Libby had been Rita's friend for most of the school year.

"Kotex is not something 'my mother' would have around the house," Rita whispered as soon as they were seated.

"How old *are* your grandparents?" Libby asked.

"I don't know. A hundred," Rita said.

"Wow," Libby said.

"I'm kidding, duhh," Rita said.

"I knew that," Libby said. "My mother's in jail."

"I thought just your father was in jail." Sometimes Libby exaggerated the reasons for living with a foster family, people she never complained about or expressed affection for.

"Mom's there, too," Libby said. She shrugged her shoulders. "Drug trafficking."

"My mother's dead," Rita said, reiterating what she'd revealed to Libby when they'd first met.

"Mine might as well be for all I see her," Libby replied. She picked up a piece of chicken.

Rita thought that if her mother were alive in jail, at least she could look forward to seeing her. She imagined a reunion with her mother *and* her father.

"My grandparents won't even let me see my father," Rita said.

"What's wrong with him again?" With the back of her hand, Libby brushed her chin-length hair away from her face.

"I think they're afraid he'll take me away with him," Rita said.

"Is that why you live in an RV? So they can always run away if he comes too close?"

"I don't know," Rita said slowly. She hadn't considered this obvious reason behind her atypical lifestyle. She'd simply accepted that this was how her grandparents had chosen to live. None of the other RVers they'd met appeared to be scared to stay in one place. All her life Rita had appreciated new places simply because they were different, not because they were safely distant from Melvin.

Rita picked through the main course and was about to dig her spoon into the shimmering red that Libby told her was curdled blood when she looked up and saw her grandfather. Clayton stood before her with such an unusual expression on his face — partly sad, partly puzzled — that she didn't know how to respond. When he held out his arms, she remained stiffly in place.

"Rita." Clayton said her name kindly. "Put your things together. We've got to get home." Rita hardly heard what he said, she was so disoriented. Clayton appeared unusually large, and the boys and girls around her were reduced to noise.

"Come on, honey," he said, pulling back her chair.

"I haven't finished my dessert," she protested.

"I'll get you a McDonald's cherry pie on the way home."

"Take it," Libby advised Rita.

"Why do I have to leave?" Rita demanded, as Clayton led her beyond the swinging doors. Rita pictured Danny, Ira, and Michael, as well as Pammie Squantz and Missy Perner, staring at her and whispering among themselves, "So that's why she's so weird. Look at her father."

"Rita, your great-grandmother died last night. We have to go to Baltimore for the funeral." After Clayton relayed the news, he said he felt guilty that he hadn't taken her back to see his mother since he'd left Maryland. Rita had no memory of Dora Vaeth, only a few old photos and the stories that Clayton had shared from time to time.

School wasn't Rita's favorite place, but there was an important pep rally later that afternoon. She was about to protest the interruption of her schedule when Clayton's unusually solemn tone of voice stilled her.

"She was eighty-nine," Clayton said. The day was sunny and warm and contrasted sharply with Clayton's mood. "It's a terrible thing," he said, "but as a young kid, after my father left, I used to wish she would die just so that she'd leave me alone. And now . . ." Clayton stopped talking the way Rita had when Libby had asked her if she lived in an RV to make a quick escape. She knew he was thinking something over. For a moment, he appeared to forget that she was with him. Part of him seemed totally out of control, and some farther-off part incredibly calm.

"We've never been to Baltimore," Rita said, suddenly understanding the implications of Clayton's announcement.

"Rita, you were born there."

"I know *that*," she said. "But we've never gone there, have we?"

Rita had mixed feelings as Clayton slowly backed out of the parking spot that had been home for nearly two years. She figured her grandmother did too; Sylvia kept folding and unfolding a stack of Kleenex in her lap. The dirt roads soon fell away, and the highway lay before them. For months Rita had been anxious to get on the road. But with Baltimore as their destination, she was reminded of all the fairy tales in which people got much more than they wished for.

If Rita was uncertain about visiting old friends and relatives her grandparents had mentioned but she'd never met, if she wasn't quite sure what it meant to be from somewhere, she was filled with certainty on one issue: Melvin. She longed to meet him. Though she was afraid of him, she wanted to see him for herself. So far, Sylvia and Clayton had been able to outmaneuver and outdistance her father. With information from Marlene and Hannah, the Vaeths had supposedly narrowly avoided him in Tennessee three years ago. But in Baltimore they would be on Melvin's turf. There, Sylvia said, he could do anything. As they drove in the direction of Clayton's hometown, Rita imagined they were moving toward a foe they were hardly a match for.

"He's probably someplace like Minnesota. Not anywhere near Baltimore," Clayton said as if he'd been reading her mind.

To see what routes they should be on the lookout for, Sylvia scanned a couple of maps. Having had no time to do her usual research for the trip, Sylvia explained that she hadn't even sorted through her collection of clippings with interesting attractions circled in red.

Rita pointed out a tumbleweed and asked if they could take it as a souvenir.

"What'll we do with it?" Clayton asked.

"Decoration," Sylvia said, winking at Rita.

"Where will we put it?" he asked next.

"I'll squeeze it in by your easy chair," Rita said.

"Great," Clayton said, grimacing.

"She wants something to remember Texas by," Sylvia said.

"Why not a key chain?" Clayton asked.

Clayton grumbled for a few minutes about how Rita had more sense when she was six years old and knew to ask for small things that the trailer could easily accommodate. "What the hell," he then said and pulled over. He sighed. "We'll be back here in a couple of months anyway," he said.

The tumbleweeds were actually much larger up close than they appeared from the RV window. Clayton wrestled with one before he gave up and lifted a smaller one. In the end, he tied the tumbleweed to the roof of the car.

As they drove away from the tan and tarnished scenery, where every blister of color stood out like a warning, they began to pass areas thickening with summer. To Rita, they were traveling deeper and deeper into a green web where eventually they would be caught. Maybe her father was somehow behind Clayton's mother's death, and this trip to Baltimore was part of a plot. But then she realized that kind of thinking was too much like Sylvia's. There had been no word of Melvin in months — no threatening letters, no phone messages via Marlene's daughter. No one had any idea where he was.

On the highway Clayton stayed to the right and did not exceed the 55-miles-per-hour speed limit. Ordinarily he would have pushed, but today, he announced, he was taking things easy. Probably he was thinking about his mother and trying to get used to the rig. He said the new RV handled much differently than the old one.

"Even with all the pillows and pads we had on the driver's seat of the old rig, I'll be able to drive hours longer in this baby," he said.

"I'll drive if you get tired," Rita said. She pictured herself merging into the left lane, then passing car after car.

Clayton laughed. "I'll bet you would," he said.

Now that their rig was all one piece, the vehicle felt more powerful and secure. Their home no longer dangled behind them like an afterthought, swaying over lines and accepting blows from the elements in a different way from the truck itself. Only the dark blue, nearly purple, Rabbit hung on behind.

150

Despite the smooth ride of the new RV, and all the improvements, like the rechargeable battery with solar panels, Rita missed the old rig, with its rust and all its mileage, which Clayton was always exclaiming over, and the map colored with accomplishment. She had never thought this way until Clayton told her, when he was debating whether to sell the old rig, that the rust wasn't any bigger deal than the lines around his eyes. It was simply what happened over time.

The old rig became another of the friends she left behind whenever her grandparents moved. Now, she would miss Libby and even Pammie Squantz. Clayton was talking about returning in a couple of weeks, but Rita's intuition pointed in other directions — new places and people.

"I want the other trailer a little bit," Rita said finally.

"It's just because we're moving, Rita. Once we stop, you'll be glad of your new bed," Sylvia said.

After a moment, Clayton said, "I do know what you mean, sweetheart."

As if she'd turned the ignition on Clayton's feelings, her comment urged him to think out loud. He said he felt no similar nostalgia for their stationary house on Garden Road. When they'd sold it, he'd thought only of traveling as far as they could from all the trouble gathered around them. Even now, returning to that area, he felt no inclination to reminisce. Sylvia mentioned gently that maybe he was preparing himself for the defensive stance he was sure to adopt around people he hadn't seen in years, people who would want to know how his retirement was going and if his lifestyle was appropriate for raising a twelve-year-old girl.

Sylvia didn't interrupt Clayton but let him go on about how funny it was that the choices agonized over one night suddenly were decided for you and threw your whole, carefully plotted routine away. Clayton said he was looking forward to doing a little boondocking. "I like the feeling of relying only on your own rig to get by," he said.

Rita wondered if they'd ever go to California like Sylvia wanted.

Out of the corner of his eye, Clayton spotted Rita's letter. "What you got there, Rita?"

"It's from my pen pal." Rita figured that even though she'd left school, she'd still want to keep in touch with Maria. Since last year, Rita had been taking Spanish in school and, as one of the top ten students in the class, she'd earned the privilege of communicating with a pen pal. Maria lived on the west coast of central Mexico and had sent Rita photographs of her village on the ocean. In the photo of Maria's extensive family, the people seemed rooted; they appeared to have sprung from the ground, grown, and never moved again.

Rita couldn't explain her feelings about the photo, not even to Sylvia. The large family belonged where they stood, the ocean and palm trees in the background. Because she found Maria's photo comforting, she kept it stuck beneath the giant clip in her notebook. In return, Rita had mailed a photo of herself with Sylvia and Clayton standing outside the new RV. Pikey had taken the Polaroid for her right after they'd gotten the new vehicle. Everyone said the photo was good of all three of them. Because the door to the RV was slightly open, the edges of a couple of Sylvia's samplers were visible, but Rita hadn't known how to explain in Spanish about the sewing projects.

Clayton hit the air horn and "La Cucaracha" sounded. Rita smiled. Her grandfather laughed and said, "This is for Maria."

"Maria wants us to visit her," Rita said, looking from Clayton to Sylvia.

Sylvia said, "Maybe we'll retire there."

Clayton said, "What the hell's that supposed to mean?" his mood suddenly changing.

"Calm down," Rita said, repeating an instruction often directed at her. Sylvia and Clayton glanced at each other.

Rita moved into the living room area and studied the billboards passing by. Some of the advertisements reminded her of Sylvia's clever samplers. But one advertisement, nothing like Sylvia's work, featured two silhouetted women in side view. The figure on the left was curvaceous, while the one opposite looked drained of every bit of air. The sign read, "For a more shapely figure at the beach: Try breast enlargement therapy." Rita tried to imagine what she and Libby might look like if they had the breasts of the "after" woman, or if they had any breasts at all. She knew Danny and his friends would look at her differently.

"Rita, does Melvin ever write to you at school?" Clayton called.

"What kind of a question is that?" Sylvia asked. "Of course not," she answered for Rita. "Rita would let us in on anything like that, wouldn't you, darlin'?"

Clayton's sister, Lucille, drove to the funeral home for evening visiting hours. Eddie, her husband, sat in the passenger seat, and Sylvia, Clayton, and Rita spread across the wide backseat of the Plymouth. The air in the car was heavy with perfume and aftershave. Lucille wore a black dress she said was new, and Eddie, a suit the color of charcoal. Clayton had put on a black Ban-lon under one of Eddie's dark brown sport coats. Sylvia's dress was black with a border of yellow and pink flowers at the hem and the sleeves. Even Rita had on navy blue.

Rita thought every one of them looked odd. When she asked

why people wore black at funerals, all she got out of Lucille was the curt phrase, "To show respect." Rita didn't understand what colors had to do with respect, but she didn't pursue the question with Lucille the way she might have with Sylvia or Clayton. Lucille was so thin that if she just touched you with her pointy fingers or arms, it felt like the jab of a needle.

Rita had heard Clayton whispering to Sylvia that he wasn't sure if his sister's new high energy level was due to her marriage or to their mother's death. Clayton said he was drained, himself, from the time-pressured trip and the prospect of running into old acquaintances. Sylvia shushed him when he said the room was sure to reek of flowers almost as strong as Lucille's perfume. But Clayton ignored her warnings and kept on, complaining that he'd have to look at his mother who, even dead, would surely be judging him.

"You know, you should think about a change," Lucille said, clearing her throat and checking her rearview mirror. "At your ages." Clayton's sister's hair was colored with a reddish tint that Rita hadn't anticipated; it reminded her of new pennies. Clayton rolled his eyes the way Rita sometimes did when he was taking charge.

"We had one heck of a time getting ahold of you, you know," Eddie said, reciting the line that Lucille had spoken repeatedly since their arrival. Eddie had a deep, raspy voice, and he smoked constantly.

"Crack the window," Lucille said as soon as Eddie struck a match. Rita guessed she demanded this of him each time they got in the car. Eddie probably never thought of it on his own, like Danny's friend Ira, who relied on Danny for instructions on everything, practically on when to go to the bathroom.

"There's just no provision for emergencies when you move about the way you do," Lucille said. Clayton had said yesterday that Lucille had been prepared for emergencies since she was a

154

girl, that she'd wasted her life in anticipation of horrendous events. In this way, Clayton said, she was a lot like their former neighbor Marlene.

"And then there was the time in Las Vegas. We didn't know what had happened to you," Lucille said. Yesterday Clayton had bet Rita five dollars that Lucille would bring up the incident of six years ago within hours of their arrival. Clayton elbowed Rita, tapped his watch, and opened his hand to indicate that he wanted to be paid. Rita giggled and pictured Lucille on her honeymoon waiting for them in some place like the Stardust. She couldn't be sure if she actually remembered the incident or if she'd been told about it so many times that she thought she remembered it.

"We had a faulty radiation detector," Clayton said.

"I don't know why you needed that thing in the first place," Lucille said.

Lucille's lips were such a bright red that Rita imagined them glowing in the dark.

"Neither did I," Sylvia said.

"Don't you start," Clayton said to Sylvia. He bent to Rita and said quietly, "I think the thing was warning us to stay away from Lucille." Rita laughed.

"Now don't go getting the child all worked up," Lucille said.

"And that poor little dog," she added.

"Let's change the subject, Lucille," Clayton said as he took Rita's hand. Rita had been asking her grandfather for a puppy for years. Sometimes she still thought about how Poco had stretched across her grandmother's lap until Clayton turned off the noisy radiation detector. She'd wanted to hold him, but Sylvia said no. The next day they'd buried him, wrapped in a towel, in the desert. She remembered how tightly Sylvia had held her hand while Clayton dug a grave. And she could almost still taste the cold milk shake they'd bought her afterward.

155

"I'm burning," Lucille said. "Eddie, turn up the air."

Lucille irritated Rita as much as the stiff tags on her new dress. Lucille chattered on until Sylvia joined in, and their words became as unintelligible as the squawking of crows. Rita understood that all of the blabber was covering over the issue that most concerned Sylvia and Clayton: Melvin. Sylvia worried that he'd be paying his respects at the funeral home, although she'd said he'd never given anyone respect the whole time she'd known him. Worst of all, he hadn't respected Janice. Sylvia said she hoped Rita would only meet boys who would respect her. Rita had never heard the word *respect* used so many times in one day.

"We could take Rita to church on Sunday," Eddie said, then looked at Lucille as if they'd already discussed the matter.

"We'll see," said Clayton. Rita had heard Clayton say he hoped to be on the road before Sunday, maybe swing up to Atlantic City for a couple of days before heading west again. Rita decided the real reason he preferred not to linger was the possibility of seeing her father.

Rita preferred to be on the road so she wouldn't have a nightmare at Lucille's. Rita hadn't had what Sylvia called a "crying jag" in months, but the incidents were unpredictable. Rita would go off to bed and wake up terrified a few hours later. She'd scream and struggle, even kick at her grand-parents. They told her she did these things. They told her what she screamed. She couldn't remember herself. All she recalled was thrashing around in a dream and trying to break free of it. All that stayed with her after was exhaustion and shame. She couldn't even pinpoint precisely what she'd been dreaming about that had gotten her so upset in the first place.

Lucille parked in front of the Boulton Funeral Home. She set the brake and turned around toward Sylvia and Clayton.

"Eddie and I have been thinking," she said in a noticeably quieter voice than they'd heard all afternoon. Eddie pointed at his wife, then rolled his eyes to admit that she was in charge, in case anyone hadn't noticed. "You're welcome to move into Mother's house with us," Lucille said.

The announcement startled Rita. Clayton had said that ever since his sister had been a girl, Lucille had been protective of her things and the space around her. The way Clayton had described Lucille had made Rita glad she didn't have a sister herself. Sylvia said Lucille had grown into the kind of person people said "liked things just so." That she would offer to share the meticulously clean and carefully arranged house with her less-than-particular brother and sister-in-law and a young girl, when they had no children themselves, touched Rita. Despite all Clayton's reports, in some ways she felt she didn't know Lucille at all.

"That's very kind of you, Sister," Clayton said tenderly. Up to this point, Rita hadn't heard him address her as Sister.

Rita had to admit the house, with its generations of furnishings and layers of useless decorations, despite the added feature of a great-aunt and uncle, was tempting. There were rooms with heavy wooden doors. A huge kitchen like she'd seen on TV served as a gathering place for friends as well as family. Lucille had even shown her the attic. It was dark and warm and full of boxes that Rita wanted to look through. If Lucille had let her, Rita would have stayed in the attic for hours. And yet, settling with Lucille would mean not moving — not having the possibility of moving. You didn't always watch TV, but you liked to have it there in case.

Her grandparents looked at her for a reaction. She didn't acknowledge their stare at first. They both seemed to be holding their breath. Then, ever so slightly, as carefully as she'd tried to apply Sylvia's eyeliner on her own eyes — to make lines thin as number-two pencil marks — Rita gave a twitch of her head to mean no. No to Lucille and Eddie's house.

Rita first saw Marlene Hinthorne on the day of the funeral. Wearing a dress with a tiny tiger print set against a navy blue background, Marlene hugged Sylvia. Then the women traded compliments. When Marlene explained that she'd just started on a liquid diet, Rita sensed that each was overtly relieved that the other had put on weight.

"I thought you'd want these." With the characteristic dependability Sylvia always praised, Marlene handed over a stack of cards identifying all the senders of flowers.

"I haven't heard from Melvin in ages," Marlene said softly, repeating information she'd already relayed to Sylvia. Marlene looked around nervously, sneezed. Then she began apologizing that she'd had to turn over her mail and phone duties to her daughter, Hannah.

"Will you look at her?" Marlene said, as if Sylvia, too, hadn't seen Rita in twelve years. Just as Rita had watched Clayton imitate her, Marlene pulled at the underlayer of hair at the back of her neck, now as white as the rest of her hair.

Rita peered down at her sandals. Every person she'd met in two days had made a big deal about her size. Like she would stop growing just because they weren't watching. She had to admit, though, that after being ridiculed in school for being a skinny minny, it felt good being told how big she was.

"You still want me to hold on to the dining room set?" Marlene asked.

"Oh, Marlene. I don't know," Sylvia said. She sighed, then paused for a second. "If you could keep it a while longer."

"What's the dining room set?" Rita asked.

158

"Never mind," Sylvia said immediately, intriguing Rita with a new secret.

Marlene turned to Rita and studied her. "You must be proud, Sylvia."

"I couldn't be prouder, Marlene." Now Sylvia looked Rita over. "Miss," Sylvia said sternly. "Have you gotten into my makeup?"

"No," Rita said. "I'm too young to wear makeup." She smiled at Marlene, then looked for Clayton. Rita thought she'd been careful applying the blush today.

"You're not too young to be lying," Sylvia said sternly. As Rita walked off she heard Sylvia telling Marlene that although Rita appeared not to *look* much like her parents, she worried that some similarities would eventually show up. The things you couldn't see were always the most frightening — like radiation. Sylvia said she didn't want a granddaughter of hers to develop Melvin's habit of lying. Rita didn't understand how they could hate her father when they hadn't seen him in so long. She wanted to examine for herself why he was such a threat to Clayton and Sylvia. Scanning the faces around her, Rita wished once more for her father to appear.

Clayton shook hands with Bud Harper.

"Same old, same old," Bud said as he held Clayton's hand. Then he dropped his hand to his side and mentioned the names of two coworkers at Evergreen who'd died in the past year. Bud shook his head. "You never can tell, can you, Clayton?"

"You can tell. You just can't tell when," Clayton said.

Bud smiled and said, "Thanks for all the postcards. We had a regular bulletin board filled with them."

In the procession to the cemetery, Rita wondered if Clayton had missed his father when he was her age. When they arrived at the cemetery, the clouds had cleared and the sun was uncomfortably hot and high overhead. Rita wanted to ask Clayton if he'd ever tried to find his father, but everyone around her was concentrating on the coffin. Rita tried to stand perfectly still in the spongy grass.

Clayton's mother's coffin was a pale pink, which contrasted with the variety of greens in the thick maples and willows and the distant hemlocks.

"She would have loved this," Marlene said.

"Who?" Sylvia asked.

"Why, Mrs. Vaeth."

"I think Marlene's right, Sylvia," Clayton said softly.

"You know as well as I do that she probably would have found fault with the color of the trees," Sylvia whispered, then took Clayton's hand. Rita, too, was surprised at Clayton's comment, after his earlier criticisms of his mother. Sylvia said she didn't want Clayton going off and romanticizing the bitter old woman; it drove her crazy when people allowed death to color a person's true nature. When she finished ranting, Sylvia looked down at Rita as if she had no idea who she was.

Sylvia pleaded with Clayton to visit with her childhood friend Pauline, who was staying at the Ramada Inn. She'd hardly talked to Pauline at the funeral, and Rita hadn't even met her. Clayton argued that it was a mistake to dig up people from your childhood, that those kinds of meetings were always a disappointment. Pauline and Sylvia had grown up in the same neighborhood in Wisconsin, and Pauline had moved to Baltimore the year after Sylvia. Sylvia countered by asking Clayton who'd ever disappointed him.

"Indulge me this once," Sylvia said.

"I always indulge you," Clayton said.

Rita listened to them lobbing comments back and forth until

they became background noise. She'd had her fill of Sylvia and Clayton's friends, but the alternative — spending the evening alone with Lucille and Eddie — was worse.

"The Ramada is ten minutes," Sylvia said. Clayton said he'd unhitch the Rabbit, but Rita asked to go in the RV.

"We don't want to do that," Clayton said.

"Come on," she said. "Please, please." Rita had slept three nights in Lucille's tidy spare bedroom.

"Pauline hasn't seen the rig," Sylvia said.

Sylvia had mentioned Pauline countless times, emphasizing that her friend had found "true love." Pauline's hair, which Sylvia had described as long and black, was wound into a loose gray knot at the back of her head. The lines in her face were deep, her eyelids wrinkled.

Although Pauline and Frederick, her husband, had been in the motel room only two nights, they had customized it. A lacy tablecloth covered a small round Formica table. Snapshots of their home in Maine were stuck into a mirror over the dresser. A container of daylilies sat atop it. And Pauline had obviously provided her own pillowcases; their tiny rose pattern didn't match the room's gold decorations.

Sylvia and Clayton sat in chairs by the table, Rita in a blue armchair. Pauline and Frederick perched so close together on the edge of one of the double beds, they appeared to grow into each other. On the other bed, Rita noticed two freshly ironed shirts stretched across it. The sleeves of the man's shirt and the woman's were positioned as though holding hands.

"I'm going to make you ladies some tea. Then you can sit here and catch up while Clayton and I watch a little of the ball game in the RV," Frederick said.

Pauline leaned against him. "A *little* of the ball game? This

man hasn't missed one Red Sox game since I've known him."
Pauline didn't seem to be teasing her husband. To Rita, she
was explaining his habit slowly, as if trying to understand it
herself.

As Sylvia and Pauline drank their tea, they chatted about
old friends and neighbors, about people who'd died, and
about their families in Topstone, who hadn't adapted to
progress.

Rita listened, wondering if she and Libby would see each
other again when they were old ladies. Maybe her friendships
were destined to replace one another time after time until, in
the end, she'd have a list of acquaintances that stretched the
breadth of the country.

"You'd think when people get on in years they'd let some of
those old feuds die off. Not my family. They'll hang you with
what they think are your shortcomings," Sylvia said.

Pauline nodded. And Rita thought, Like we hang on to
Melvin. The small room began to irritate her. The only things
moving were her grandmother's voice and Pauline's. Their
words swirled in the air, bits of conversation bumping against
the stiff drapery.

"I don't want to get married," Rita said suddenly, just as
Clayton and Frederick came back into the motel room.

Pauline spoke gently. "It can happen when you least suspect
it."

"It will feel like it was meant to be," Frederick said.

They were all quiet for a few minutes.

"You think it will happen to *me?*" Rita asked, now glancing at
Sylvia.

Pauline and Frederick sighed simultaneously. "Who can
tell?" Pauline said and patted her husband's hand. "It'll soon be
fifty years," she added.

"My God," Sylvia said, looking up at Clayton. "Ours is

162

coming up, too." She paused and looked around. "How could I have let that slip my mind?"

"I want to go to the rig," Rita insisted, tired of all the nostalgia.

Alone in the RV, she imagined it was all hers. In bed with her window open to the dark summer air and noisy insects, she wondered if Pauline and Frederick would want to be Libby's foster parents. Then she considered whether, for the short time her mother and father were married, they'd loved each other like Pauline and Frederick. Or if she had broken their tight circle of romance by being born.

Sylvia and Clayton said their good-byes to Lucille and Eddie, with Clayton promising to return to help Lucille sort through their mother's possessions.

"I've been meaning to ask. What in God's name is on the top of your car?" Lucille asked.

"A tumbleweed," Rita volunteered.

"If you change your mind about moving in with us, just give us twenty-four hours," Eddie said. He flicked a cigarette onto the small lawn, which looked just vacuumed.

"What do you need twenty-four hours for?" Lucille asked. Her eyes were trained on the cigarette butt.

Once Clayton had driven out of the city limits and gotten on the beltway, the fears and pressures of the last few days began to blow away. "Hey, Vee, why don't we go by the old house? It'll be on our way."

"We don't want to do that, Clayton."

"Why not?"

"Yeah. Let's," Rita said. Sylvia had described in detail the house where her mother had grown up. Rita remembered Sylvia inventing bedtime stories, using the rooms of the

Garden Road house as the setting. Over the years, Sylvia had described the flowers and trees she'd planted, the slipcovers she'd sewn for the couches and chairs.

"Yeah," Rita repeated. At last she would see the place where her mother had been a baby, walked to school, gone on dates. She would visit her mother's room. That enclosed space with a door that clicked shut, a window that looked out onto a yard with a chain-link fence for a border. Lately Rita had been fascinated with her mother's adolescence.

"You're acting like it's Disneyland or something. It's only a little house like every other one on the street," Sylvia said.

When Clayton signaled and pulled off at the highway exit he said he'd taken so many times in the past he could do it in the pitch black without headlights, a dark green car that Rita had been watching for miles did the same. She peeked past the yellow curtain, beyond the Rabbit hitched to the rear of the RV, and through a windshield at a man whose face was partially hidden by the visor. Rita couldn't tell if the man had a beard or if the lower half of his face was covered with shadow. The car followed the RV swerving along the rolling road.

Clayton said every small thing looked the same, and yet the composite picture appeared very different. As a result, the individual landmarks and signs and stores confused him.

"Look at the plaza," Sylvia exclaimed. The original three-store, ground-level shopping area had been transformed into an extensive two-tiered complex with signs announcing a country-French restaurant and gourmet food market.

Clayton shook his head at the changes. "I can't wait to see what the old block looks like." His voice sounded not excited, but sad.

Rita was intrigued with the progressive pileup of new details decorating her family's old life. Sylvia, however, voiced her worry that the house she'd lived in much of her life would be disfigured by the pressures of change. "Can you believe we once considered this the country?" Sylvia asked no one in particular.

"Look over there," Clayton said suddenly, startling Rita. "What in the hell is that?"

"Cool, a mall," Rita hollered, forgetting about the green car that still hadn't passed them, even though Clayton was driving like a turtle. She wasn't used to seeing so many different conglomerations of stores in one area. Malls and plazas and strip malls.

Sylvia felt someone had shaken her up, along with all the old parts of her life, and then spilled the pieces out in a new arrangement. If something new showed up, something else had to be missing.

"Clayton, I think they've taken down some of the houses."

"They don't just take down houses," he said and laughed. "But something does feel out of place. I know this sounds goofy, but I wonder how all these new buildings fit where they are."

"Mr. Fritch's orchards," Sylvia said, referring to the fields of apple and fruit trees, which she had described over and over to Rita. After a long day at work, Clayton said he had always been relieved to spot the expanse of carefully spaced trees. The orchard had made him feel happy that he was almost home. During picking time, Clayton could smell the ripened fruit that had escaped the harvest and fallen to the ground. When he'd first described these sensations to Rita, he'd been more serious than she was used to. Now, not one of the trees remained. In their place were fields of retail establishments.

"Great," Rita squealed when she spotted the golden arches of McDonald's. Had she known that her grandparents' old house was near not only a mall but also a fast-food restaurant, Rita would have pushed for them to return sooner. "Maybe there's a campground near here," she called.

Garden Road had not been plowed under to make room for Herman's World of Sporting Goods. But its houses looked old compared with the neighboring streets' sprawling ranches and slate-blue colonials. The house Sylvia pointed out as the one that had been theirs, the one where Rita's mother had lived, appeared neglected. The grass badly needed cutting, Clayton noted. Despite all the brick, the place appeared to have lost its crisp lines and softened.

"It doesn't look all *that* much bigger than the RV," Sylvia said of the house that, except for its tan trim, was a replica of all the others on the street.

"Now, Vee," Clayton said.

"Well, you might as well stop as long as we're here," Sylvia said.

Clayton turned the engine off and they sat in the RV and stared until Rita came up front and said, "Can I at least look?"

"You can't remember this, Rita. You were only a baby," Sylvia said. She was angling her head like a bird.

"You've told me so many times I feel like I remember."

Clayton got out of the rig, put his arm around Rita, and together they walked to the sidewalk, from which paths veered off toward the front door of each house. Rita thought of the puzzles where you tried to find your way out of a maze without letting your pencil cross any solid lines.

Sylvia walked up to the old front door and peered in the lowest of three small windows.

"Sylvia," Clayton called. He reminded her that on the way in he'd seen a sign indicating a Neighborhood Watch Community.

"Nobody's home," she said. "I'm just looking," speaking the words as she did when approached by salespeople while shopping. Sylvia went around to the back of the house. "I can't believe she still has my curtains up. I must have made them twenty years ago." Things you bought these days just didn't hold up like the old stuff, Sylvia was always reminding Rita.

Sylvia walked to a ladder against the side of the house. "Come help me, Clayton."

"Your grandmother's going crazy," Clayton said to Rita and slowly shook his head.

"Please," Sylvia pleaded. "Just let me have one look."

As Clayton held the ladder, Rita counted her grandmother's deliberate steps. What would people think if they spotted two senior citizens casing a house? Rita wondered if any of the old neighbors Clayton mentioned would even recognize them. The Schaeffers or the Walshes.

"Let *me* see," Rita insisted.

"In a minute," Sylvia said.

"I'm going to say hello to Marlene, then," Rita said.

Clayton grabbed her hand. "We'll all go over there together, Rita."

"OK, Sylvia. You've had your look. Now let's get going," Clayton said. He slid his hands down the ladder and stood back. "I said I only wanted to swing by the house, not make a big deal of it."

But Sylvia couldn't get enough of the house. She called out features of the rooms as if naming old friends. Looking through the windows, she described the swinging Dutch door that led to the tiny kitchen, the new dining room table and hutch and four chairs completely filling the room. Sylvia said she'd sewn all of Janice's clothes in that small room, spread the crinkly patterns over lengths of cotton and corduroy, then cut and stitched and hemmed. She pointed out where she'd kept her sewing machine in the corner. Trying to catch a glimpse of one of the bedrooms, Sylvia bent slightly to the right. Clayton immediately tightened his grip on the creaking ladder.

As if it were a secret he was sharing with her, Clayton

whispered to Rita that probably the owners were at work. He noted that the Pinches had made a number of cosmetic changes to the house, nothing structural. New gutters had been installed, and the trim, now chipping, had been repainted an unattractive tan. Rita tried to imagine her grandparents moving through the rooms of the small house and fussing around in its yard.

"Come on, Sylvia," Clayton insisted. He said to Rita, "She's bending all over the place. The next thing I know she'll fall on her ass." He turned away from the house, but continued holding the ladder.

When Sylvia reported on the china lined in grooves along the polished hutch shelves, Rita thought of their own plastic dishes, deeply scratched with wear. Clayton mumbled below Sylvia and chided her, but Sylvia ignored him.

"She's in a trance," Clayton said. Rita had to agree that she wasn't used to seeing her grandmother so mesmerized.

With the mall looming so close by, Rita could see the back entrances to a few stores and the employees' cars. The man in the green car had parked and now stood between his car and the RV. When Rita pointed him out, Clayton explained that he was probably part of the Neighborhood Watch patrol. Then he turned and stared at the man. When Clayton reached for Rita's hand, she pulled away.

"I'm going to tell him we won't hurt anything," she said, running off.

"Rita," Clayton called, as she approached the green car. She felt odd, pulled to this clean-cut stranger wearing a suit like filings to a magnet. The pounding in her heart reverberated to her fingertips. She looked back at Sylvia, with difficulty making her way down the ladder.

"Rita!" Sylvia called across the bright green lawn.

The man had turned to something in his car. Rita stood

curbside and thought of what to say. Perhaps she'd simply blurt out hello, then when he raised his eyes to look at her she'd study his features for her own. She couldn't be certain exactly what she wanted. Maybe just to touch the man to determine if he was real. But even the thought of simple contact made her stomach harden into a metal ball.

When the man straightened up and looked at her, she saw that her father was handsome. Melvin's large round face projected intensity; he could start a fire with his eyes.

"Hello, Rita," he said. His voice was steady, but he smiled awkwardly. "Want to go for a little drive with me?"

"Where are you going?" she asked cautiously.

Her voice seemed to encourage him to take a step closer to her. "Where would you like to go?"

She shrugged her shoulders. Appearing not to know what to do or say next, he ran his fingers along the side of his face. She stayed on the curb and studied him.

"Rita!" Clayton called out again as he hurried toward them.

"I'm calling the police," Sylvia hollered. "Marlene," she screamed.

Her grandparents' voices seemed to startle her father, reminding Rita of a lion she had once seen in a zoo. The animal was confidently strolling through his cage until a teenager jumped the guardrail and ran up to the bars. Instantly the animal let out a growl and lurched at the boy, who jumped back. The animal sent one paw through the bars and batted violently at the place where the boy had stood.

"Melvin," Clayton said, not as if he were just recognizing him, but challenging him.

Melvin jumped at Rita. Then everything speeded up. She felt her father grab her. She screamed, but only a squeak eked from her mouth.

She felt a hardness, maybe a knife, at her neck. With her eyes closed, she pictured the weapon shiny, picking up every trace of available light and turning it dangerous. She took a deep breath. This time the sound came out in a howl. When Melvin covered her mouth with his hand, she bit him. "Shit," he said, pulling his hand back from her mouth. She didn't see a knife.

"Let her go, Melvin," Clayton said. He was at the driver's side of the RV. Holding the gun, Clayton's hands were shaking.

"Let her go, Melvin," he repeated. Rita stared at the weapon pointed in her direction.

"Not on your life," Melvin called. "She's my daughter, not yours. I've found her, and now I'm going to keep her."

"It's not that simple," Clayton said. "She's not an umbrella. She's not a glove somebody lost. We've raised her."

"She's my daughter," Melvin said again.

Without turning his back to Clayton or releasing Rita, Melvin opened his car door, pushed Rita onto the front seat, and shut the door. Standing defiantly beside the car, he appeared to invite an encounter.

Clayton advanced on Melvin.

"I said she's mine," Melvin said. Then, "Kidnapper. Old goat." He lunged at Clayton and the gun went off just as Sylvia grabbed Clayton around the waist.

The three fell to the ground in front of Melvin's car, the gun discharging a second time. Pressing her face against the windshield, Rita anxiously looked from her grandparents struggling on the ground to the figure of her father. Melvin jumped up and ran toward the mall.

Rita kept her eyes trained on the man who was shrinking smaller and smaller by the second. By the time she opened the car door and knelt next to her grandparents, her father was completely out of sight.

"Are you OK?" Sylvia asked.

"Fine. What's with Clayton?"

"He shot his foot," Sylvia said, her voice and lips trembling. Clayton's shoe and sock oozed bloody red. His face was pale. Blood stained one sleeve of Sylvia's white blouse.

When Rita had looked at her great-grandmother Vaeth's face in the coffin, the features had been coated with makeup and colors that weren't real. But her bluish lips had given Rita the impression that she was very cold. Clayton's lips were the same color. Her grandmother was crying, and Clayton was now leaning against the RV, staring in the direction of the sirens. A few people opened the doors of their houses and came running.

Marlene rushed out her front door, yelling about having been in the basement doing the wash. Oblivious to the outside world, she had missed seeing Melvin in time to avert the crisis.

Clayton said his foot hurt like hell, and Sylvia said, "If you hadn't been wearing those damn cutaway shoes your foot wouldn't be so tore up." She wiped at her eyes with her fingers.

Clayton said things could have turned out worse — much worse. Something could have happened to Rita. Rita's fear that he was going to die quickly faded. Then he voiced a realistic reaction to the incident. "Looks like we'll have to stay put for a while now," he said, mimicking Lucille.

Rita wondered if Melvin would come back for the green car.

Clayton was lifted onto a stretcher, then fed into the wide mouth of an ambulance. Sylvia and the paramedics worked over him as Marlene took Rita's hand and pulled her out of the way. Then the ambulance drove off, lights flashing but no siren. Rita watched her grandfather disappear like her father.

A policeman closed the door to Melvin's car, then stared in the direction of the mall. A neighbor collapsed the Pinches' ladder and leaned it against the foundation of the house.

171

EIGHT

———◆•◆•◆———

The police didn't find Melvin. But they found all kinds of
paraphernalia in his green car, including an album of photographs taken of Rita as a baby. In a couple of the photos Melvin
must have set the automatic shutter and run to squeeze into the
picture. Pressed up close to Rita's face and Janice's, he appeared
a little out of breath. A collection of toys, many still in their
original packaging, was in the trunk. Some of the toys, like the
miniature tea set and the nurse's bag, were meant for someone
younger than Rita. Rita liked to think that he'd been looking for
her ever since she was young enough to play with that baby
stuff. She imagined the toys in the trunk of the green car were
an accumulation of his hopes to find her.

After Clayton and Sylvia talked to the police about Melvin,
and Clayton's foot had healed enough for him to drive, he
dropped his Atlantic City plans and said it was time to head
back west. He told Rita that the delay in Baltimore worried
him. He was concerned that once Sylvia got with Marlene for

any length of time, she wouldn't want to leave. Plus, the shooting had unnerved him.

Sylvia didn't cry when they left Baltimore, but before they crossed the state line, she started in again about Melvin.

"Doesn't that look like his green car, Clayton?" she asked. And she kept on until Clayton said, "Vee, he's gone. The authorities are on the case."

"I know all about *authorities*," Sylvia said.

"Melvin," Clayton said, "won't bother us again."

Rita felt a strange combination of relief and sadness. Her father had terrified her one minute and then completely won her sympathy. She remembered the image of Melvin running, smaller and smaller, into the background. On TV, the enemy always seemed bigger and stronger than anyone else. And ready for revenge.

"How's your foot?" Sylvia asked.

"It's still there," Clayton said.

In her dream, Rita was on her way to California with her father. They weren't driving an RV with Rita's space partitioned off like a kennel, but in his dark green car. Sitting in the front seat beside him, she crossed the entire country without lingering in one place for long. Each of the stopovers — house after house, hotel after low-lying motel — was filled with friends who told them stories about Rita's mother. Everyone had their own nicknames for Janice. They called her Jade for her favorite color; Miranda because it meant extraordinary; Eve because that was the way "everything" started. The dream names came at Rita like rain and confused her. Even her father didn't say "Janice." Instead, he called her, "Janet, my favorite planet."

In between stops thick with music and faces and smoke, Rita

and Melvin drove. Stretches of desert expanded and contracted like a monster was breathing deep inside the earth. Cities small as toy models grew when approached, then cars and horses turned to dots as Melvin drove off from the farmlands patterned with crops. The sun crept over the crests of mountains and maneuvered straight overhead, then guided them with the angle of its descent. Rita and Melvin didn't stop at a single place because someone had read about it or someone else had recommended it or because it was reasonably priced or close to some weird museum, or because it was free of radiation. Her father stayed at places because they happened to be there when Rita said it was time to stop driving.

As much as Rita wanted to see California, she insisted that she and Melvin end up on Garden Road — near the mall and a selection of fast-food restaurants for every day of the week. If only for a day, Rita wanted the two of them to actually *be* from some place that had no possibility of moving. In the small house where her mother had been raised there would be enough space for a piano, a telescope, an easel surrounded by giant canvases, a loom if she wanted it, a full-size oven . . . Rita would have room to do anything, become anyone.

When she woke up, deep in West Virginia, Rita remembered Melvin's hands at her mouth and neck. Strong and sweaty, they'd been insistent on wanting her in the car. No one had ever held her with such determination. The interior of the green car had smelled of old cigarettes and plastic. It made Rita think back to when Sylvia had loaded a roll of used film into her camera. The result had been a bizarre montage of faces and locations. She and Sylvia had spent hours trying to identify the different aspects of each shot. Sylvia had said what she frequently did when she was threading a needle to work on samplers, "My eyes aren't what they used to be." And Clayton had said, "What is?"

Before Rita could figure her father out, Clayton had scared him off. Even though she hadn't actually examined all the toys in her father's car, she imagined all those doll faces that had never been kissed, board games that hadn't been won or lost.

Rita quietly opened the RV's door and sniffed the pungent odor of cedar. With only the forty-seven dollars that she'd stashed under her mattress, she walked away from the RV.

She was going to California by herself, without getting distracted by museums or mementos or Clayton's favorite spot in Texas. She was going to California alone. Before she reached her destination, she would pause in the desert, where everything leveled out. There, she imagined, she could let her mind drift away from its tight knob of confusion and spread all across the expanse of sand. She imagined building a house in the desert. Her dream of meeting her mother she took as a sign; perhaps Janice was really alive somewhere.

Before she reached the main highway, she'd spent nearly six dollars on candies, snacks, magazines, and soda at Tom's Deli. Rita was delighted to be doing what Clayton would have called wasting good money.

All morning she walked, careful to avoid cops and trucks, which might have CBs. Clayton would have sent out an emergency message on his CB. She remembered Pikey using a CB to find Dot's glasses when they blew out the rig window.

The higher the sun moved into the sky, the more Rita wondered if she had done the right thing. By midday she was hot and confused. She considered that her grandparents must want her very badly and love her very much to even think about shooting Melvin. But her father must have loved her just as much, because he'd pursued her for so long and risked his life to get to her. She thought, too, about why her grandparents would want to keep her from that kind of courage.

Late in the afternoon, she stopped by a farm. The cows bunched together under a tree made her think of campers congregating at the end of the day. Row after row of corn stood as orderly as a marching band.

Once when she and Sylvia and Clayton had stopped for the night alongside a raspberry patch, Sylvia hummed as she picked berries in the last of the daylight, and a little later sang as she rolled out a piecrust for the fruit. If they lived in a house with a raspberry patch alongside the driveway, Sylvia said, she wouldn't have gotten so much pleasure from the task. She would have expected the berries to be there, the way the farmer counted on the corn he'd planted. It was the unexpected that made life interesting.

Before long, the police came with Sylvia and Clayton. In the distance, Rita saw the farmer who must have reported her. His arms were folded and his dark hat was pulled down into his eyes. Rita supposed she looked like some overgrown pest about to eat his crop.

Sylvia and Clayton checked her over, but Rita could tell they didn't know quite what to do. Neither did she. She'd frightened them, the person they loved best in the world. Sylvia and Clayton looked tired. And old. They stared at her, their mouths slightly open. Suddenly she realized that, studying her, they were remembering her mother.

And how they'd lost her.

"Melvin killed your mama, honey," Sylvia said as if apologizing for the gun and the panic and all their efforts to protect her.

"With a gun?" Rita asked. She'd only heard the word *accident* associated with her mother's death. "Tragic recklessness" had been the extent of Sylvia's description of the accident.

Clayton shook his head sadly and looked at Sylvia to explain.

"He took her away from every careful thing we did for her."
Sylvia paused. "Like peeling the skin off a piece of fruit."

Rita didn't know what to say, but she knew she had to divert
Sylvia from talking about her mother's accident. "What's for
dinner?" she asked.

Sylvia got down on her knees and opened her arms as if Rita
were still four feet tall. Clayton shifted on his temporary
crutches. "Get ahold of yourself," he said to Sylvia.

But Sylvia just kept squeezing Rita, until Rita finally said,
"Vee, aren't we close to Kentucky?" She was thinking of Hazard. Although she was glad her father hadn't been hurt, Rita
thought Luke Duke would have been proud of Clayton.

IV

THE TREE, THE CARAVAN, AND THE GOLD MINE

NINE

———◆———

When they finally crossed the state line into California, Sylvia said, "I was beginning to think I'd never see this day."

"Now you can color it in," Clayton said. California was the only state in the lower forty-eight they hadn't visited. He'd hated giving up the free parking in Nevada, which they'd qualified for by being seniors. Still, Clayton figured, the final frontier was worth it. Plus he was afraid if they'd stayed another day in Las Vegas, Sylvia and Rita would have lost every penny the camping fees had saved them. Rita loved sneaking into the slot machines. The girl could go through money like water.

"We don't have that map anymore. It was on the old rig," Sylvia said.

"We sold that trailer without all the states colored in?" Momentarily confused, Clayton lightly touched the side of his head as if he were only now noticing that some of his hair was missing.

Along the highway ran a ragged line of weeds. A few white

and orange wildflowers appeared intermittently, briefly catching his attention. Up ahead in the middle of the highway, a group of blackbirds strutted out across the asphalt to feast on a road kill, then flew off as the RV came up on them. By keeping himself in motion, Clayton worked his worries out of his system. Since "the Melvin incident" — the term Clayton preferred to any mention of shooting himself — he had gotten a second wind; he and Sylvia and Rita moved almost as frequently as they had their first days on the road.

Sylvia found it comforting when old patterns began to reestablish themselves. And she didn't object to Clayton's frenzied pace, even though there was no rational reason for it. They hadn't heard from or of Melvin since the encounter four years earlier. Not even a letter. Nothing was certain except that he wasn't in Maryland.

Rita had learned to deal with transience; she seldom became tearful at leaving new friends and familiar classrooms. She wasn't interested in team sports or extracurricular activities, which would only have been disrupted. Because she mastered concepts quickly and memorized events and dates easily, Clayton no longer concerned himself about her schoolwork. When Rita took her year-end tests, she made a near-perfect score.

To keep in touch with her growing list of acquaintances from different schools, Rita became a letter writer. She regularly wrote pages to Libby in Texas and shorter, informative notes to her Mexican pen pal, Maria, as well as to new friends. Lots of the kids sent her bumper stickers, which Clayton stuck to the RV, even the risqué ones like "Bitch on Wheels" and "Honk If You're Horny." He didn't make an issue of those because if you raised too big a stink, kids became even more attracted to what was forbidden. Rita's stickers covered the entire back and half of one side of the RV.

Sylvia had waited so long to visit southern California that

she didn't want to zip in and out like they were making an obligatory visit to relatives. She had her mind set on seeing Hollywood and Venice Beach, and maybe going on a bus tour of the stars' homes.

"I thought we could visit Little New York. It's near San Diego," Sylvia said, explaining that the attraction was a palpable version of New York City. Little New York had no crime, pollution, or noise.

"Is this going to be another Talking Animal Farm?" Clayton asked. He shook his head at the idea of Little New York and was glad to hear Rita voice his own concern.

"How could it be like New York if it's not dangerous?" she asked.

Rita had heard how in New York City twenty dollars could easily buy a phony ID, which magically transformed a sixteen-year-old into a twenty-one-year-old. She loved the idea of jumping ahead to an age when people would respect what she said; when she could legally drink a whole beer; when, hopefully, she'd be holding the hand of a handsome man a couple of years older than herself.

"I think there's a small Empire State Building and UN," Sylvia added. "I'll bet the Twin Towers are cute."

"I'd rather see the real thing," Rita said.

Lately, Sylvia worried that Rita had developed a combination that could get her into trouble: Janice's curiosity and Melvin's determination. She supposed it was inevitable, healthy even, for the girl to want to establish her individuality. Sylvia only wished her old age hadn't made her so sensitive to everything Rita said.

Janice had gone through a similar rebellious stage. The difference was that Janice hadn't sided with Clayton, as Rita was now doing, but turned away from both of them. Rita enabled Sylvia to understand that lots of things Janice had done as a child weren't normal but signals of disaster. In spite of her inquisitiveness, Janice had been extremely reclusive, even when approached by children her own age; she'd methodically ripped apart three stuffed animals; she'd always been apathetic toward family activities.

"I thought of another one," Rita said as Clayton pulled off the highway for gas. " 'We travel around from coast to coast.' " She paused. " 'You bring the bottle, we'll be the host.' " Sylvia glanced at Clayton before smiling at her granddaughter.

"Or else, 'We'll make the toast,' " Rita added.

"What do you know about bringing bottles?" Clayton asked, his right eyebrow raised.

"Oh, Clayton," Rita said, "relax."

"And you just watch the signs for me, Miss," he said. Rita was always telling him to relax. He thought it would be some joke if, with all the years he and Sylvia had spent running away from Melvin, he now sat behind them in the form of a sixteen-year-old girl. Clayton liked to think he'd put an end to Melvin's bad influence the day he'd shot himself in the foot and Melvin had run off like a rodent.

In the years since the clash with Melvin, Clayton had turned different possibilities over in his mind. He could have wounded Melvin; the doctors found only one bullet lodged in his left foot, and Clayton had fired twice. For a while, Clayton's only regret was that he hadn't killed Melvin outright. But every so often, when Clayton recalled pulling out the gun, then spotting the look of surprise, of almost innocence, on Melvin's face, he had a hard time sleeping.

Santa Barbara was Clayton's idea of the perfect town. Bricked walkways down the center of the shopping district led from one unique shop to another. One store sold only baseball paraphernalia; another, different shaped and scented soaps. There was something for all of them. And not one sign for a familiar chain store broke into the charming picture.

He usually had about a twenty-minute tolerance for shopping with Sylvia, but in Santa Barbara he walked along with her for an hour. He and Sylvia trailed Rita into record shops and shoe stores and along counters displaying lengths of gold, silver, and plastic jewelry. Sauntering among the racks and rows of merchandise, Rita appeared to know exactly what she was doing. Clayton, on the other hand, could become confused by the rush of color and cloth and chrome and music.

He liked the pier area best. Each day that he and Sylvia and Rita went down to the waterfront, the area was alive with young, tanned people jogging, walking, or roller-skating. Above him, the wings of seagulls beat up and down against the air. In the distance, sailboats stripped of their sails looked to be all bone. He walked along the pier and often dropped a fishing line into the expanse of water. The regular slap of the tide and the shades of blue-gray along the horizon reminded him of Ocean City on Maryland's Eastern Shore.

They had been in a trailer park just outside Santa Barbara for five days when Clayton ordered the tree. From his wallet, he unfolded the full-page ad from a Denver newspaper with its drawing of a miraculous tree. In the rendering, a man stood with his arms crossed under a thirty-foot tree, his house dwarfed in the background. The prospectus, guaranteeing a half foot of growth after each weekly watering, said, "Plant now, and next summer reach out and touch lush branches from your second-story window." The tree was perfect for someone who couldn't wait fifteen years for it to grow to a decent size. In addition, the plant was offered for only $3.95.

"Why would you want to plant a tree?" Sylvia asked. She was

anxious to head to LA, which they'd only skirted after running into intense traffic.

"Because I'd like to wake up in the morning and see a tree outside the bedroom window, all right?" Clayton pictured looking out of the RV at a thick, green tree instead of his neighbors' webbed lawn chairs and laundry.

"It's cool here," Rita said. "I wouldn't mind staying. School doesn't start for three more months."

Sylvia said, "By then, the tree should be about your height."

"Very funny," Clayton said.

A fortune-teller who called herself Madame Tooley lived in a trailer ten spots down from the Vaeths. She had invited Sylvia into her rig on three occasions before Sylvia finally went. The trailer's interior was decorated in mauve. Newspaper accounts of Madame Tooley's uncanny predictions and notices of her accomplishments hung on every available section of wall. Sylvia studied a clipping describing how Madame Tooley had been instrumental in helping three men locate treasures from a ship that had sunk centuries earlier off the coast of Mexico. A faint jazz tune floated out into the trailer's main room.

The tall, thin woman in her sixties commanded an unspoken respect. Rita said that Madame Tooley looked like some exotic bird from the rain forest.

"I wonder if I could ask you a question," Sylvia said. When Madame Tooley hesitated, Sylvia suggested paying for the advice with one of her samplers.

Somehow she couldn't bring herself to tell this stranger the whole story of Melvin. After all, Madame Tooley was the one who knew all.

"My granddaughter won't eat," Sylvia said instead.

Madame Tooley said, "What's the question?"

"I wonder if you have any . . ." Sylvia paused, "any insight on this." It worried Sylvia when Rita said she didn't feel like chewing.

"She's seen a doctor?"

Sylvia briefly explained the eating problems in the past that had recently reappeared, the tonics that hadn't worked. She didn't mention Rita's crying jags that, for a time, had unpredictably shattered their nights.

"How are you feeling yourself?" Madame Tooley asked Sylvia.

"I'm fine. It's Rita I'm concerned about."

"I understand that," Madame Tooley said, her voice covering Sylvia like a gentle wash of water. She mentioned objects and people from Sylvia's recent past, then back and back all the way into Sylvia's girlhood. When Madame Tooley spoke the initials of key people from Sylvia's life, a flood of comforting images surrounded her. She remembered the bouquet of irises she'd carried on her wedding day, and the first day that Janice had gone to school. Sylvia could feel herself smiling until she heard the psychic speak about someone Sylvia needed to forgive.

"Melvin," Sylvia said with some difficulty.

"Melvin," the psychic repeated. "You should learn how to forgive him."

"Forgive him? Not me." At first, with Madame Tooley, Sylvia felt she'd been given a full body massage. And then, just when she was perfectly at ease, her body all loose and liquidy, the masseuse had stuck her with a pin.

"It's not so difficult. Just think of the child," Madame Tooley said. "Your husband will help."

Clayton. Sometimes Sylvia forgot how they had worked together, how their combined wishes for a family had finally borne them a child, and how their mutual determination had made it possible for them to gain custody of Rita. And yet, when it came to Melvin, they had gone different ways, hiding letters, holding back their fears.

"I feel his presence all around you." Madame Tooley spoke in the low, gentle tone that, Sylvia imagined, aides used in an insane asylum.

"My husband's or Melvin's?"

"Maybe both of them."

Sylvia wanted to scream, "Jesus, don't you know for sure? You're the one with 'the gift.' " But instead she politely asked Madame Tooley how long she'd lived in the trailer park.

Then Madame Tooley said, "Did you ever consider that maybe you made Melvin stand for houses?"

Houses? Maybe the woman *was* nuts. Melvin stood for trouble.

"Just think about it," Madame Tooley said.

Sylvia couldn't take this beating around the bush a second more. "Melvin killed my daughter," she said.

Madame Tooley stood up and ground some coffee beans, their nutty odor filling the space around them. Sylvia thought maybe the woman would somehow manipulate the beans to coax more information to light, but Madame Tooley only pulled a coffee filter from the cabinet.

"Do you know where Melvin is?" Sylvia asked.

"He's close by," Madame Tooley said, her back to Sylvia.

"In California?"

"I wouldn't go so far as to say California." After a long pause, Madame Tooley said, "Make your peace with him."

Sylvia felt lightheaded as she walked back to her own rig. The moon was full, the air beginning to cool. She heard voices and preparing-for-bed noises coming from the trailers she passed. A pay phone rang insistently in the distance.

"Well, you get all your questions answered?" Clayton asked

as soon as she opened the door. He appeared to search her for answers. For a few seconds she felt herself the fortune-teller, holding the news but not delivering it. Guarding the huge secret of people's whereabouts and shortcomings and potential. Knowing that it was not the information itself but what was done with it that mattered.

She'd been gone longer than she'd anticipated. "Did you have dinner?" she asked.

"Grilled cheese," Clayton said.

"Did Rita eat?"

Clayton shook his head.

"It's no big deal," Rita called from deep inside the trailer. "What did she say about me?"

Sylvia eyed the short yellow sundress that Rita had bought the day before. "I didn't talk about you," she answered.

"No?" Rita asked surprised. "Come on, Vee." With her index finger, Rita twirled a strand of her long dark-brown hair.

"Madame Tooley asked me about myself," Sylvia said. "Want some chocolate milk?"

"Maybe I could go see her," Rita said. She could ask about her father and why they hadn't heard from him. She could ask when she would finally find a boyfriend.

"I don't think that's such a good idea," Clayton said.

At Mission Santa Barbara, everywhere Clayton looked he found signs that his desire to stay in the area and plant his tree were good instincts. When he first pulled up to the adobe building, Clayton remembered himself as a boy staring at just such an exterior bathed in blinding sunlight, though he had no idea where he might have been. Then, when he actually entered the mission building, he was certain he was being given specific signs. In the chapel's book of prayer requests, the line above where Clayton prepared to write said, "Tim Bristol, Baltimore, MD, Tijan Industries, Inc." Tim asked for a blessing for his new company, named after his children, Tim Junior and Janet.

Clayton walked into the small courtyard cemetery that, except for the skulls positioned above the chapel's doorway, resembled a normal garden with plants in different shades of green, many thick with large leaves. A huge fig tree grew from the parched ground. Below the stone paths, beneath the mass of gnarled and partially exposed tree roots, were buried ten thousand Indians. Imagining all the dead below him, as well as generations still to come, Clayton felt a profound, if momentary, ease.

"You're blocking the panels," Clayton said, shielding his eyes and looking at Rita sunbathing atop the RV.

"There's plenty of sun for both me and the old solar panels," Rita called back. She wore a pink bikini and the Walkman Clayton had bought her for her sixteenth birthday. Clayton could smell her tanning lotion.

"Why don't you do your sunbathing down here?" Clayton asked.

Rita didn't answer. She liked the heat of the hard surface under her towel and her position well above ground level. And she wanted a little privacy to concentrate on the letter she was writing to Maria in Mexico. In a recent picture, Maria's skin and hair were very dark, and, although she wasn't overweight, her cotton dress was stretched tight across her chest and hips. The backdrop of ocean and palm trees looked exactly the same as in the first photo Maria had sent nearly five years earlier. Miguel, her boyfriend, wasn't in the photo, but Rita envisioned his handsome black eyes and his strong hands. Maria said he worked at the docks whenever something needed to be loaded or unloaded.

Rita fantasized about a visit to Maria. She pictured a young child clinging to the back of Maria's legs and an infant in the crook of her arm. They'd sit on plastic chairs and eat rice, beans, and chilies. Maria's little boy, maybe his name would be Miguel like his father, would run into the small waves on the nearby beach, then hurry back to his mother. The baby would work her tiny mouth in the cloud of shade Maria provided. The sun would sparkle on the water, and Rita would catch flickers of passion in Maria's eyes when she brushed sand from little Miguel or spoke of her husband.

In the distance, someone was mowing grass. The droning background noise seemed to gather momentum and race right for their RV when Sylvia heard a crash. She turned to find that Clayton had fallen against the shiny black body of their new Weber grill. She leaped toward him. Clayton said nothing as she helped him up and brushed his shorts clean of dirt. Relieved that he appeared fine except for a bad humor, Sylvia stood back as he bulled by her and then slammed the RV door.

"You'd better get down, Rita," Sylvia warned.

"Oh, he's probably mad because his tree hasn't come," Rita called, climbing down from the roof.

When Sylvia went inside, she saw that Clayton was pacing through the RV with the same fervor that had stomped the carpeting of their Garden Road house into an obvious trail. He'd regressed to that state of mind where he would throw things out for no good reason, or wake her in the middle of the night just to point out that a neighbor's bathroom light had been left on.

"Is it the tree?" Sylvia asked.

"What tree?" he asked, not looking at her.

He began to pick up appliances, books, clothes.

"When in the hell did we get this?" he said of an electric juicer.

"Why, Pikey and Dot gave us that one anniversary. I've been making juice with it for years," Sylvia said.

From the bathroom, Sylvia heard Clayton yell, "And just what in the devil's this?"

"He's got my curling iron," Rita whined as she came through the door. She'd never seen her grandfather so agitated.

Sylvia realized she was holding her breath.

"It's weird," Rita whispered.

Clayton ignored his wife's pleas and his granddaughter's squeals. All the possessions around him were taking over, pressing at him, building up to his chest, his mouth. He began to toss everything he picked up into the center of the RV. Sylvia yelled when a just-completed sampler joined the heap of plastic dishes, utensils, pot holders, books, and shoes. He strode into the bedroom and came back with the sky-blue bowling ball. Then he sat down in his favorite chair. Almost as an afterthought, he took off his orange and black Orioles cap and tossed it onto the pile.

As soon as Clayton took off his cap, he heard the music. It circled him like water those times he'd sat in the middle of the Little Pipe River and loaded a fishhook with bait. The music grew louder, so loud he couldn't think of fish or the glossy, dark surface of tiny ripples. The melody pressed through him, then moved his body. Though he remained in his chair, he knew he was dancing, but he'd never danced like this before. His arms and legs were manipulated at a feverish pace. Pulled through a sleek current of music, he sensed everything dropping off from him, finally even the final notes.

"Put on another," Clayton said. He waited for the next song to start.

"What did he say?" Rita asked. Clayton didn't move.

Sylvia approached Clayton, who sat perfectly still. He didn't move when she touched him, blink when she called to him or even when she screamed.

"Doctor," Sylvia said to Rita. "Call a doctor." She briefly cursed for not pushing Clayton to spend the money for a car phone like she'd wanted. When Rita remained staring at Clayton, Sylvia grabbed her arm. "Hurry," she said.

Racing outside, Rita almost ran into their next-door neighbor, Cliff Hamm, the man Clayton called a blowhard. Cliff caught Rita by the shoulders.

"My grandfather," she said, gesturing at the RV. "He was acting crazy and now he's not moving." Cliff stopped; he appeared to be making a diagnosis. Rita pulled him toward the RV door. Sylvia pointed to Clayton, immobile in front of the huge pile of things topped off with the Orioles cap.

"What's wrong?" Sylvia pleaded as Cliff touched a spot on Clayton's neck just below the ear.

"Most likely a stroke," Cliff said.

"A stroke?"

"I once saw a tiny old lady who could barely walk break an entire set of dishes. One by one she threw them against her kitchen wall, using profanity all the while. Her husband couldn't believe she knew the words she was using." Cliff rocked back on his feet. "She was having a stroke."

"Aren't you going to do something? Like blow air into his mouth?" Rita asked. Clayton's hands lay limp in his lap.

"I'm afraid it's too late for that, honey," Cliff said.

Rita moved toward her grandfather. Clayton was just taking what he called a "breather" when they used to play catch or run around the rig. She'd make him all right in a few minutes. She'd blow air into Clayton's mouth herself. Her own air.

TEN

———◆◆◆———

Sylvia wanted to leave Santa Barbara immediately, but Rita insisted on waiting until Clayton's tree arrived. Rita planted it, fertilized it with a handful of Clayton's ashes, and surrounded it with a plastic-coated piece of fencing, a shield against Jim Pilot's bush hog. Jim regularly maintained the campground with a gas-powered, metal-blade weed whacker that Sylvia said could easily take a kid's leg off.

Everybody offered to put up Sylvia and Rita: Sylvia's brother and sister in Wisconsin, Lucille and Eddie in Baltimore, Bob and Carol Melnick in New Mexico. Marlene suggested flying out to meet Sylvia and Rita and then the three of them driving back to Baltimore together. But Sylvia and Rita set off for LA on their own.

Sylvia had driven the rig on occasion, but not for any length of time. Concentrating on the highway, she imagined she was on her way somewhere to pick up Clayton. In the early years of their marriage, when she needed the car during the day she used to drop Clayton off at the gates of Evergreen, just before the long blast of the horn that officially began each workday. In the evening, she'd wait for the same sound and then watch for him to appear among the rush of men. Usually she spotted his energetic gait before she recognized his face or his jacket. Clayton's strong presence had always made an impression on her. Even now, settled in the container by her bed, the gray grains and clumps of his remains were heavier than she'd anticipated.

"I'm just going to take it easy," she said more to herself than to Rita as the traffic rushed by them on either side. "We don't have to keep up with these maniacs."

"Let's call Triple A and see what they have to say about traffic to LA," Rita suggested.

"Never mind about that," Sylvia said. Just yesterday she'd bought a phone, which Clayton had never agreed to, and enrolled in the AAA. Sylvia thought she'd gotten a good price on both.

Rita didn't regret driving away from Santa Barbara. She craved the speed of leaving, the sensation of moving off. She wanted to be far away. She wanted to picture Clayton's tree growing into a size that would surprise everyone.

Rita and Sylvia didn't talk much about Clayton, each reluctant to get the other crying. Rita held her sadness back the same way she'd learned to hide her desire for large things, toys that wouldn't fit into the condensed, tight quarters of a travel trailer. The RV couldn't contain the emotion Rita felt at losing Clayton. If those feelings spilled out of her, they would fill an entire state. Maybe two states.

Besides forcing her to drive, Clayton's absence made Sylvia view things in a different way. She saw this picture of a young girl and an old woman toughing it across the landscape, yet as vulnerable as wounded animals when they stopped. Like the scent of blood, their sorrow seemed to reek around them, sending out messages of weakness. Sylvia began carrying Clayton's .38 in her purse.

That day in the desert when Clayton taught her to shoot, she couldn't have envisioned eventually holding a pistol in her lap. And when he first taught her to drive their old Pontiac, she hadn't any idea that she would someday be steering her entire home through the western states. Everything had become larger than she'd ever thought possible.

The first stop they made was at Rita's suggestion, the Museum of the Snake. With feigned enthusiasm Sylvia agreed, but neither she nor Rita could park the RV. Sylvia drove on past the museum until she found a stretch of curb long enough to accommodate the vehicle. She wanted no part of backing it up and wiggling into a space, as Clayton had been so adept at doing.

"Rita, we've got a walk back that will kill me."

"It will be good for you, Vee."

"In this heat, it's not good for anybody."

Sylvia knew that Rita had no sense of her age, even with all her wrinkles, poor eyesight, and arthritis, even with Clayton dying.

"Let's drive the Rabbit down there," Rita suggested.

"I don't want to fool with unhooking it," Sylvia said.

The museum was a single large room filled with all sorts of snake paraphernalia, which appeared to have been gathered from a more ritualistic world. One wall was covered with snake skins pinned to a cork backing. Near the cash register sat a wooden bowl full of snake teeth, which looked delicate as jewels, hardly capable of inflicting fatality. The museum featured an array of items made from the skin and teeth of snakes, as well as ordinary merchandise decorated with reproductions of snakes: welcome mats, mugs, T-shirts, socks, hats, shot glasses. Some snakes appeared threatening; others smiled or grimaced. The most incredible souvenirs were things Rita and Sylvia would never have expected to see covered with snakeskin: a top hat, a cane, the handle of a toothbrush.

The shop owner, a large-faced man wearing a cowboy hat, explained that all of the snakes had been farm raised. As Rita and Sylvia exclaimed over the various gifts and collectibles, the man recounted "a rattler sting operation" that had put one of his competitors out of business for trapping snakes illegally.

Sylvia touched a snakeskin-covered cow skull and recoiled. "What else will they think of?" she said to no one in particular.

"This," Rita answered, pointing to a snakeskin-covered doorknob. Everything in the place was for sale. Sylvia said she didn't think Clayton would have enjoyed the Museum of the Snake.

They made other stops on their slow and roundabout way toward Los Angeles. When there wasn't much traffic, Rita took over the driving for short stints. Rita had gotten a learner's permit in Colorado, but Sylvia said she wasn't sure it allowed driving in other states.

Rita remembered when she had to wiggle to the edge of the seat to reach the gas pedal, back when Clayton first allowed her to start the rig. Sitting beside her, later standing outside the driver's door and looking in through the open window once she'd learned the routine, he had watched over her. She thought he'd be proud to see how she'd learned to handle the rig. She wished he was with her again; she'd settle for the amount of time it would take to drive the mile to the next exit.

Sylvia insisted on joining the caravan. She cut the long-awaited LA visit short when she read a flyer that Marlene had sent, promoting travel in a caravan. The caravan featured a wagon master who led the pack, set the itinerary, and guided the tour, as well as a tail gunner who brought up the rear and helped repair any RVs that ran into trouble. In between, thirty or forty RVs would press out of southern California toward a common destination: Idaho.

"It defeats the whole idea of RVing," Rita said. "What happened to the individual forging on alone through the natural world?"

"No more boondocking," Sylvia said. Her voice wavered as if she were tuning it for the best effect. "I'm getting too old to get dressed in the dark and crap in the woods."

Rita looked at her grandmother as if she might be losing it.

"The opening of the frontier," Sylvia said. "A caravan of RVs is simply a modern version of the wagon trains that first thrust into the West."

"Only they didn't charge $250."

Ignoring Rita's comment, Sylvia said, "There's a nice feeling of security with all those other RVs around." As much as she tried to suppress it, an image of Melvin still pushed into Sylvia's consciousness often. She no longer had Clayton to keep her thoughts of Melvin at a distance. Madame Tooley's words still spooked her: "I feel his presence all around you."

"I hope the wagon master's cute at least."

The wagon master was Jeremy Jugg, whose thick, shiny brown hair was swept back and ridged from the teeth of a comb. His sideburns resembled sharpened arrowheads. Jeremy called Sylvia "Darlin'," and the men older than himself he designated "Pop." When he named Rita "Little Girl," she immediately let him know she disapproved.

One breezy afternoon before the caravan took off, Jeremy invited the group to an outdoor get-acquainted buffet. After making herself a sandwich, Rita retired to the rig to read. But it was hard to concentrate on the story for long without thinking of Clayton. Her grandfather had to be out there somewhere. Like her father.

Each time Rita heard the wind whine through the parking lot, she'd drop her book and look out the window. The gusts made the people talking and eating outside rush to hold down their napkins and plastic forks and Styrofoam cups. When Jeremy lifted his arm, seeming to explain something off in the distance, his sandwich blew right out of his hand.

"You used to enjoy meeting people," Sylvia said when she returned to the rig. "I don't understand why you'd want to stay cooped up here on such a sunny day."

"I didn't want to get hit by a sandwich."

"Did you see that?" Sylvia said and laughed. "People were chasing food and paper products all over the parking lot." It felt good to laugh, and to see Rita smiling, too.

"Well, let's just hope Mr. Jugg has better control over the caravan." Even as Rita spoke, she thought the comment sounded eerily like one of her grandmother's.

The leisurely caravan drive to Idaho featured a sing-along, games of bingo and cards, and a potluck breakfast each morning. Though it felt like camp for seventy-year-olds, in one way Rita didn't think the caravan was too bad; it was how Sylvia had initially described it — almost protective. People were friendly and helped Sylvia focus on things other than Clayton and Melvin.

Sylvia drove the highways in the middle of a great metal herd, watched the directional signal of the RV in front of her, checked the mirror for the RV behind. The owners of each one waved periodically.

Occasionally Rita envied the small, sleek bodies of the cars they met on the road. Impatient with the size of the RV procession, the little sports cars swerved in and out of the caravan at slow spots on the highway with all the determination of fingers on buttons and hooks and zippers. Sometimes it seemed like everything Rita thought about was small. Small and concentrated. Everything could be reduced. Probably she should have collected stamps instead of bumper stickers.

Some of the caravan travelers reminded Sylvia of people she'd met at other times. "That fellah is the image of Bud Harper," Sylvia said of the thin, dark man who'd been designated the tail gunner.

"Who's Bud Harper?"

"An old friend of Clayton's. They used to work together at Evergreen." Sylvia paused. "You remember. He was at the funeral." She paused. "Clayton's mother's funeral."

Rita wasn't used to Sylvia reminiscing so much. Sylvia's stories of their recent adventures in LA gave way to a string of recollections, especially stimulated by the fertile company of the caravan's storytellers. One tale spun off into another, and when she and the other RVers ran out of incidents they knew firsthand, they relayed the stories of friends, then friends of friends.

Jeremy Jugg made a business out of memories. He videotaped the RVers starting out in the morning, stopping during the afternoon, and socializing during specially planned activities at the end of the day. At about nine each night, Jeremy pulled a large TV from his rig and then showed the tape of that day's adventure. Often, a couple of the elderly RVers with short-term memory lapses were genuinely surprised by a few of the morning's events. All the travelers watched one another and the road and the traffic for a second time. They critiqued one another's clothes, the way they walked and ate and drove, and how much they smoked. And everyone went to bed as exhausted as if they'd been on two voyages — an actual one and one that could be improved upon. Jeremy took orders for copies of his completed tapes, available for $19.95 apiece.

When their fellow RVers pressed their stories and their food and even their clothes on Rita and Sylvia, it was all very friendly; even the air felt cozy around the caravan, as if it had blown out of a calico-patterned room. But there wasn't a trace of the focused urgency Rita had detected in her father's hands the day he'd snatched her to him in the bright sunlight of suburban Maryland.

The morning after they reached Idaho, Sylvia and Rita followed the hardiest of the caravan members to the top of a mountain to witness the sunrise. By the time they reached the peak, the sky was pale as a just-dusted room, with clouds blowing in, pushing off.

Taking Sylvia's arm, Rita walked over the cracked sloping stone at the summit until she found a good spot to view the spectacle. She pulled an old wool blanket around her grand-mother's shoulders.

Without the distractions of stories and roads, the place of smoothed stone lulled Sylvia into feeling peaceful. She imag-ined herself and Rita seeing the sun first, before it thrust its light on to buildings and parking lots and empty cars.

"There's so many clouds," Rita said in a whisper.

As she spoke, the clouds cleared briefly and she could discern what looked like a body of water, but no sunrise color. Rita had never been to sea, but she pictured it this way, end-lessly light and gray and the air too tight to hold much sound.

Rita spotted Jeremy setting up his video recorder about two hundred feet away. He began his commentary, surprising her with how far it carried: "Here we are, waiting for the show while the rest of the group is still snug in their beds . . ."

"Clayton would have hated this," Rita said.

"Let's get the hell out of here," Sylvia said, but she didn't move as Jeremy's voice curled over the mountain like the clouds, which, now and then, rolled in and obstructed the view. Jeremy Jugg said, "Oh, *yeah,*" dropping his voice on the second word as if a stage curtain had been pulled back.

Sylvia ignored Jeremy and concentrated solely on the sun — a magnificent red omen in the sky. *This* she wished Clayton could see. With her and Rita. This essential phenomenon, stopping the day before it began. She sat quietly and watched the circle rise higher in the sky. Beside her, Rita was speechless.

The few people who'd come to observe daybreak now moved off toward their vehicles. RVs and cars started up in the parking lot, and soon Sylvia and Rita were alone. After a few minutes, Sylvia turned to her granddaughter, who was studying a man walking in their direction. Rita angled herself directly at the sun and closed her eyes. When she opened them, she saw the man still coming toward them.

The last time she'd seen him, he'd become smaller and smaller until he had dwindled into a spot, a period, then only a memory.

The moment he got close enough for her to really take in his face, Rita loved him. Her father was unshaven and thin. Melvin's jeans and olive-colored shirt hung off his body as if they were of little importance. His hands appeared hardened with work. His hair was graying. And his face wasn't nearly as round and shiny as she'd remembered. Rita thought he looked like someone who'd dropped out of the pages of her history book.

He began to speak rapidly, as if he feared Rita would run away. He said he was a new man. He wanted her to come live with him and his friends on a tract of land in nearby Brighton. He said he'd known they'd be coming his way because, anony-

mously, he'd sent Marlene the flyer about the California caravan adventure.

Sylvia squeezed her purse up close to her waist. By now most
things in her life had worn out or died off or simply stopped
working, but not Melvin. If at times she'd fooled herself into
thinking the threat of him had disappeared, she knew now that
he'd only grown larger and larger, like a tumor — and here he
was, ready to devour her.

Sylvia spotted the taillights of Jeremy's rig dipping out of
sight down the mountain.

"Hey!" she shouted.

"There's no need to shout," Melvin said. "I only want to see
my little girl, Mrs. Vaeth."

His voice was almost soft, startling from such a rough
exterior.

Hearing him call her Mrs. Vaeth made Sylvia realize just how
young Melvin still was. Part of him had fallen and never totally
escaped the pit of misdirected youth.

All Sylvia's thinking and rethinking about Janice, about the
idea that maybe Janice hadn't been as innocent as she'd
dreamed, disappeared when she faced Melvin. Every old ha-
tred and disappointment resurfaced and attached itself to him.

"I thought maybe you were dead," Sylvia blurted out.

"Vee," Rita said. Yet the man before her didn't seem affected
by Sylvia's comment. Rita studied his eyes, dark and steady like
the deep water where Clayton had caught the best fish. Once
more he both scared and intrigued her.

"No such luck," he said, grimacing. He glanced at Rita. "I
thought you'd look more like Janice."

"No such luck," Rita said, then instantly regretted being so
smart-mouthed. As she continued to stare at him, she heard the
screech of a lone bird and her own heart beating.

Melvin's sigh broke the silence. His tone changed once

again. He opened his arms and hands in Rita's direction. Rita thought, My father has no money or anything else except need for me. Wanting to hold on to a little trace of his relationship with my mother.

But she didn't move.

"We've got a nice setup in our compound, Rita. I live with a pretty good group of people. There are young people your age."

He mentioned that the compound was called Brown's, out of tribute to the original landowner. "Mrs. Vaeth," he said. "Why don't we let Rita decide? I'll take her over to my place, let her check it out."

He went on talking about where he lived.

He described animals and stretches of evergreens, a lake so beautiful it stopped you every time you looked at it.

Sylvia felt the bulk of the .38 through her purse.

She wished she possessed Madame Tooley's soft voice of universal understanding. Or the forgiving tone of Dot, who could pick up with Pikey exactly where he'd left her behind. But Sylvia's anger and fear had been with her so long they were almost essential body parts. And if Melvin took Rita, even if he simply talked her into going off with him, the discarding, the paring down that had begun when she and Clayton had sold their house would finally be complete.

"I don't want her to have to choose," Sylvia said, playing up the last word. "A sixteen-year-old is too young for an ultimatum."

Melvin reached for Rita.

Sylvia remembered his cramped letters spelling out, "I'll get her no matter what." She imagined one swift movement that would look as though she'd practiced it for years — pulling Clayton's gun from her purse and doing what she knew Clayton regretted not doing, shooting Melvin in the heart. Reducing him to the colors and confusion of the car accident.

But when she reached into the purse, her hands shaking like she was coming out of a deep freeze, everything was a jumble of emotion and purpose. She groped for the bullets. Her hands jabbed deep at the corners of the bag until she remembered she'd stored the ammunition in the zippered compartment. How could she have forgotten? The purse fell from her lap, the handle of the gun exposed.

She heard Rita yell, but before Melvin could grab the gun, Sylvia leaped at him and circled his neck with both of her hands. Instead of resistance, she felt him going with the fall, dropping back until she lay atop him. Squeezing her hands against his throat.

"Vee, Vee." She heard her name and felt Rita pulling her off. And then she was crying — for Rita, for Janice, for Clayton, who wasn't here when she needed him most. Rita's voice rose above the chaos. The girl was apologizing for her, explaining about Clayton, as the sun, now golden, crept higher above their heads.

When Melvin stood up, Sylvia saw immediately that he favored one leg. "Did I hurt you?" she asked, then looked quickly at Rita.

"No, ma'am," Melvin said.

He fingered his knee in the silence. He said he'd gotten a bad infection that spread through his body. "I got shot," he said. "Didn't bleed much, but I didn't take care of myself." He coughed.

Sylvia said nothing after that. Mutely, she followed Melvin and Rita to the parking lot.

The sky clouded over as they drove down the mountain,

Melvin and Rita in his truck ahead of her. Surprised that Melvin hadn't taken her gun, Sylvia entertained the possibility that he admired her being prepared, especially considering that he'd asked her where the gun belonged and then slipped it back into its place beneath the RV seat.

If things had turned out differently, Melvin's body would have been flown out over the evergreens and lakes to his parents in Baltimore. But instead here she was, thankful to be trailing behind him along steep winding roads she barely noticed.

When they reached Melvin's compound, Sylvia watched his truck amble off down the dirt road. Rita turned and waved from the front seat. This could go on for years, Sylvia thought, camped out at the gateway to Melvin's home, boondocking at the edge of her granddaughter's life.

The bedroom with its brown curtains that drooped in a couple of places on the bent rod, the ceiling's chipped paint, and the door marked with fingerprints weren't part of Rita's idea of the perfect sanctuary, and yet the room was all hers, tucked among the different buildings and barns that made up the compound. As long as she wanted it.

Hundreds of questions swirled in front of her, but she didn't want to scare her father off or make him angry with her curiosity. Where was his room? Where did people eat breakfast? What had happened to all the toys in the trunk of his old car?

"That's your mother's yearbook picture," Melvin said, pointing to one of the two framed photos in the room. Janice's hair was puffed high on her head, and she wore a funny-looking sleeveless top, yet her face was calm and pretty, her smile genuine. She stared right at Rita.

"Who's this?" Rita asked of the second picture.

"That's Janice when she was a baby," Melvin said.

The man and woman holding her looked oddly familiar, yet it took a few seconds before Rita recognized them as her grandparents. Clayton was cradling the baby and Sylvia stood to the side of him, her eyes focused on the child.

Her grandfather's face was young and happy, his features distinct, eyes determined. For a few minutes, she missed him intensely.

"You didn't know Janice when these photos were taken," Rita said.

"No," Melvin said.

Rita saw how when someone died, people spread their grief over the entire life of the deceased.

"You want to help me feed the dogs?" When she hesitated, Melvin said, "Why don't you get settled in then, and I'll go feed the dogs. Tomorrow I'll take you horseback riding."

One morning in her second month at Brown's, a wasp woke Rita. It buzzed and bumped against the upper part of the window nearest her head, then dropped down and began a random crawl up the screen. The wasp had no idea where it was, yet it was determined to escape.

Since she'd first heard about her father, Rita had hoped he'd want to take her off with him, letting her choose the destinations. They might stop at Garden Road for a day or two, but it was on the road where they'd get to know each other. She had never imagined Melvin would want her to settle down in a commune with posted schedules, where the clanging of a large metal bell divided each day into three parts. Brown's seemed to Rita like a tiny speck surrounded by hundreds of miles of deserted land, connected to nothing. Only one thin wriggly line led to freedom.

Her uneasiness had nothing to do with unanswered questions. Rita approved of the large, impeccably clean bedroom, which Melvin shared with four other single men, and at meals her place was right next to her father's designated chair. Although Melvin hadn't mentioned the toys in his trunk the day Clayton shot him, she suspected her father never saw them *or* his car again. She now knew all her father's friends and even their dogs. Melvin appeared happy to have her with him; her first week at the compound he said proudly several times a day, "This is my daughter, Rita." Still, there was something missing — something that prevented her from really being a part of Brown's.

Their daily routine was fixed and placid. For most of the day, Melvin disappeared to do chores, including caring for the compound's animals. He left Rita to read, hike within designated parameters, or ride a horse.

That morning after breakfast, Melvin helped her saddle and mount Stout, a golden horse with a black mane. As she trotted in the fenced area, she thought for probably the hundredth time about being on the road, the steady pace of getting away. Once she had asked, "Now where are we?" so many times her words had dissolved with countless stores, campsites, and road signs into blotches of color, smudges of light.

Trees, houses with barbecue grills and basketball hoops, people mowing lawns, planting flowers, shoveling snow, all had moved at the speed of fast forward. And she hadn't minded, because there were others just ahead. Whatever Sylvia pointed out, Rita was sure to see again. There was an unlimited supply of everything. Except fathers. And she'd finally found hers.

And boys. On the road, the boy she would fall in love with could never catch up with them. They moved too fast. Rita pictured herself in McDonald's, him in Burger King, and every day each just missing the other by a store, a traffic light, a highway exit. At night, from her bed in the rig, she had watched the taillights of passing cars. In those two red glows, she imagined the lit ends of cigarettes smoked by lovers in the dark, conjured up slow, sexy conversations.

Rita urged Stout into a trot. In a wash of brown and green and blue, a man rode up and introduced himself without slowing his horse. When they dismounted outside the barn, Rita noticed that Gary Kennecott wasn't much taller than she was, but she knew he was older.

He had sandy-colored hair and a thick mustache that almost looked red. Green eyes. Once inside the barn, he put a raw, bruised hand on the feed counter. With his undamaged hand, Gary reached over and took Rita's forearm, which he held to the counter. Thick bands of dirt showed under each of his nails. Slowly, one by one, he straightened the fingers of the wounded hand to reveal a shiny lump the size of a misshapen grape. There were indentations on his palm from the nugget and from his fingernails.

"Gold," he said, as if naming it for the first time.

"Wow," Rita said, trying to wriggle her arm free.

"Wow's right. It's a good-size piece." Then he said, "Sorry," and released his grip. He acted like they'd known each other a long time.

He asked her if she was Mexican. She smiled and shook her head, but they exchanged a few phrases in Spanish anyway. Then he returned to his excitement over the gold, his mustache moving as he talked and gestured. The way he spoke of rocks, they could have been the names of old girlfriends: sandstone, chert, shale, quartzite. In a hushed voice, he told her of his plan to extract gold from seawater.

When they had unsaddled the horses and were walking in the direction of the dining hall, Rita asked Gary what he was doing at Brown's.

"My brother's here." Gary wrinkled his brow. "I'm trying to get him to go down to Blue Mountain with me. Another pair of hands and I know I could hit it big." He patted his shirt pocket where he'd stored the piece of gold.

Rita briefly told Gary about Melvin to explain why she was at the compound.

Gary shook his head. "There's too many crazies here for me." He paused. He said that his brother was now more interested in guns and politics than in Gary's gold.

"They seem friendly," Rita said, thinking of how the strangers had known her name before she'd been introduced to them.

"I'll bet you haven't watched any of the 'maneuvers,' " Gary said, accentuating the last word. He whistled one sharp tone. "It sounds like World War III around here when they get going."

Rita tried to picture her father taking part in practice warfare. She hadn't considered the people in the compound that bizarre. "There's plenty of nuts out on the road, too." She told Gary about the RV.

"I've always wanted to do that," Gary said.

"Do what?"

"Rent an RV and go cross country. Where are you from anyway?"

"From everywhere," she said. "That's where I grew up."

He whistled softly through his teeth, then turned and, for the first time, really looked her over. She could feel him sizing up her scrawny legs, dark hair, her small hands and breasts.

"I'm impressed," he said. "You want to go to Blue Mountain?"

"What?"

"Let me show you my claims." He looked directly into her eyes. "Let me show you all the gold I've found."

Rita and Gary stood outside the communal kitchen. Through the window she watched the cook's fingers curl around a carrot and retreat before the approaching foot-long knife. He swiped vegetable bits into separate mounds on the wooden work surface.

"What about your brother and my father?" she asked.

"They belong here," Gary said. On a napkin, he carefully drew a map to Blue Mountain, Nevada.

At first, explaining about Blue Mountain to her father was easier than Rita had anticipated. Melvin sat on the edge of her bed and ran his hand across the spread while she talked about Gary. He didn't interrupt or protest.

"His brother's good people," Melvin said, nodding. But he avoided looking into Rita's eyes, and she knew she'd hurt him. He stood up quickly and squeezed her to his chest, the stiff shirt scraping at her face. In the khaki-colored cloth she smelled tobacco and the outdoors.

Rita wanted to question him about the "maneuvers," not only because she was curious, but to change the subject of her leaving, yet it felt awkward. She wanted to ask, "Do you want me to go?" but that query felt too large and direct.

Melvin didn't seem to mind not being questioned. He was more at ease in silence. It spread over him like clear weather.

Why won't he say something? Doesn't he care? Rita thought, wanting to put words in her father's mouth.

Melvin placed his hands on her shoulders and gently pushed her away from him. He looked at her directly, his eyes soft, his face as bewildered as it had been the time Clayton shot him. Rita thought of years earlier when she'd spent all morning planning to snare a chipmunk. When it eventually crawled beneath the box to take the bait, she pulled the string that crashed the trap down over the scrabbling little animal. But she had not known what to do next.

Dealing with Sylvia the next morning was a relief.

Every other day, Rita had visited her grandmother at the rig, still positioned at the gateway to Brown's. Rita brought Sylvia fresh water and occasionally desserts from the compound's dining room. Sometimes they took a walk together along the boundary of the property and afterward shared a quick lunch.

"Blue Mountain?" Sylvia said. "I think I saved something on that town." Humming, she rummaged through clippings until she found a piece on The Salt and Pepper Museum.

Without going into detail about Gary, Rita said simply that while Sylvia was at the museum, she wanted to explore the gold mine she'd been told about.

"Fair enough," Sylvia said. "What about Melvin?" she asked cautiously. For weeks she'd fought back her nagging concerns about the compound.

"We left that open," Rita said. "He said my room would always be here."

"That's nice," Sylvia said. Though she wanted to shout with happiness, she held herself in check. Her tolerance had been rewarded. The long fretful nights without her granddaughter were about to end. Rita had come back to her, would travel on with her at least to Nevada. In time, perhaps, Rita would understand that Melvin needed a daughter only to forgive himself.

ELEVEN

Now that Melvin was behind them, Sylvia felt full of light. When she and Rita left the compound, all she wanted to do was drive. The night before, she'd dreamed she was standing over Melvin's dead body. After all these years, his face was still greasy. She'd placed her palm on the side of his face, the spot from the nose to the cheekbone that remarkably resembled Rita's.

The motion of the RV and the purr of its engine soothed Rita's concerns, too. The landscape was intoxicating. The scenery they passed was all dry hardened surfaces, then loose and marked with fallen rock. They drove through a tunnel cut into one of the mountains. Some of the rock appeared lacquered in black from unexpected moisture.

Sylvia directed the RV down a slope into a wide vista of mountains, and at the bottom, the town of Blue Mountain, Nevada, suddenly blossomed from the barren surroundings.

They boondocked outside town. They hadn't talked over where they would go next, or whether she'd go back to her father. For the first time, Sylvia realized that Clayton had been the one to provide a schedule for their lives.

To compensate for failing to give Rita some structure, the next morning she ordered her granddaughter to secure the interior of the RV.

"I already checked," Rita complained.

"Check it again," Sylvia insisted.

Rita looked over the door and windows to be sure they were locked, and examined counter surfaces for loose objects. She rolled up the unraveled toilet paper and encircled it with a rubber band.

They drove the RV into town. While Sylvia scoured the Salt and Pepper Museum for the most ingenious pairing, Rita walked around Blue Mountain and considered when she should phone Gary. She was drinking a Coke in a diner — exactly like the diners in Garland, Tennessee; Flat Rock, Texas; and Pleasant Valley, New Mexico — when he came in and sat down beside her at the counter.

She imagined that since she'd pulled into town he'd been watching her like a cat, camouflaged against the places he knew well. But he told her it was a coincidence that he'd run into her.

"You aren't here trying to lease one of my claims, are you?" he asked Rita, one eyebrow raised.

"I have no idea what you're talking about."

"Of course not," he said, shaking his head sharply. His passion for gold was so singular that he made Rita think of Melvin.

"I guess I better get back," she said, figuring Sylvia had probably seen every salt and pepper shaker the museum had to offer.

"Where's back?"

Outside Rita pointed to the huge pale rig in the distance.

"Sylvia, this is Gary," Rita said at the trailer.

"Show her the gold," Rita said. Gary laughed, but slid the nugget out of his pocket.

"Would you like something with your Coke?" Sylvia asked. She was unsure of what to do next. Rita had never brought a guest home unannounced. Sylvia checked her watch. It was five-thirty.

"I got an idea. Why don't I take you ladies out to dinner? Celebrate my good luck today?" he said as soon as the gold was safe in his pocket again.

Sylvia and Rita looked at each other. Rita explained that she'd met Gary at Brown's and that his brother was a friend of Melvin's.

"Rita and I had other plans for tonight," Sylvia said, irked that she hadn't been told about Gary earlier.

"What plans?" Rita said, pulling away from her. "TV and Campbell's soup?"

"Rita!"

"Nothing wrong with Campbell's," Gary said, "except tonight's a celebratin' night."

"Maybe *I* could go with Gary," Rita said.

"Well," Sylvia said, glaring at Rita, "let me go make myself a little more presentable." She gave Rita the look that meant, Let's talk this over in private.

"Hey, forget about it. Go as you are," Gary said, then held his hands out as if to say, Look at me. "There's not one place in Blue Mountain you have to dress up for."

"We'll meet you at the restaurant," Sylvia said.

215

"I'll escort you ladies," Gary said.

"We'll meet you," Sylvia said, this time as firmly as she used to talk to Clayton.

"OK, OK," Gary said, holding up his hands in surrender. "Whatever you want. How about six-thirty at the Oasis?"

"The Oasis," Sylvia said, sounding like she and Gary had just made some deal.

When Gary left, Sylvia said, "You mean he just came into the diner and started talking to you out of the blue?" Rita nodded. "You must have encouraged him," she said. "At Brown's."

"I didn't *encourage* him. I looked up and he was there."

"He drew that map," Sylvia said.

"He drew that map," Rita repeated.

"He's a good ten years older than you."

"Relax, Vee. I'm not going to marry the guy. He just asked us to dinner."

"Relax, nothing. I swear you're just like your father."

Sylvia had never said anything like that before, and all Rita could do was gape at her. Then Sylvia put her fingers to her mouth and her eyes turned watery. "What does he do?" she said softly.

"He mines for gold."

"Food's not bad here," Gary said as he led Sylvia and Rita past the bar and deep into the dining room. "But better 'n that, I've got credit in this place."

"Credit's a good thing," Sylvia reminded the young people. "It's hard to get when you don't have a permanent address."

"Exactly," Gary said.

"They must know you mine gold," Rita said.

"Sweetheart, just about everybody in Blue Mountain mines gold. They give me credit because I work here."

"You do?" Rita asked. The word *sweetheart* felt like he'd just presented her with a rose.

"Cook?" Sylvia asked.

"Not quite. I clean up after closing. Then I hit three more places. The last one's in Laurel about twenty minutes south of here. I'm done by eight A.M. Perfect hours so I can mine all day."

Gary kept his elbows on the table while he chewed, as if his chicken might get away from him if he let down his guard. He didn't shift the fork back to his right hand after he sliced the meat, but stuck it immediately into his mouth. His mustache moved with his mouth and held the froth of his beer after he took a swallow. Whenever Rita looked up from her plate, Gary narrowed his eyes at her. She could feel Sylvia studying her, too. Rita finished her plate off by imitating Gary, wiping up the last bits of garlic sauce with a piece of bread.

"Rita's not normally such a good eater," Sylvia said to Gary.

Rita couldn't believe Sylvia embarrassing her. She nudged her grandmother's knee under the table a little harder than she'd meant to.

When she and Sylvia were back in the RV, Rita pleaded, "Do we have to leave tomorrow?"

"No," Sylvia said quickly. "But we should decide what we want to do by Friday the latest." Sylvia tried to sound as if she had an agenda, like Clayton.

She said, "It's funny, when I married your grandfather I didn't even love him."

"No?"

"It's true. I was lonely and far from home. I liked him fine. And in time I loved him. But there was no fireworks. Nothing like that."

Sylvia went on, to Rita, longer than necessary. Sylvia said she had never been overwhelmed by love or made crazy by its passion. She hadn't met someone like Miguel, Rita thought, with strong arms and eyes almost bits of polished coal. Rita tuned out her grandmother and daydreamed *she* was Maria, bound to a man who proudly took her hand on their daily walk into the village, then carried all her purchases home because she was so overburdened with love she couldn't lift a single thing herself.

Gary pointed out the Four Winds Range, which he said was filled with gold dust. He explained how erosion had already done much of the initial mining by flushing gold from the mountains and down into the valleys.

"You can still pan for gold the way people panned 150 years ago," he said, demonstrating by shaking sand in a strainer as he poured water over it. "I found that nugget less than three feet from where we're standing." He stopped talking for a minute and looked off into the mountains. "I could pan here the rest of my life and maybe never find another thing. You just can't tell."

As they walked, Rita felt grit gather in the folds of her pants and shirt, and stick to her hair and skin. Specks of gold were sure to be hidden there, Gary said. Spread out, the gold was inconsequential. Rita thought for a moment of her conversation with her grandmother. Passion meant every emotion coming together in a crucial place, like the gold dust into one solid clump.

If Rita moved into Brown's with Melvin permanently, she wouldn't be *that* far from Gary.

"How old are you, Rita?"

"Eighteen," she lied.

"Eighteen," he said, still studying the mountains with the resolve of someone who's directed and redirected his actions toward one purpose. The landscape was baked hard with unrelenting, unfulfilled dreams, which, he told Rita, he planned to realize. She thought about what it might be like to live with a gold miner so rooted to what sat below him he could dedicate his entire life to discovering its most intimate parts.

He took Rita's hand and directed her to a pit where big-time excavating was going on. His hand was callused and warm. More gentle than her father's. Huge black crows perched high on the walls of the pit and now and then swooped at food possibilities. The rough tooth marks of the excavating tools were gouged into the sides of the hole.

Later, Gary took Rita to his upstairs room at the Oasis. He pulled back a scatter rug and, just like in the movies, lifted a floorboard to reveal a small metal case.

"Can't be too careful," he said. "This is my savings account." He gently unlocked the case, which held a collection of gold pieces ranging in size from a speck of gravel to the piece he'd shown Rita at Brown's. Gesturing at a particularly pointy piece, he said, "I found this first one the morning my mother died." Gary appeared sad only for a moment. "I find a piece on every important day of my life." Pointing at the piece Rita recognized, he looked up at her and smiled. He lifted the gold from its place among the others, ran it along his fingers, kissed it before setting it back.

"What happened on this day?" Rita asked of a shiny raisin-shaped lump.

"I got my job at the Oasis," he said without hesitation. He took her hands in his and confided that he'd never shown someone his entire collection.

"My only problem is cash flow." As he looked around the small room, Rita took in the single window, the beige bedspread pulled perfectly smooth across the single bed, the lopsided lamp shade. He pointed to the case. "If I sold some of this stuff, I could have plenty of money." He took a deep breath. "But I can't bring myself to do it."

Then he kissed her. Long and hard. Rita heard the clatter of dishes being readied for customers below, glasses clinking together, the clash of silverware and voices. Someone hollered, "Oh, shit," but Rita didn't flinch.

On Thursday, Gary found another piece of gold. He was sweating, and his sun-bleached hair was disheveled.

"Doesn't it look like a heart, Rita?"

"Looks more like a garlic clove." She was remembering the garlic chicken special she'd had at the Oasis.

"It looks like a heart. I've never found two pieces of gold in one week."

He took her hand, placed the gold in her palm, and folded her fingers over the prize. "You know what this means, don't you?"

What Rita was certain of was that something crucial had been decided without her. Like the moment Clayton died and the instant Sylvia jumped at Melvin. With Gary, Rita didn't feel capable of interfering with a natural sign laid down right in the center of her hand.

"This is why I go after this crazy stuff," he said. "You never know what you're going to find when you set out for gold. At the Oasis, I know. It's always the same crap — full ashtrays, empty bottles."

Rita wondered if her father would ever grow tired of Brown's.

With the gold still in her hand, they drove out of town. Rita had told Sylvia they were having dinner with Gary's aunt and uncle, but Gary had no relatives in Nevada. Rita's hands started to sweat, so she switched the gold piece from one hand to the other and wiped the empty one hard against her jeans. Gary kept driving and whistling softly; now and then, he looked over to smile.

The woman at the reception desk of the Owl Manor Motel was friendly to Gary, not like she knew him, but like he reminded her of somebody. They were assigned the honeymoon suite, and Rita thought the room was one more sign that what was about to happen was out of her control.

Room 24B was as elegant as anything Rita had seen in a magazine. The walls were painted white with the exception of the one behind the bed, papered with a delicate pattern of leaves and flowers in gold, white, and peach. The entire room was carpeted in off-white. And the bed — she'd never been this close to such a huge bed — was covered with a thick white quilt.

When Rita looked at Gary and he shrugged his shoulders and grinned in amazement too, she felt, for a second, that they might be equal. But as soon as he kissed her lightly on the forehead, she knew she couldn't match his confidence.

"Almost as good as finding gold," he said, looking around.

"Don't worry," Gary said as he helped her unbutton her clothes. Then gently he told her she was so small he could break her in half, then into thousands of valuable gems.

"That's supposed to make me relax?" she asked beneath him. He was heavy against her and pressed at her chest so hard that she worried her heart would stop. She would become a part of the bed on which he slept. A lump he would press flat to make himself more comfortable.

"Rita," he said with a sigh, "you are so lovely."

Rita didn't feel lovely. She felt confused, scared of the insistence in his body, the resistance in her own. She did the last thing in the world that she wanted to, the thing she hadn't done even after Clayton died: she started to cry.

Gary pulled her head to his chest and put one hand in her hair. He told her how once he was sure he was going to die.

"I was working for this guy, Trent, on his claim. There must have been about eight of us blasting and moving the rock. I was driving this big-ass truck when all of a sudden a huge boulder came loose. The damn thing was moving right at me. I jumped out of the truck just in time. But rocks were rumbling all over the place, then rolling and sliding, and guys were hollering. When the dust finally cleared, Trent said he was surprised I was still alive. I was pretty surprised myself. I had this one flash where I was holding a purple and white marble up to show my mother. I saw myself all happy, displaying the marble. For a split second I saw myself the way my mother had. Anyway, the truck was a mess. The windshield was smashed out completely."

Gary turned to Rita. "You feel better now?" Before she could answer, he was on her again, urging her legs apart with the weight of his body, pinning her arms and hair to the bed. This time he was actually making love to her, though making love hardly seemed an appropriate phrase to Rita. With his body, he seemed to ask her a question over and over again. What feels good? What do you need? What do you want? Forcing the question deep inside. It was a question she didn't know the answer to, in a language she didn't speak. Because she didn't know how to respond to him, she lay still and let him move within her. She freed her arms enough to hold onto him.

"That wasn't so bad, was it?"

"I guess not."

They lay against each other for a long time. She had the urge to speak to him in Spanish, to bring some romance to what they'd done, but the only Spanish phrase that came to her was, "What time does the next train leave for Guadalajara?"

"Have you ever been to the Gold Museum in Colorado?" she asked, describing a life-size mural of a cancan dancer with her garters and eyes and fingernails made of gold ingots. She'd gone there two years earlier on Clayton's birthday.

"Some day I'll have my own gold museum," he said, his voice deep and sleepy.

"I'm thinking of moving to Brown's," she said. Maybe love had to stay in one place.

"You don't want to move there," he said, then fell off to sleep still holding her.

The sun set in beautiful gold stripes through the venetian blind. As Gary stirred, kissed her on the cheek, and turned away from her, Rita thought of Sylvia marrying Clayton without loving him. Then she thought of her mother, who must have been "crazy in love" to exchange Sylvia and Clayton and college for a place with Melvin.

And what happened if you obeyed the wild pull of your heart? You could die on the highway with your baby on your lap, cheated of all the journeys ahead. Rita could see everything her young mother never had.

> I come to the bed
> Get under the covers.
> If you're not the right one,
> I'll have plenty more lovers.

There's a sampler idea that would shock Sylvia.

When Gary woke up, Rita was fingering the piece of gold that he'd found earlier that day. "We better get back," Rita said.

"Yeah, I have to go to work." He took the gold piece, moved

it among his fingers, then returned it to her hand. "You may be right about this. It really doesn't look like a heart, does it?"

Early the next morning, even before breakfast, Sylvia and Rita hit the road, traveling east. Rita kept her hand on the gold nugget deep in her pocket, but neither of them mentioned Gary or his relatives, except when Sylvia said, "At least he got you eating again."

Ahead of them, a truck loaded with bales of hay clipped along the highway.

"It's yours," Rita said.

"We can both wish on it," Sylvia said.

"I know, but you get this one and I'll take the next." Rita thought it was more likely a wish would come true if only one person concentrated on it.

"How do you know there'll be a next one?" Sylvia asked.

"We're in farm country, Vee."

As they got closer to the truck, bits of hay rained back at the RV as a reminder of all the good luck that was possible. And then Sylvia stepped on the gas and passed the truck.

She wished a double wish. She hoped Rita would be happy and she hoped Rita would forgive her.

Less than half an hour later, a second hay truck came into view. Rita claimed it and wished for another boyfriend, one who would follow her all over the country. Maybe he'd grown up afraid to leave his room. Rita imagined the boy hoping to make himself small as a salt shaker so that he could hide in a coffee cup or in his mother's skirt pocket. Maybe he'd grown up dreaming of traveling. With dark eyes like Maria's husband's.

His name might be George, the imaginary playmate she'd had as a young girl.

"*Venga acá,*" he would say.

"Heme aquí," she would answer.

They would lie back on a bed, touch each other lightly on the face, on the arms and fingers, as if to prove that this was about even more than passion. He'd know there would be plenty of time for pounding out desires, like precious metal, into a small shiny jewel to be worn over and over again.

When Sylvia pulled to the side of the road for a little break, she said the rig must have crushed a branch of sagebrush. An odor like cedar from a trunk that hadn't been opened in years floated about them.

Once her rooms had held the scent of fresh-cut wood and newly painted sheetrock. Their faces free of lines, their bodies not yet dimpled, she and Clayton had been a young couple moving in before their little plot of land was green with grass, before they knew their place was small.

Had she cheated Rita by not letting the girl grow up in a neighborhood with regular dimensions — an ordinary yard, clear-cut symbol of the natural world, and a house planted right in the middle? Where she wasn't constantly thrown up against new surroundings and people? Maybe I should have let Rita be disappointed by houses herself, Sylvia thought.

"I guess we can start with that," Sylvia said, pointing at the urn she'd positioned behind Rita's seat.

"While we're moving, you mean?" Rita asked and Sylvia nodded.

When they were on the road again, Rita perched beside the open passenger window and flung a handful of the thick ash at accessible spots. She blew at the dust that stuck to her fingers almost as hard as she'd blown into Clayton's mouth. Then she switched positions and Sylvia tossed the silty material into the air at intervals.

Clayton had given Rita driving tips as far back as she could remember. "You were in training pants the day he said, 'Never wiggle the steering wheel,' " Sylvia said.

Even though they were flinging Clayton off in all directions, Rita couldn't help but think they were driving to meet up with him. Her sadness blew off along with the window-size images of the world. It was impossible not to imagine Clayton, fishing pole in hand, at the end of some distant highway exit. Sylvia said she pictured him like Pikey and Dot, Alvin, Bob and Carol Melnick, waving as they pulled into a new trailer park, then approaching, and calling something like, "Long time, no see." Later, when Rita was dozing, she saw Clayton with his arm around Melvin, two tiny figures waving gently in the rearview mirror.

While Rita pumped fuel into the RV, Sylvia walked to the station building and bought cigarettes for herself, a candy bar for Rita. The cashier rang up the purchases and Sylvia stared out at the RV. Home. Battered with bumper stickers and mileage and road dirt. It didn't seem large enough, somehow, to accommodate everything that had happened.

"Rita, do you want to quit all this?" She suddenly appeared at Rita's side.

"The ashes?" They were making an outline of Clayton's life, state by state. He would be everywhere.

"Not the ashes. The traveling, boondocking. If you want, we can buy a little house some place nice, and in a couple of years you can go to college." She paused. "Unless you'd rather go back to your father." Sylvia held her breath.

Rita studied her watch. At the compound, people would be washing off the dirt of the days' activities in preparation for dinner. Someone would be filling the coffee urns with water, someone else setting out serving platters and clean silver-ware.

Melvin had a built-in family there. In the dining room full of friendly chatter and the aromas of food, people automatically passed him seconds of mashed potatoes because they knew he enjoyed them. During a ball game, he'd argue over a call with another man the way siblings contested the size of their pieces of cake.

Rita looked at her grandmother, at the wrinkles like seams on her face; at her hair, a mix of blonde and white; at her gnarled hands.

"I don't have to think about it. Who wants to live in any old house?"

"Where do you want to go, then?" Sylvia felt suddenly confident, relying on Rita for a destination.

"How about Mexico?" Rita asked as she opened the RV door for Sylvia and helped her climb up. Already Rita was thinking of the letters she would write to her father. The first one would be hardest, but the rest, she imagined, would flow with the details of her new adventures. She heard Melvin reading her letters to his friends at Brown's as proudly as he had once introduced her.

"A little excursion south of the border?" Sylvia asked. "You could use your Spanish."

After lunch Rita took over the driving, breaking through the brittle landscape as they headed south. From her shoe box of articles, the special section on Mexico, Sylvia read aloud about the dangers of *bandidos,* night driving, and tap water, and about an incredibly hot chili pepper. You had to wear gloves to handle it, but it could cure the common cold.